FIND ME

BOOKS BY CARLA KOVACH

FIND ME

Carla Kovach

bookouture

Published by Bookouture in 2022

An imprint of Storyfire Ltd.
Carmelite House
50 Victoria Embankment
London EC4Y 0DZ

www.bookouture.com

ISBN: 978-1-80314-327-9
eBook ISBN: 978-1-80314-326-2

I dedicate this book to the lovely people and businesses of Looe and Polperro. Their warmth and love for these stunning seaside towns shines through.

PROLOGUE

'Have you seen a little girl? She's gone missing.' The woman runs across the road and into the gift shop, searching through the aisles before wiping her brow and running back out onto the path. 'Someone help us.' Her arms are in the air as she turns in a circle, not knowing which direction to go in. 'Have you seen a little girl. Someone must have seen her.' She shouts so loud her throat hurts.

The other little girl tugs at the hem of her T-shirt. Tears run down her cheeks as she points to her ice cream that has dropped out of the cone onto the pavement.

The woman grabs her hand and darts into another shop, then another. It's no good. The child is gone. Her heart is breaking as she gasps for air. It's as if the life is being sucked out of her. She can't breathe, her vision is blurred and her whole body feels heavy, like it's being weighed down by an anchor.

Passers-by stare through windows. Some stop to take photos, others stop to readjust shopping bags as the straps dig into their arms, but not one of them stops to ask her why she's so distressed. For her, time stands still. If only she could go back five minutes and prevent what had happened but it's okay saying that now. Especially as it's too late.

'Someone help us!' She collapses onto the road and the man she was helping is crying too. The screaming child is almost bursting her eardrums while all she can think about is the missing child. 'We can't find her. Please help us.' People keep walking by, most not willing to stop.

A woman runs over. 'I've called the police.'

The police.

It's real now, the police are coming and the little girl is missing. Her gaze darts up and down the road in the hope that someone is bringing the little one back, but no one is coming towards them carrying a child. She glares at *him* as he stands there looking helpless. What can he do? What can either of them do?

All the woman can keep repeating is the little one's name followed by, *she's gone* and *we lost her*. That's the truth.

'Please find her,' she yells. *Please find her*. The woman would give her life to find the child. She places an arm around the man.

'I've lost her,' he cries and he has. He lost her.

ONE

KATE

Monday, 10 October

I'm up out of bed before six, as I always am in the week. With a huge mug of coffee in one hand, I enjoy the silence that only exists in this house before seven in the morning. This is my time, when the children are asleep and my husband, Damien, is still lying there, waiting for his alarm to go off. It's also a day where I need a bit of time to think about the past.

My finger presses the Facebook app on my iPad and I flick straight onto the Remembering Baby Jess page. Jess died twenty-five years ago to the day, which means I will do what I always do on this date. I will start the day by posting a photo of Jess. Selecting one I love, I start making a post. My gaze lingers on her gummy smile as she rattles the ladybird that is attached to her wrist. I don't know what to type underneath because I'm running out of things to say. Every year, I write how much we all miss her but that's not the truth. I'm the only one left who misses her. I type in a simple *Thinking of you, Baby Jess*. I can't say things that come so easily to other people like I know she's with Nanny in heaven or the angels are looking after her. I don't believe that to be true but I can see why thoughts like this give people comfort. They won't help me.

I've noticed that some local businesses have started advertising underneath the very occasional posts that I make and I slam my fist onto the kitchen table. This page is for information about her, not for spreading the word on the catch-of-the-day special. I want to know if anyone knows more about how she died that day. I bite my lip and delete the offending post.

My mind mulls over what Jess would look like now if she were still alive. She'd probably have light-brown hair, like mine. Maybe it would be longer or shorter. She'd have the darkest chocolate brown eyes; wait... were Jessica's eyes more of a hazel colour? My skin is more like my mother's with her Spanish roots, but Jessica was fairer with her pink cheeks, more like our father. I'm athletically built and strong. I wonder if she would have been built the same, or would she have hated running and swimming?

How long do I keep this up? Maybe it's time to close the page and leave her memory be. I know that would make my husband, Damien, happy. He's uncomfortable with me bringing this up, every year.

I turn the screen off just as he walks in. He whistles as he ruffles his damp hair with a towel. His chirpiness annoys me slightly. We've been married long enough for him to know what today means to me.

He looks at me with his lips pressed together. I don't always say much about the Jess page because he worries that she's the reason I won't give our children any freedom, and he's right. A life can be lost in a matter of seconds and I won't let that happen to my girls. I'm their mother and their protector, and I will do my job to the best of my ability, even if it kills me.

'I'll get breakfast started if you want to go up and shower.'

He leans in and kisses me on the head. 'I haven't forgotten. I know what day it is.'

I grab my iPad, anger still showing in my face from the advert that was posted.

'She wouldn't want you to be like this.'

Damien's right, I know he is but I'm not ready to let her memory die too.

'I can't let her go.' That's as much as I can tell him, the rest I will keep to myself.

Damien sees my mind whirring and my bottom lip trembling. He hurries over and wraps his strong arms around me. 'Please, Kate. For our marriage and our children you have to stop dwelling on the things you can't change or do anything about. Look what you're doing to the kids.' Instantly, I know he's not talking about me keeping this Facebook page, it's about how I am with our children.

I pull away from him. He doesn't understand what guilt is like and I will never be made to feel that bad again. The burden I carry is more than enough. 'I just want to protect them.'

'You're smothering them.'

'I love them.'

'I love them too but I don't stop them going out with their nan or going to birthday parties. You won't even let them play in our neighbours' gardens with their kids. It's getting ridiculous and my mum is starting to take it personally. All she wants to do is take them to the park or for a picnic.'

He's right. My children barely have any friends. I don't trust anyone. My father has never seen them and he never will. He gave up on finding out the truth about Jessica. I would never give up on my children.

'You won't even let them play in our own bloody garden because you think a psychotic killer is going to climb over our fence and snatch them. Children need a bit of freedom. What are you going to do in a few years when they're teens? Lock them up.'

'They're only four and five. They're still babies.' I can't think about them being teenagers, it's too far away. That's something I'll have to deal with when the time comes.

'They are not babies any more! They need friends. It's not normal to keep them cooped up the way you do. This is getting ridiculous.'

He's right but I don't know how I can change. By overprotecting them, I'm hurting them but I can't let what happened to Jessica happen to Millie and Rosie. They're my world.

My phone rings breaking the silence and I'm glad. It vibrates across the table and I reach it before it falls. 'Hello.' I nod and make a few noises to show that I'm listening before ending the call and gazing over at Damien. 'I have to go into work early. Brett is going to be a bit late in and there's no one to supervise the pool for the early sessions.'

'Great. We'll talk about this later.' Damien kisses me on the cheek. 'You go and get ready. I'll make you some toast, then I'll take the kids to school. I don't have to be at my first job until half nine.'

I swallow. 'Can you make sure you wait for them to go in? Don't leave them. Watch them actually go through the door.' Millie is in a nursery class so security is a little tighter but Rosie has to wait in the playground.

He shakes his head and his body language becomes rigid. The vein on his temple twitches, a sign that he's getting aggravated. 'This is exhausting, Kate. I'm their dad. What do you think I'm going to do? Leave them and run before I've handed them to a teacher. Please, stop this and if you don't delete that page, I'd say our marriage was going down the pan. I can't do this for much longer. It's exhausting.'

That's the first time he's said those words about our marriage but he's always blamed my page as if that is the cause of my overprotectiveness. I want to scream at him. It's not the page, it's what happened to Jess. It pains me but I must leave him to deal with the children so that I can get to work. I want to scream and shout. If it was down to me, I would never have gone back to work yet. The children are still so young but Damien thought it was for the best and that it might cure my anxieties. He can't see how much I'm already sacrificing.

A tear trickles down my cheek. 'I'm a terrible person.'

'Look, no you're not and I didn't mean to say what I did. I love you, okay, but I want you to start thinking of ways to find closure. Twenty-five years is a long time.'

'I'll delete the page.' The last thing I want is to lose him. I wipe my wet cheek and check the time. The hotel awaited me and I'd soon be running late.

'You'll feel better for it. Letting go of it will help, I promise. Now go and get ready before we're all late.'

I force a smile and check the time again on my iPad. Unless I get a move on, I'm going to be seriously late. 'You're right. I'll delete it later.'

After showering, I put my tailored shorts and polo shirt on over the top of my swimsuit, ready for a day of work. I quickly log on to Facebook and check the page. There are no new comments or messages so I swipe it away. Before heading out to work, I creep into the girls' bedroom and kiss them both gently on the cheek.

'Mummy loves you,' I whisper as I remove a hair from Millie's mouth. I step gently down the stairs and back into the kitchen.

'Bye, love.' Damien pulls me close to him and kisses me. It's like everything he said to me earlier has all been forgotten. 'See you later. Here, I made you this.'

He reaches towards the table and passes me a slice of buttered toast. 'Love you.' My face and smile tells him that I'm not the same person that he was speaking to only a few minutes ago, but inside, she still exists, gnawing away.

Before I pull off the drive, I pretend to eat my toast with one hand and I check the page again with the other. What he doesn't know won't hurt.

My heart bangs as I click on the notification. It's an article in a local Cornish paper about Jess published today. As I scan through it, my blood begins to boil. How come they contacted my dad when they were writing it but missed me out? I'm the one who cares about what happened to her. I'm the one who keeps her memory alive. It's me, all me, and they left me out. I hate them.

Then a message pops up and as I read it, I go cold.

I know what happened to your sister.

TWO

KATE

I check my watch as the pool starts to empty. Some of the parents dawdle with their fussing babies as they say their good-byes. Today was another success for the baby swim programme but I can't revel in my success at suggesting it, not with that message on my mind.

Will Wilcox, the name is as ordinary as any. He has no photos or information that I can see on his profile, which is why I sent him a friend request. He still hasn't accepted so I must conclude that, once again, someone is playing about with me. The account is probably fake. So many people have done this to me over the years. They don't realise how cruel they're being.

What would Damien say if I told him about the message? Firstly, he'd be angry that I didn't close the page so telling him isn't an option. Secondly, he'd tell me that we've been here before, lots of times, and each and every message had turned out to be nothing. Sad people with nothing better to do. Some turned out to be teenagers playing a joke, others were untrace-able fake accounts. Heartless, I know, but it's true.

Years ago, I'd call the police with every message but they soon tired of me. They followed them all up but every one of them turned out to be nothing. I can't call them again. Hearing the pity in their voices as they offer me numbers of helplines for bereavement charities merely makes me angry. I don't want their pity again so I won't call them. I realised a long time ago that I'm alone. Jess is nothing to them. She's a closed case. Besides, the messenger hasn't given me anything of any use.

No, I'll sit on the message and see if I get another and if I do and it looks convincing, I'll follow it up myself. At least I'll do a proper job. Jess deserves that. The article runs through my mind. I wonder if my dad has read it yet. I take a deep breath as I gaze across the pool again. I need to forget the message and the article for now.

I try to fill my head with more positive thoughts. It's the only way I'll get through the rest of my shift. I'll be finishing work soon and I can't wait to pick the girls up. They're always ecstatic to see me. My muscles twitch with anticipation. I want to hold them and ask them how their day was. I hope they had a lovely time but I also hope that they missed me and tell me that they'd rather be with me all day. The more I toil about that message, the more I think of my girls and how much I need to be with them all the time. Maybe I could tell them to tell Daddy that they want me to be at home all the time. No, I stop that train of thought. If I carry on the way I have been, I will definitely lose him and I don't want that to happen. We've been a bit divided lately. He wants me to loosen up as a parent, focus on getting a life of my own back and I want to keep a closer eye on the girls. It was easy when they were babies, but now they run off when we're out. They hide in our large garden and they keep asking if they can go to friends' houses, but all I want is to keep them within my line of sight. Even just the thought of all that is giving me palpitations.

I inhale, taking in the smell of chlorine, feeling sweat beads forming at my brow. The chatter is dying down as some people have left for the changing rooms. I glance at the pool where one of my mothers is smiling at her baby, little Jake. She throws him in the air, and then she catches him. His giggles are a delight to watch.

As the other parents leave the pool, cradling their babies, I smile. Only the one woman still remains waist high in the water. Everyone loves baby swim and I'm really starting to relax into my job more. Seeing the little ones gurgle and laugh brings me a sense of joy that I didn't know I could feel.

The tiniest baby lies in the arms of a muscular man and I smile as the baby reaches for his beard and begins tugging his hair. Sadness washes over me because all I can think about is my own children – again. I'm obsessed, I know I am, but I can't help it. I'd still rather be at home than here, working.

I hear a scream, then I see the woman splashing in the water with her baby. Without a second thought I dive straight in to the deep end and swim towards them. I can't see. I reach around for the infant and miss. For a flash of a moment, I see Jessica's fine baby hair and that red hat, the only thing left behind. Everything seems dark now, like I'm being whirled in the water and weed is gathering around my ankles pulling me deeper. I jolt back into action and come up shaking. I can't let this baby down, not like I did Jessica. My heart pounds as I reach out and snatch the little one in my arms.

I can't stop shaking and I hold the baby closely, fearing that I might drop him or I'll slip. For a second, I thought that the baby might die and it would be my fault. If I'd had my eye on the pool instead of being consumed with my own thoughts, I'd have been in there quicker. A tear builds up in my eye but the water dripping off me conceals it as it bursts and runs down my cheek.

'What the hell are you doing?' The mother snatches baby Jake from me and holds him to her chest.

'He was drowning. You shouted. I saw—' The eye sees what it wants to see. I realise what I've done.

'We were playing and you scared the life out of us.'

Baby Jake begins to bawl, his face getting redder with every piercing scream.

'Playing. I'm so sorry. I just heard you scream and—'

'And you didn't think to look.' She stroked her baby's head. 'It's okay, Jake. Shush.'

I had Jess on my mind but I couldn't tell her that. Glancing around, the muscular man shakes his head and leaves. The woman gets out of the pool bouncing Jake on her hip, grabs her towel and heads towards the changing rooms, shaking her head and muttering to herself.

'I'm sorry,' I call again but it makes no difference. She tuts and hurries away. I can still hear the baby bawling his eyes out from here. What have I done?

As I reached into that water, I saw Jessica. It was as if I'd entered another world, one where I had a chance of saving her. But then... it wasn't her. Tears slip down my cheeks. If Jake had died, or I hadn't been able to reach him on time... Swallowing, I wipe my face. That didn't happen. In fact, all the upset had been my fault.

If only someone had done that for Jessica. If only I could have saved my sister.

As I close my eyes to get my breath back. I imagine jumping into a bottomless ocean, so vast that it would be impossible to find anything or anyone. It's not blue like people always imagine. It's more like the waves have disturbed the seabed. Sand and grit are coming at me from all angles. Through the murkiness, I see my baby sister and the more I swim towards her, the further away she gets.

'Kate.' Nadine, the receptionist, is standing at the door. 'Oh, Kate. What happened?'

I go to talk but instead I sob. Nadine runs over, her hair escaping into my sodden eyes as she hugs me even though I'm soaked through and smell of chlorine. 'Come on, sweetie. It's all going to be fine.'

'It's not going to fine. I'm in such big trouble. What have I done?' Gripping her arm, I'm so thankful that she's here. I want to tell her about the message I received and the article, but she doesn't know the significance of today.

'Erm, Kate.' Brett stands at the door and Nadine releases me. 'Boss told me to step in. He wants to see you in his office.'

I swallow, knowing that I'm in huge trouble. My manager won't care one bit about my personal life, not when the safety of our customers depends on me being present. I lost concentration in a job where losing concentration can cost lives, and now I have to accept the consequences.

THREE

KATE

I hurry out of my manager's office in my soaking wet clothes before bursting into tears. The woman made a complaint and I have been issued with a first warning. From now on, I get to stay behind a desk, booking people in, while Mr Croft decides what to do with me.

'Kate, what happened?' Nadine brushes down her smart grey hotel-issued suit and furrows her brows.

'I got a warning.'

'Kate, everyone here has had a warning at some point. Croft is a miserable git. You misread a situation but better to jump in and help than to sit back and wait.' Her concerned smile warms me slightly. At least she's on my side. She's trying to make me feel better but I also appreciate that Croft was right. I should have had my mind on the job. 'Come through to the back, you look like you need a drink.'

She leads me through to the office behind reception, then she flicks the kettle on. I remain standing, not wanting to dampen her chair, and check my phone while she spoons some coffee into the cups.

'Are you okay?'

What am I meant to say? I'm dwelling on a message about my dead baby sister. My dad knew that an article was going to be published today, on the anniversary of her death, and he failed to tell me. Should I mention that I spend all day anxious about my children? That I think the nursery will lose Millie or that Rosie will escape from school. I want to be with them all day, all of the time. I trust myself and I trust Damien to look after them. If anyone else were to look after them, I'd feel like my insides were churning. 'I will be. I just want to forget today. I feel like such an idiot.'

'You're definitely not an idiot.' She places the hot steaming drink in front of me.

'I totally lost it and I don't know how I messed up so badly.'

'It can happen to the best of us.'

'And now I'm on desk and cleaning duties. I'm going to spend all my time picking up dirty plasters from the changing rooms and checking people into the pool, and I'll never get another job.' I realise I've gone off on one.

'Just keep your head down and it'll all blow over. I'm sure you won't be picking up plasters forever.'

'Thank you.' I've only spoken to Nadine a few times but I like talking to her. I open my phone again and she catches sight of my screen saver.

'Aww, they're gorgeous. How old?'

'Four and five.'

'Lovely ages. Wait until they turn into teens. My two spend all day hating me and glued to Minecraft. Hold on to them for as long as you can. Are they enjoying school?'

Nodding, I take a sip of coffee. 'Yes. Rosie started primary in September and Millie is in the nursery class still.' I stop talking and stare at the floor.

'I can tell there's more bothering you. You know how good I am at listening.'

'How did you feel when yours started school or nursery?'

Nadine let out a snort followed by a little laugh. 'It broke my heart into a million pieces. With each of them, I cried like a baby.' She pauses and looks at me. 'Then I realised that they were having the time of their lives. They'll be playing with other children all day, getting tired out so you can enjoy some downtime at night, and I hate to say it but they're probably not missing you. My little terrors didn't even want to come home when I picked them up. Ungrateful gits.' She shrugs. 'I don't think I've asked you this before but what got you into swimming?'

'In my teens, I swam for my school and I loved the thrill of the race. I have a few medals. I trained as a swimming teacher. It's all I ever wanted to do and now I've ruined my career.'

Damien had encouraged me to take up swimming again and I did for awhile when I was teaching the girls. I remember them kicking their legs while holding on to the pool gutter. Within weeks, they progressed from using the pool noodle to doing the doggy paddle. At their young ages, both can now do breast-stroke and front crawl. They will never drown, I have made sure of that.

Nadine places a hand on my back and tilts her head. 'It'll all be okay. No one was hurt and you haven't blown it. Things will feel better in the morning after you've slept on it. If you had really put any lives at risk, he'd have sacked you. All you did was startle a mother. No harm done.' She paused and smiled. 'A swimming pro. I should have known, I mean look at you.' Her sleek black hair falls forward as she points. 'Those arms, I can tell they have strength. Not like mine.' She lifts hers up and wobbles the flesh just below her blouse sleeve. 'I jiggle and I can tell you don't. I see the way you lift those crates of towels and I totally covert your toned legs, but I covert cake more.'

'You're funny.' Nadine does cheer me up.

'I know. I'm definitely the funniest person in this building so if you want to have a laugh, always sit with me at lunchtimes.'

I know I'm frowning as the tension in my forehead is a clue. I should leave her office and take a shower before I head out to pick the girls up.

'Have I upset you?'

'No, sorry. It's me.' I blurt it out. 'My sister drowned, twenty-five years ago today. My mind was on that while I was watching the pool. She was only a baby.'

Nadine tilts her head. 'I'm so sorry. That's why you learned to swim so well.'

'And that's why I can't bear my children being out of my sight. Leaving them kills me every day but I have to try to make things normal for them.' I shake my head and force a smile, hoping that I haven't said too much. 'Look at me with my pity party. I've only been here a few weeks and I'm already sharing my life's misery with you.' Shaking my head, I smile.

'I know what will help. Cake. I know there's a stash in the cupboard. Chocolate or carrot? Say carrot and we can't be friends. Vegetables don't belong in cake.' She turns around to rummage through the snack cupboard. Crisps and packets of biscuits begin to fall out.

'What's the time?'

Nadine checks her watch. 'Almost three-thirty.'

'Damn.' I grab my keys and bag. 'I'm late picking the girls up. I have to go.'

'Then go. We can do cake another day.'

'Thank you.'

I run out of the door in my damp clothes, passing several people entering the hotel. My car is at the back of the car park in the staff area and I can't get there fast enough. My girls – they need me. Millie can't get out of nursery until I actually get there, but with Rosie, it's different. I know a teacher normally waits with the children but what if they left her because it's so windy and chilly. Maybe the teacher didn't notice her because I know Rosie likes to sit on the dwarf wall that is enshrouded by bushes. She's on her own and scared, I can feel it. My heart pounds as my mind's eye feeds me images of her leaving the playground to look for me after the teacher has gone back into the school. My worst nightmare is coming true. She knows the route home. Maybe she tried to walk. A twig almost hits me as a gust of wind propels it in my direction. A few raindrops begin to fall. Rosie – someone has taken her, I know it. It'll all be my fault if she's gone.

My phone rings so I answer on hands-free as I start the engine. 'Hello.'

'Kate, where are you?' Damien sounds concerned.

'I'm on my way. Has the school called?'

'The nursery has. I'm just leaving to get Millie now.'

'Something's happened to her, I know it.' My heart is banging in my chest.

'Kate, calm down. I'm sure Rosie's—'

I cut the connection. She's not fine. The school hasn't called. I press my foot on the accelerator and speed out of the car park, nearly crashing into a car entering. Slamming on my brakes, I take a deep breath and start again as the man mouths angry words at me.

When I take my mind off the things that are important to me, bad things happen. Really bad things.

FOUR

NATALIE

Natalie started to pack up for the day. Every man and his dog had wanted their finest Cornish ice cream, despite the wind howling the way it had been all week. That's what happens after a death. People sympathy buy. She thought people might avoid her with them not knowing what to say but they'd all come out, buying ice cream in support and now she was exhausted. She needed time to nurse a glass of whisky alone while she thought about how Alan's life had been cut short.

He was fit, always up with the birds and ate a healthy diet, but a heart attack got him in the end. Natalie slammed a lid on the chocolate chip, then she pressed it hard as if it were to blame. Ice cream – that had been his only downfall and he'd eaten lots of it. All that sugar and fat got him in the end.

She grabbed the local rag and skimmed the pages until she stopped on the article.

Community in shock as much loved ice-cream man, Alan Thomas, dies of a heart attack.

Why wouldn't the local paper run an article? He'd been a pillar of the community all his life and his parents had owned the shop before him. She scanned through it, all of it good. They didn't see what she saw. Alan was far from the perfect husband.

All day people had popped in with cake. That's what people do when they face the grief of others, they give food and sympathy, both of which made her uncomfortable.

She stared out of the shop window. Transfixed by the power of nature. With this savage landscape on their doorstep, Alan finally died of a heart attack. Not from boating, sea swimming or abseiling – all dangerous pursuits of his in the past.

Danger splashed up the harbour walls, spray hitting any unsuspecting person who strayed too close to the edge. She'd watched the fishing boats being cleaned after their catch, the workers on them swaying back and forth as they washed away the blood and grime of the day.

During happier times in their marriage, they loved to walk around the fish market, taking in the boxes of mackerel, lemon sole and John Dory. That's what it was all about. The dangers and perils of the sea gave them the best seafood. It didn't come much fresher. She reached into the fridge and grabbed the pale and lumpy cottage pie that Laura had made for her. That was as good as it was going to get. She shook her thoughts away. Even after all the accusations she had thrown at Laura when she thought it was her who was having an affair with Alan, Laura had proved she was still her friend. She should be grateful and she was.

She checked her phone to see what the weather was going to be like the next day. Sun always equalled ice-cream sales and she hoped for sun, even in October. If only Alan had life insurance but both of them decided not to bother. Big mistake. The stormy outlook could do one or it was going to be a frugal winter for her. Frugal and now lonely. What a combination. She grabbed a flaked chocolate out of the jar and began eating it as a tear slipped down her cheek. Had he ever loved her? That was a question she'd never be able to ask him now.

She flicked over to another page in the paper and an article caught her attention. Baby Jessica. Twenty-Five Years On. That case had broken her heart at the time. It had broken everyone's heart, but now Jessica was no more than a lesson that the media rehashed now and again to remind people to watch their children when walking by the harbour and on the pier. Today, they were going for it large with it being a big anniversary date. She almost choked on her chocolate as she read it and held the sobs back.

'Damn, Nat. Pull yourself together.' She closed the paper and scrolled through Facebook. So many condolences, she didn't know how she was ever going to get through them, then she stopped on the Remembering Baby Jess page.

Many people believed it was the father's fault for not supervising his baby properly, others speculated as to whether someone else was involved in her drowning. An accidental drowning was believable. Drunk father left in charge of tiny baby. It's so easy to lose concentration for a moment. Shaking her head, she scrolled down the other posts on the page, clicking on some of the comments. Two restaurants had planted adverts under the posts on the page, telling tourists about their daily specials. She let out a sigh, wondering when it became okay to be that morally bankrupt but then again, social media was morally bankrupt in many ways.

She clicked on another picture. A tiny baby with swirls of wispy brown hair and her gummy little mouth filled the profile picture box. Bright eyes and peachy skin. She was a beautiful baby and if she and Alan had had children, she'd have wanted a baby that looked just like Jessica. She often wondered what it would feel like to cradle her own little baby in her arms, a warm bundle that she'd do anything for, but it wasn't to be. After several failed attempts at IVF, their souls had been destroyed and they chose not to try again.

The bell rang and Mary entered, her fifty-five years on the planet not showing on her face at all. Natalie stood erect behind the counter with folded arms.

Mary's black leather jacket had half-slipped off her shoulders to reveal a low-cut leopard-print top. She pulled it back on properly. 'I'll take a box of your finest salted caramel for the pub.'

'Right.'

She looked through her dyed blonde fringe. 'I'm really sorry about Alan. We all loved him.'

You more than most. That's what she wanted to say but instead, she quietly said, 'Thank you.'

Natalie grabbed the large tub and passed it over the counter. 'I'll put it on your account. How's your husband?' She emphasised the word husband but Mary didn't take any notice. Kyle co-owned the local pub, the Old Smuggler, with Mary who often worked in the kitchen or behind the bar.

'Same as, living it up as usual while I do all the hard work.'

'I saw what you put on that page, on Facebook.'

'What?' Mary's neatly defined brows furrowed.

'The Remembering Baby Jess page. It's not the best way to advertise your specials menu. I just had to say, I thought it was heartless.'

'Heartless! I don't know what you're talking about.' She tucked her hair behind her ears.

'This.' Natalie pulled her phone from her pocket and scrolled to the offending post.

Mary grimaced as she read the whole spiel. 'But... I didn't do this. I would never do something this horrible. Damn, what must everyone think of me?'

'It's your pub. You manage social media and it's come from your page.'

She exhaled and shook her head. Blotchy pink patches began to spread from her cheeks. 'Kyle does it now. Damn that drunken prick of a husband.'

'That post needs to go, especially with it being the anniversary of her death. It'll be bad for business. It's in bad taste and I think everyone around here will think so too.'

'I'm sorry that you saw that, but believe me, I had nothing to do with that post. I'd never post something like that. I've got to go.' She headed towards the door shivering as she gripped the tub of ice cream.

'Wait. I thought we could catch up.' What she really wanted was to lure Mary into talking about the things on her mind. 'How's Rachel?' She always liked to talk about her daughter, like any proud mother would. Maybe she'd stay for a chat now.

Mary paused. 'Fit to drop, hormonal, tired. As to be expected. Anyway, I'm sorry again, about Alan, but I have to get back. I need to remove that post.'

'Maybe we can have a drink soon. It's been a long time.' Her once best friend looked sheepish, but then her shoulders dropped.

'Kyle's playing golf on Thursday. Call me later, about nine thirty, the pub should be quieter then and we can arrange to do something.' With that, Mary was gone.

Natalie opened the Facebook page again and looked at Jessica, her insides gnarling, making her nauseous. With one swift press of a button, she closed the app and popped the phone into her pocket. No sense in dwelling on the past, but then again, there was no sense in contemplating the future either. Alan had gone just like that, and so had Jessica.

She stared out at the harbour again, hypnotised by the

stormy waters. The sea was unforgiving of any mistake, no matter how momentary it was.

As she went to lock up, a sandwich board flew across the road outside as a gust of wind caught it. Just like that, the sign had gone from outside the tiny souvenir shop.

Just like that, Jessica had gone all those years ago.

FIVE

KATE

Finally, I pull up on our drive and Millie waves out of the living room window, her coppery waves of hair framing her face.

'Mummy, why are you wet?' Rosie asks, as she waits patiently for me to assist her out of the car.

'I fell in the pool, sweetie.' My hair is firm against my face and clumped together in a block, like I'm a Lego figure.

'Are you mad at me?'

I hurry out of the driver's side of the car and I unbuckle her, then help her out. 'I'd never be mad at you, my beautiful Rose. Mummy's mad at herself for being late.' I bend down to her level and hug her closely. All that panicking was for nothing.

'Mrs Clay said it was okay. I went back in and made you a drawing. You smell funny, Mummy.'

Swallowing, I pull away from her realising how cold I am as my polo shirt sticks to my torso. I shiver. Right now, I stink of chlorine and I know I need to get in and have a shower. I don't know what fear and adrenaline smell like, but I'm probably oozing those too. Getting a warning had been a shock, and it wasn't something I was going to tell Damien. He'd think I was purposely sabotaging my job so that I could stay at home and smother the girls.

'I know I smell, baby. Come on, let's go in and see your dad and sister.' I grip her hand like I never want to let her go.

Damien opens the door, a shocked expression on his face as he takes in the state I'm in. Eyes red and I'm shaking. 'Has something happened?'

He leads me through to the living room. Millie and Rosie run upstairs together, stomping on the landing like baby elephants. I burst into tears and go to sit on the couch but stop myself. I don't want to make everything stink as bad as I do. Damien dashes out into the downstairs toilet and comes back with a towel. I pull my wet polo shirt over my head and wrap the warm towel over my torso. He places another towel on the settee and I sit.

'I thought a baby was drowning, that's why I was late.' I pause. 'I was so scared something had happened to Rosie.' My hands tremble.

He places a hand under my chin and leads my gaze to his. 'You didn't let Rosie down. Rosie's fine, you only have to listen to them playing.' Giggles came from above. 'You saved a baby. That's amazing. You are amazing. Come here.' He wraps me in his arms and I allow all my upset to spill out as I allow him to believe that I saved a baby. 'Do you want to talk about it?'

I shake my head and sniff. What I want to do is talk about how it felt like I was rescuing Jessica from the sea. I want to tell him about the message, but I can't. I promised him that I'd find a way to get over Jessica so that our children would not feel stifled, not dig things up in such a big way. I should have got a different job. The burden of being protector at this level terrifies me but it's all I know. Being a swimming instructor is all I've ever done, but the lifeguard responsibilities, they might be too much.

'Baby Jake is fine.' My sobs subside as I think of his little

face as his mother angrily snatched him off me. 'I'm fine. It was
a shock, that's all. I think I just need a shower, a hot chocolate
and snuggles with my wonderful husband and children.'

He pulls away, a large smile on his face. I take in the
freckles on his fair skin, the same ones that I fell in love with all
those years ago. He's ruggedly handsome with his stubble and
I'm a mess. I inhale the scent of paint that always lingers on him
after a day's work.

'I can make the hot chocolate happen. Why don't I order us
a pizza and we'll have a film night. You go and get cleaned up,
I'll sort the rest out.'

'I love you.'

'I love you too. Now go.'

I feel like a fraud now but I'm comforted by his affection.
Before heading into the bathroom, I peer into the bedroom and
I see the girls playing hospital and bandaging a teddy up. They
really melt my heart. Damien's right. I need to let the past go. I
need to give my girls more freedom to grow. I will find a way to
finally allow Jessica to rest in peace and that message is just like
the rest. Nothing I do will bring her back but I stand to lose all
the precious things I have if I carry on the way I have been, and
I will never risk losing my family.

Before checking my phone, I make sure the bathroom door
is locked. Several messages from work light up. Nadine and
Brett are checking on me, asking if I'm okay. After turning on
the shower, I send quick replies telling them that I'm fine and
that I'll see them tomorrow at work.

My finger brushes on the web browser and I type in Facebook. It's no good, I have to check the page. As I click into that
message, I see the three dots which means the sender of the last
message, Will, is about to reply. The pulse in my head is
banging louder than ever and all I want to do is shout at the
screen for the sender to hurry up. The three dots vanish and my
heart drops. My friend request still hasn't been accepted. I click

onto his profile again. It could even be some bored teenager, like before. *Shut up!* It's probably not even a real profile. I'm getting needlessly carried away again. It's a troll messing with my head. People are like that, they'll revel in your deepest misery. I've seen the darker side of humanity too many times, yet I fall for it over and over again. Even the police have wiped their hands of me on this. He's gone, for now.

Just as I go to step into the shower the three dots appear once again and I stare in hope that a message will come.

I flinch at the knock on the bathroom door. 'Kate, you okay?' Damien waits for an answer.

I drop my phone on a pile of towels face down just in case he walks in, before realising that the door is locked. 'Yes, I'll be five minutes.'

'Great. Pizza will be here soon. I've ordered it. Kettle's on.'

'Thanks, love.'

As I lather my body up, I wonder if Will has finally replied. I'm struggling to dismiss the message as nothing more than a troll. I'd never forgive myself if I didn't take it seriously. My heart is telling me I need to find a way of going back to Looe so that I can find Will. There is something I need to do and the very thought sends sickening flutters through my stomach. I need to see my dad. That article is awful, so awful I don't even want to show it to Damien. Why did my dad have to speak to them? I'm going to have to talk to him about what happened that day and I'll get my answers, once and for all.

SIX
KATE

Wednesday, 12 October

My heart bangs as I pull up at the house I grew up in. Once it had been pretty, with window boxes and flower beds dug into the front lawn. Now, dried up weeds are entangled against the front of the house and the lawn is mud.

I haven't seen my father since my mother's funeral, three years ago, and that was enough. After Jess died, he did nothing but drink. My mother and I were made to feel like intruders in our own home as he slurred and shouted. I couldn't help but resent him as it was his drinking that lost Jessica. As soon as I turned sixteen, I left them, choosing to live in a room above a shop. Mum stood by him and I'll never know why. I remember seeing her brave face as she brushed over his hurtful comments or tried to cover up their arguments, but he had a nasty tongue.

As I take the mossy steps and open the creaky gate, I stop and peer through the bay window. I can't see him but I know he's in. He never went out much when Mum was alive and from what I'd heard from the neighbours I'd kept in touch with, he barely went out now. I glance back, he still has his car but it's parked under a tree on the road, covered in dried up berries and bird muck.

He must have seen the article. If he had, I know he'd be drinking himself into oblivion and I dread what I might find behind that washed-out wooden door.

I move his old rusty pushbike out of the way and hurry to the door. It's not like I have all day, I have to be in work for midday. I swallow, wondering if I did the right thing in not telling Damien that I was visiting Dad. If I told him about Dad, I'd have to tell him about the message and the article. Knowing how I've reacted to things like this in the past, he'd have put his foot down. The last thing he needs is me going off the rails.

Knocking on the door, I step back and wait.

'What?' My dad's angry voice bellows along the stone hall. 'Go away.'

I lift the letter box. 'Dad, it's me. Kate. Please open the door.' I expected to smell alcohol and bodily fluids but I'm surprised to smell lemon.

As soon as I drop the letter box, he's there. 'Kate, come in. I wasn't expecting you.' He has a towel wrapped around his neck, like he's just been having a wash. 'Go through.'

I step further in, not knowing what I'll find but I'm surprised. The kitchen shines as a ray of sunlight glints off the draining board. Taking a seat at the kitchen table, I nervously shuffle. It feels strange to be back and I can't believe I grew up here.

The dink in the wall is still there. My dad can paint over things like that but he can't paint over the terrifying memories of him throwing things around the kitchen, destroying not only the walls but my mother's happiness.

'Do you want a drink? I've got tea and coffee.'

I shake my head. 'No.'

He puts the towel in the washing machine and sits next to me. 'I think I know why you're here.'

Nodding, I unzip my hoodie. 'I saw the article. Why, Dad?'

'I needed to tell my side.'

'And all you did was open it all up again.'

'I know, I know.' He shakes his balding head.

'So why did you do it? You should have told them to call me and ask me about Jess.'

'I needed the chance to put my side over. I'm sick of the hate mail I've received over the years. I've lost friends and even jobs. I know I was a bad person, but that day—'

'I was there.'

'But you were so little.'

'I still remember bits.'

'That argument I'd had with your mother, it got to me. I know I drank too much on that boat and I know I was in a state. She shouldn't have left me with Jess.'

'So you thought it was okay to blame her now that she isn't here.'

'No.'

I flinch as his hand hits the table.

'Sorry, no. I didn't want to live with it any longer and the reporters wouldn't stop calling. It got too much, Katie.'

The moment he calls me Katie, I'm transported back to early childhood. When things were going well, I was always his little Katie and he'd play dolls and ball games with me. How has he gone from the dad I occasionally remember to a bitter and angry alcoholic? 'Are you—?'

'No. I haven't had a drink in a year now. Not a sip. There's none in the house, you can check every cupboard if you want. This is the new me.'

I glance at the cupboard under the sink, the place he used to keep his vodka and cider.

'Have a look.'

Walking over to the cupboard, I open it. Bleach, disinfectant and a few packets of over-the-counter tablets.

'I wanted to call you so many times, Katie, but I knew I needed to prove myself. I'm clean of that poison. I know that I hurt your mum and you and I regret every minute of it. This new me is an honest and open me. I am to blame for everything and I know I can't make amends, but I want to try.'

Staring right into his creased blue eyes, I wonder if he is truly capable of changing. He looks away and walks over to the patio doors, staring out at the overgrown garden. 'How are the little ones? I still have the photos that you texted me.'

'They're great. Growing up so fast.'

'I'd love to see them.'

My muscles tense. He'd have to do a lot more than have a ten-minute chat with me to prove that he was responsible enough to see his grandchildren. I lived in fear as a child at his outbursts and I'll never put Millie and Rosie through that.

'Dad, someone sent a message to Jess's Facebook page. They say that they know what happened to Jess.'

'I've had loads of those. The police don't want to know.'

All these years, my dad has been forwarding messages to the police too.

'They take the details and that's it. As far as they are concerned, Jessica is a closed case and I have to accept that. I was drunk, I fell asleep and I let her fall to her death. I've spent too many years blaming everyone else but myself. A part of my recovery is owning my mistakes, which is why I agreed to speak to that reporter. I can't make up for losing Jess but I can accept my role in her death.'

'What do you remember from that day, when we got off the boat?'

'After getting off, your mother led me to the bench. I was so drunk, I could barely stand. I closed my eyes to try and quell the nausea from the drink and the boat, but I fell asleep. It was only for a couple of minutes. When I opened my eyes, Jess was gone and we were so close to the edge. I rummaged around her baby seat. It wasn't strapped. I couldn't remember whether your mum had strapped it or whether I had.'

I feel my eyes filling up with tears. 'Were Mum and me in the ice-cream shop?'

He nodded. 'You must have been. When your mum came back, she saw me calling up and down but I could barely stand. The police were called but they seemed to take a lifetime to arrive. There was a huge search at the time. Then everyone said that too much time had been spent working on the idea that someone had taken her. CCTV through the town had showed nothing, no stolen babies being carried away. Too much time had been wasted when they should have been looking for her in the sea. The police concluded that Jessica had probably got caught up in rope or net under a boat, before being dragged out to sea. She drowned, Kate. I let my baby drown all because I got drunk after having a stupid argument with your mother.' He began to sob.

I've never seen my dad like this and a part of me wants to go over and hug him. I want to feel like his little Katie again, but I can't. I blame him and I can't get that out of my head. I blame him for Jess and my turbulent upbringing. I blame him for making Mum miserable. 'What did you and Mum argue about?'

'She didn't want to go on the boat trip. That's all it was. She was fed up because I was already half drunk before we got on. My fault. She was right to be angry at me.'

'I miss Mum.' I want to tell him how much it hurts that I never came to see her after I left, that I didn't come because of him. She chose him and his drunken moods over me and I resented that. I shook away the other reason, the one that pointed the finger at me. Maybe my dad was all about facing up to his wrongs but I wasn't there yet.

'I miss her, too. I wish she were here now so she could see

how much I've changed. I am now the husband she deserved but she's no longer here to see it.'

He places a hand on mine as I weep but I pull it away. Instead I get my phone out of my bag and see that I have a missed call from Damien. A message pings through telling me that he'll pick up some more milk on his way home and that I don't have to.

'What are you going to do about that message?'

'Not go to the police, that's for sure. I have to go there, to see for myself if it's real. I just don't know when.' Or how, I forgot that bit. How can I convince Damien that we need to go to Looe? Something about this message feels different, so certain. The message is to the point, not like the others. Besides, the police don't want to know any more and I can't let this message go without knowing if it's real.

'Don't do anything dangerous. This person could be some sort of weirdo. Jess is dead, love. Nothing can be gained by going back.'

Tears fall and I can't stop them. I leave my Dad and run upstairs to the bathroom so that I can sort myself out. I don't want his love or his tenderness, not now. It doesn't feel right. I need some space. Slamming the door behind me, I sit on the loo seat and blow my nose. Gazing around, I can see that the bath shines and the sink is clean. I've never known my dad to be like he is now. Never.

Hurrying back down, I walk into the kitchen and see him holding my phone and scrolling through photos.

'Sorry, Katie. I saw your screen saver and I wanted to see what the girls look like now.'

I snatch it back. How dare he invade my privacy like that? He only had to ask. My dad pulls out a small box and in it are some photos. 'I thought you might like to look at these. You can take them with you. Your mother kept them in the loft and refused to look at them again after that holiday.'

I pick one up and it's of my mum holding Jess with me tugging on her skirt. 'Where was this taken?'

'Outside the cottage where we stayed. Will you come and see me again?'

I grab the box and hurry to the front door. This is all too much.

'Will you?' he calls as he catches me up.

I can't answer that. Glancing back at him as I open the front door, I try to see right through him but I can't. Can a man like him ever change?

Everything's closing in on me. I need to get away from this house, from the memories and from him, so I run as fast as I can as he calls after me. No, I won't be coming back – ever.

SEVEN

NATALIE

Thursday, 13 October

Mary said she'd visit her apartment above the shop but that didn't happen and now it's too late. She'd be working at the pub now. She checked her messages and not even a sorry had come through. Tonight should have been Natalie's opportunity to air all that was whirring in her mind but she'd been denied that.

Slamming the door closed, she locked up, ready to go for a walk, leaving her lifeless shop and apartment behind. Grief did that, made a home feel empty. So-called friends had come and gone for days but now, her loss was really starting to hit. Laura hadn't called her back. Maybe Natalie was destined to be stuck with that old ceramic pie dish forever. Mary was a no-show.

Loss, that was a joke. She'd lost something that wasn't real. Their whole life together had been one great big lie.

'Alright, Nat. It's good to see you out and about.' Cody stepped off his boat and zipped up his jacket. His peppered hair mussed up from a day running boat trips.

'Yes, I suppose.' What could she say? No, I'm not alright.

'Good day for October.' He patted the money pouch that was tied around his waist.

'Yes, it's been mild. I wish this stormy weather would do one though. How's your dad?'

Cody shrugged. 'Getting worse, but what can you do?'

'Sorry to hear that.'

'You know, no one ever asks about him. Thanks. I appreciate it.' Cody paused and momentarily bit his bottom lip. Natalie hadn't asked for years and suddenly a pang of guilt washed through her. Soon people would start forgetting to ask her how she was. Alan's fatal heart attack would be history. Cody continued. 'I miss working with him on the boat, before all that... you know. He never stepped on the boat much after. The trauma of the car accident, his health problems and that poor little baby drowning. Bad memories. I read the article, brought it all back for me.'

'That was a long time ago.'

'I know and I wish we could all be left to move on. I was just thinking about it, about him before the accident. It used to be great hanging out at the harbour. It was us, Mary and Kyle, and Old Mr Pritchard back then, bless his sweary soul. Mr P was a character. We dominated boat trips around here. Such good times and Dad, he used to love taking the families fishing. It's what he lived for.'

'Yes, it was a shame that everything happened the way it did. Tell old Archie I send my regards. I do think about him.' Truth be told, Natalie had spent the whole night thinking about Archie and she knew she needed to visit him, but first she needed to straighten things out in her head. Archie had a lot to answer for but she had to keep what she'd heard to herself for now.

'I can try. He does have the occasional lucid moment but they're becoming few and far between. I tried to tell him about

Alan but it didn't sink in.' Cody stayed silent for a few seconds and checked his watch. 'Is that the time? Best get home. Missus wants me to be back for tea tonight and our Daisy is cooking, which makes a change.' He let out a laugh.

'Have a good one.' Before Natalie had finished speaking, Cody was heading home – to his lovely home and his daughter who always sat down to tea with him. Natalie swallowed, wishing that she had that warmth at home, but that was never going to happen and it was Alan's fault. If only she could have her time all over again, adopted maybe. Seeing all of his texts and emails had opened her eyes. Her whole life had been a lie and she'd sacrificed so much.

Darkness had fallen and the tide was getting higher. The slight breeze blew the fairy lights that lit up the harbour, casting twinkly shadows on the pavement. Before she knew it, she was striding down the narrow paths, passing all the closed shops and bustling restaurants and takeaways. She stopped in an alleyway, watching through the window of the Old Smuggler. She wondered if Mary was in there, or whether she was upstairs with her husband. No pain was greater than that of knowing that someone you love had been giving their all to someone else.

That's why Alan had avoided the Old Smuggler and he'd told her not to go in too, stating that he didn't get along with Kyle. It had nothing to do with Kyle. Mary's husband had been deceived as much as Natalie had. She was going in. Alan was gone and he couldn't tell her what to do or where she could go. She was sick of secrets. She wondered why people were happy to live a lie. Mary had been living a lie; Archie had too. Everyone she knew was putting up a façade. This town was carrying a sickness and it was getting sicker by the minute. Too many people had been hurt and that article had probably already started to ruffle some feathers.

She hurried across the road and pushed open the door, stepping in with all the bravado she could muster. Her gaze flitted across the room. Several families, a bar that was two people deep and a group of people with dogs sitting around the fire-place, filled the pub. Frank Sinatra sang about New York on the jukebox. She inhaled the hoppy smell and her mouth watered slightly at the thought of downing an ale. Maybe she should have a couple of drinks for Alan. He did like a drink.

There was no sign of Mary, Kyle or Rachel. The staff who worked for them were quite happily running the place alone. She nudged her way through the drinkers, before grabbing her purse and waiting to be served. Her planned outburst was now choking in her throat. With no one to tell, the sick nerves cloying in her gut had fallen flat. All she was left with was an emptiness that had become so familiar it was spreading like mould. Besides, Kyle didn't deserve that. It was a good job they weren't there.

'Mrs Thomas, you don't come in here much. What can I get you?' The girl's blonde ponytail flicked as she turned to her. She couldn't remember her name but she'd been buying ice creams from Alan since she was a nipper.

'Thought I'd check this place out. I never come in. I'll have a Hell's Stone, make it a double.' Only a large whisky would cut it tonight. Forget the ale.

'Coming up. We're all really sorry about Alan. He was a top guy. We all loved him.'

She pressed her lips together in a smile. 'Thank you, that means a lot.'

As the young woman grabbed the bottle and began to measure out the whisky, Natalie continued speaking. 'Is... err, Mary around tonight. She was meant to come over to mine earlier.'

'I'm afraid she's not.'

She swallowed. 'Do you know when she'll be in?'

She scrunched her nose up. 'Nah. That would be tricky to tell. Rachel was taken into hospital after going into labour earlier. Mary and Kyle left several hours ago and we haven't had any more news yet.' She grabbed a jar. 'We're having a collection to get Rachel a gift for the baby. Wanna contribute? We're trying to get her a car seat.' The girl smiled.

She fished around in her pockets, her anger evident as she poked in the corners. Had Alan turned to someone else because she couldn't give him what he wanted more than anything?

'You don't have to.' The girl went to withdraw the jar just as she pulled out a ten-pound note from the depths of her pocket.

'Wait. It's not much but I want to wish Rachel all the best.' She dropped the money in the jar, swigged back the whisky in one go and left enough money to cover the drink and a tip on the bar. None of this was Rachel's fault. She didn't even turn around when the girl said bye and thank you.

The hum of chatter became distant as she navigated the tight windy roads, finally ending up by the lifeboat centre. She gasped for breath as she hurried towards Banjo Pier. The lapping of waves normally calmed her but now, all they did was make her anxious. Everyone was getting on with their lives except her, and she hated it. She didn't want to be alone.

She could end it all now by plunging into the cold sea. It would take minutes as she could barely swim. Everything was gone so what was the point? She stared down into the swirling inky darkness as she walked further up the pier, her balance a little off after necking the strong liquor. Warmth flooded her face although her nose was numb. Ferocious splashes of sea spray slammed against the rocks creating a flurry of light as the moon caught the crests. Edging closer to the sea she stood still, toes over the side of the pier. All she had to do was fall and it would all be over.

She shivered at what she knew about the day baby Jessica went missing, and it wasn't just about Mary and Alan. She knew who was spotted with Jessica's red sun hat in this exact spot. She alone had heard the conversation that let that bit of information out of the bag and maybe it was time to tell. Reading that article had brought her to tears. Jess's parents hadn't even mentioned the hat back then, not until it had washed up in the harbour. Again, she thought of Archie.

The burden of keeping what she knew a secret was crushing.

A gust of wind sent her heart to her mouth as she almost toppled over the side to her death. Instead she fell back onto her bottom and lay there on the wet path staring up at the stars. Her phone buzzed. Without hesitating, she snatched it up and answered. 'Mary.'

'I'm so sorry, Nat. Rachel went into labour and I barely have a signal at the hospital.'

'Congratulations.' She listened to the sound of crying babies in the background and wondered if one of them was Rachel's. Her heart felt hollow as she thought of something pleasant to say to the woman who'd been sleeping with her husband. She'd suspected for a long time. Not having a life outside the shop has its advantages. Natalie had time to watch people, to hang around corners listening to other people speak, to follow people; to follow Mary when she thought she was meeting with Alan and vice versa. She'd heard all Cody's phone conversations while the man set up in the mornings. Mary didn't realise how her voice carried out of her backyard. And with Kyle being merry all the time, he talked too loud. Natalie never had to be that close to hear everything. The burden she was carrying was weighing her down and the only way she'd be able to breathe again was to talk. A person can't live with these kind of secrets, or they'll eventually explode.

'Nat? Are you okay?'

She had slurred a little. As someone who never really drank, that whisky had gone straight to her head. 'I know things.'

'You know what?' Mary paused.

'I know this town's dirty little secret, Mary, and it's not just your affair with my dead husband. This is big but you all know that. Everyone knows. I can tell by the way you give each other those knowing looks. Archie, he knows, doesn't he?'

'Nat, what are you talking about?'

'Nothing.' She ended the call. She would show them all but to do that she'd need to book a visit with Archie at his residential home. Reaching out, she let her fingers sink into a puddle. She wept for Jessica, for herself and for all the time she'd wasted on her cheating husband.

EIGHT

KATE

Saturday, 15 October

Five days have passed and I haven't had any more messages from Will. I shouldn't have sent him a load of messages but since visiting my dad and looking through those photos, I feel spurred on to find out more. Several times I've checked and quite often I see the three dots come up. Someone is at the other end reading all the replies that I've sent. Maybe I've scared him off.

Please if you know something about my little sister, I need to know.

Will, you want to tell me what you know or you wouldn't have messaged me. Jessica needs to be laid to rest. My family and I need closure.

Will, do you have children? Do you have grandchildren? Imagine if one day, one of them vanished and you never heard from them again. Imagine the heartache and the hurt. Nothing hurts more than losing a child whether that child is your sister, your baby, your grandchild.

Will, if you need to tell me something in confidence, you can? We don't have to meet. I can give you my email address or my phone number. Whatever it is you need, you can have it.

Please, Will, please. I can't bear that you're not replying. I can see that you want to say something. You keep going to reply, then you don't. You know how Jessica really died and you want to tell me, I know you do.

Will, who are you?

Talk to me, Will.

This is killing me. I beg of you, please tell me what happened.

I hit send on another message.

Did you hurt her, Will? If you did something by accident, I'm sure you didn't mean it. The police don't need to be involved.

I glance over all my messages to Will. Not one reply. I sound desperate because I am desperate. The more I tell myself it's a hoax, the more I disbelieve it. If the sender was some joker getting off on my misery, I think they'd be long gone. The little dots wouldn't keep coming up. To me, that says whoever is at the other end of this profile wants to talk but is finding it hard. I might even be talking to the person who killed Jessica. Maybe as someone passed they accidentally knocked her in. Either way, what I really need is the truth now. I'm prepared to communicate with a potential murderer to find out what happened. *I know what happened to your sister.* Those words don't leave my head. I stare at the ceiling in the middle of the night, in the dark, wondering who sent them. Just as I'm about to close Facebook, I see those three dots again and the words I've longed to see. Will is typing. As I wait, I find I'm twiddling the gold bracelet with the word Mum engraved on it, the one the girls got me for my last birthday.

A message flashes up.

> *I will only speak to you in person. Come to Looe and message me when you arrive. Tell no one about me, or I'll vanish and you'll never know the truth.*

'Hey, I called you three times. The girls are ready.' I flinch and stand as Damien enters. I wonder if he can hear my heart banging away as I feel the weight of what Will has said.

'I was just coming.' I pop my phone in my coat pocket, frustrated that I can't see if I have a reply.

'What were you doing?'

'I, err, ran out of my hand cream, you know the stuff I use. I was just ordering some more.' I rub my hands and grimace. 'My skin is itching a bit from all the chlorine at the pool.' Forcing a smile I hurry towards him, kiss his lips and hurry down the stairs. The lies are coming too easy now. I should tell him that I saw my dad, instead I hide the photos under my bed. I should tell him about the message I've just received, but I can't.

'Come on, Mummy. We've been waiting ages.' Millie sucks the end of her ponytail after ticking me off.

'Yes, Mummy. You promised you'd push me on the swing.' Rosie's bottom lip covers her top lip as she fakes a grumpy look.

Damien zips his jacket up. It's not the best day for the park but at least it's not cold.

'I am so going to push you as high as the sky on those swings. Come on, let's go.'

As I walk through the estate with my family, the urge to pull out my phone and reread that message is driving me mad. The girls run ahead, chattering away in their high-pitched voices and Damien grabs my hand. My fingers lock into his as if they've always belonged there. As the girls skip, I'm reminded of how lucky I am and they deserve for me to be present.

'They're beautiful, aren't they?'

'Just like their mother.' He kisses me as we walk, his lips meeting the side of my head. I wish that I could fully immerse myself in this moment, but my other hand grips my phone and all I want him to do is give me a few seconds to check my messages again.

'Daddy, come and get us.'

Millie runs away screaming, then Rosie follows. My opportunity is about to come.

'I'll count to three and give you a head start. One... two... three!'

They scream and he runs.

'The daddy monster is coming to get you.' He runs with his arms outstretched making the monster noises that always make the girls giggle.

As they turn onto another path, I slow down on purpose. I can still hear the girls screaming and Damien roaring. With trembling fingers, I click onto my messages and read Will's reply again. It isn't a hoax; it can't be. I have to find a way of getting Damien on board for a trip to Looe. Reaching out, I grab someone's garden fence and take a deep breath as I read it again.

'Mummy, hurry up.' My red-cheeked Rosie runs up to me and barges into my side.

'Coming, sweetie.' Dropping the phone in my pocket, I stop and try to control my emotions before I turn that corner and

Damien sees me. Exhaling, I proceed to paste a smile on my face.

'Hurry up,' Damien calls back as he runs towards the round-about with Millie, his face full of glee. I couldn't have asked for a better father for my children. I only hope that I don't let him down as a mother with my lies, but I need to know the truth. The park will give me time to figure out how I get us all to Looe. More lies, but is it a lie when you only want the truth?

NINE

KATE

'I've got a bit of a sore head, do you mind if I go for a lie-down for half an hour?'

I grab two paracetamol and down them with a glass of water. I've set my lie up nicely by telling Damien that I wasn't feeling too well at the park. It feels calculated and that's not me but it's the only way I can try to find more out about Will, who doesn't have anything useful for me to see on his Facebook profile. No posts, no visible friends. Nothing at all. He's like a ghost. That last message won't leave my head though and I can't concentrate on anything else.

''Course, love. Go up. Me and the girls can watch a bit of telly. I'll put dinner on in about an hour.'

'You're wonderful, do I say that often enough?' I'm grateful that he gives me space if I need it. I kiss him and smile.

'I'm proud of you.'

Scrunching my brows, I wait for him to say more. If he knew what I'd been doing he'd be as mad as hell. 'Don't be silly.' I'm not proud of me, I don't see why he would be and if he knew what I was going upstairs to do, he'd be disappointed. I clear my throat and step back a little.

'Closing that page must have been hard and I know you're probably thinking about it all the time but it'll get easier, I promise. The last thing you need is all the cranks coming out of the woodwork all the time.'

Now I feel awful. I have my nose buried in that page more often than ever. I have changed its settings to secret, which feels even more deceitful. If he's tempted to set up an account to check on me, it won't be there.

'I've been thinking about that.'

He pulls away and his stare meets mine. He's worried that I've let him down so I need to reassure him somehow. 'You know you said I need to find closure, with Jess.' My voice crackles a little as I say her name.

'Yes.' He scratches his stubble.

'I want to go there, to Looe, to say goodbye once and for all. We never have to go again after that. It's been twenty-five years and I want to say a final goodbye.'

He leans on the door frame and I stare out of the kitchen window, focusing on the barely used playhouse that looks like it's seen better days.

'Don't you think that would be too painful? Won't it just bring everything up again?'

'I have to be there to say my final goodbye. It will be painful but it will also help me. I need this and I need you there with me. We can tell the girls about Jessica, too. I know we said we never would but I want them to know about my little sister. She's a part of who I am and it feels wrong to never mention her, even if it might upset them and me. Maybe we can all say some lovely words and throw some petals in the water to remember her by.'

He pours a glass of water from the filter jug and drinks half of it down. 'If you think it would help.'

My heart is thrumming. I throw my arms around his neck, kissing him on his cheek, nose and mouth. 'Thank you.'

'It's half-term soon, why don't you see if you can find us a cottage to rent? Book the week off work and I'll rearrange the jobs I have on that week. Let's do this, then we can finally start looking to the future.'

'I love you.'

'Now, go and have that lie-down. We'll tell the girls later.'

I hurry up to the bedroom and check my messages again but there's nothing more. Adrenaline surges through me. I pull the photos out from under the bed and I look at the photo of me, Mum and Jess again. Not only do I need to go back to Looe, I need to go back to that cottage and stay there. The name plaque is prominent. Sea View Cottage. I search the net and find that it has its own website and it's also my lucky day. It's available for that week. I quickly put all my details into the booking form and then I pay the balance.

Losing my sister like that has left a huge hole in my heart. Too many people have said I should move on but growing up was painful. The loss she left behind hung in the air. Every birthday party I had was a reminder to us all that Jess never had one party. We'd gone from having a cooing and crying baby in the house to this deafening emptiness. My mother would lie in bed for days on end around Jess's birthday. No one saw any of that. And, of course, my dad would drink even more as he'd sink into a guilt-ridden stupor.

Going back might all be for nothing but I have to know that for sure. I'm going back to where it all started and I'm going to find out the full truth of that day. That article has led Will to contact me and I'm not letting this lead go.

TEN

KATE

That message – *I will only speak to you in person. Come to Looe and message me when you arrive. If you talk to anyone about me, I'll vanish and you'll never know the truth.* It won't leave my mind however hard I try. I wanted a reply, I badgered Will for a reply and, now I have one, I don't know how I feel.

All this might be a lure, maybe whoever took Jess wants me now. I shake those thoughts away. It's probably someone who's burdened by the guilt of what they know. Guilt works like that. It never stops reminding you that the course of tragedy could have been averted if it wasn't for you. Again, guilt gnaws at me. It's easy for people to say that it was a long time ago and that I was only a child, but that doesn't stop me thinking about my part in Jess's disappearance. My mother was never the same with me after and her coldness continued up until her death. That was another reason I had to leave home as soon as possible. Every day was a reminder of what had happened to Jess. I could never match up to the baby girl that had died and I tried so hard to be loveable, but my mother's grief won in the end.

The way everyone saw it was my father was so drunk that he shouldn't have been left in charge of himself by the harbour's edge, let alone a baby. Although my mother stayed with him, she could never forgive him for losing Jess, so he drank even more to blot out the memories. I couldn't forgive him and I know Mum couldn't forgive me.

A rush of panic chokes my lungs and I let out a yelp. The hurt I felt growing up is still there. It never leaves. Quickly, I place my hand over my mouth to muffle the sounds of the sobs that I'm trying to suppress. I never want to go back to that house again. It's a sad house, full of sorrow, full of past memories that I can't get past.

I don't want to think back to that day, but I can't help it.

When my mother left Jess and Dad to take me for an ice cream, there was a man in the shop. I don't remember what he looked like but I do remember his necklace as I said loudly that I could see the boobies on the female figure pendant that dangled from his neck. The memories are vague and I think had mostly been filled in by my mother, who went over what happened that day with me many times. She says that she told me to shush before she apologised, but the man said something about a pixie called Joan. I read up about her, hoping for a clue. Joan the Wad is the queen of the pixies or piskies, which is how it's said there. Joan carries a torch, which is the wad so she can light the way. He must have seen something. The necklace wasn't the only thing about him, he wore a silly pirate hat and held his elasticated eye patch in his hand. I think he may have been skipper on our boat but I'm not sure. He was there that day and he left the shop before we did. Maybe he is Will.

Damien has given his full blessing for us to go to Looe. I will speak to whoever is calling themselves Will and I will finally get the truth. This can't be a hoax. It has to be real.

Can I trust Will? I ask that question again. What if over the years I've got a little closer to the truth and someone is luring me there to finally shut me up. I shake my head. Even I don't think anyone could be that cruel. I have to have some faith that Will is trying to help me or what's the point. A part of me is shouting, don't go, but I will. I have to.

It's getting chilly in the bedroom so I pull the quilt over my body and reach down under the bed. I push the box of photos that my dad gave me aside and I reach for my jewelled memory box. My nan gave it to me when she was alive. As I open it, it releases a musty smell that takes me back to Nan's living room. Photos of her and Gramps when they were younger spill out. They provided such a loving home for my dad. I feel around the bottom and pull out an old brooch and an odd pearl earring. Then, I feel the cardboard surround at the bottom, the photo of Jess. Pulling it out, I hold it up. Then I grab the family photo. Some time ago, it must have got damp. The edge of the photo is tainted and my mum's face is almost blurred out. I hate this photo as I look miserable. I'd been crying. My mother is gripping baby Jess in her arms and I am pulling her hard, like I want her to hold me too.

'I'm sorry for being miserable, Jess.' I don't know why I said that. It's not like she can hear me.

My dad looks distant, his pupils dilated and his nose a veiny red. I hope he's finally faced his demons and changed.

I shove that photo back under the others and I stare at the one of Jess. She's positioned on her front, knees tucked under her tummy with her sleeping head gently placed on her doll-sized hands. Her flower headband and frilly nappy cover make her look like a tiny cherub and I just want to hold her and take in her baby smell. Instead I smell the photo and all I get is Nan's cigarette smoke-filled lounge.

'Love you, Jess.' I've missed out on having a sister to play with, to fight with, and to share make-up with.

The door bursts open and Rosie runs in and jumps on the bed. I place the box on the floor and pop the photo of Jess on my bedside table. 'Hello, sweetie. Is everything okay?'

'Millie won't play with me. Will you play with me, Mummy?'

I hold her tightly and kiss her tangled mass of hair. Her hands are wandering and before I know it, she's reached for the photo of Jess and her red-tinged brows furrow.

'Can Mummy have that?' I don't want to take it from her in case I tear it. The photos I have of Jess are precious as I have very few.

'This isn't me or Millie.'

'No, sweetie.'

'She looks like a dolly, Mummy. Is it you when you were a baby?'

I shake my head. There's no time like now to introduce Jess to Rosie. I'll take the photo downstairs later and show Millie too when Damien and I tell the girls about our half-term plans. 'That's my sister, Jess.'

'Don't be silly, Mummy. You haven't got a sister.'

'I did have a sister. I'm sorry I never told you about her.'

'Where is she?'

I shrug.

'Did she run away or get lost?' Her child's mind makes things sound so simple. 'Maybe she'll come back.'

'She was in an accident not long after this photo was taken.'

Rosie places her finger on the photo and traces Jess's outline, then she places that finger in her mouth. 'What kind of accident?'

'She went missing a long time ago.' I grip Rosie harder as I think of how dangerous the sea is. I swim like a champ but even I don't go in the sea. The very thought makes me sick to the stomach after what happened. My daughter seems unaffected by the news as if Jess isn't real. Then, I remember, Jess isn't real to her. I have to bring her to life.

'Jess was a smiley baby and ultra-cute, just like you. If she

was alive now, I know she would have been a lovely aunty and
she would have loved you and Millie.'

'That's sad. Can we put her photo in a frame?' My child's
lovely comment touches my heart and I have to bite back a sob.

'Yes, that would be lovely. We'll get a special frame for
Aunty Jess.'

'A sparkly one?'

'Yes, a very sparkly frame.'

'Did she die in the accident?'

I shrug my shoulders. 'People think she fell into the sea. She
was never found.'

Rosie grips me and buries her head in my chest. I drag a
snuggle blanket over her and hope that I'm doing all I can to
make her feel safe. 'That's very sad. Maybe she swam out and
she lives with the mermaids.'

'Maybe.' I need answers and I'd like my children to know
what happened too. While cuddling Rosie, I flick through
pictures of the cottage again. I can't remember much but I'm
hoping that being there might bring everything back.

I'm coming to find you, Jess.

ELEVEN

KATE

Saturday, 22 October

'Can we see the sea today, Mummy?'

I smile at Millie and pass her a banana. Rosie scrunches her nose and shakes her head when I offer one to her. We've been in the car hours and they're getting agitated.

Millie begins to peel it and I scrunch my nose at the smell.

'We are staying in a cottage right by the sea. We'll be able to see it from our windows. How lovely is that?'

'Wow. I can't wait.' The excitement across her face warms my heart. 'Can we walk on the beach even if it's still raining?'

'Yes we can.' I nod animatedly and smile widely.

'Then we can buy some flowers for Jess.'

My daughter warms my heart again. 'That's right, Millie. We can choose some pretty, colourful ones.'

'Are we nearly there?'

'We are here.' Damien navigates the car through the narrow town, driving slowly as tourists step off the pavement and onto the road. We finally find our allocated parking space. Sea View Cottage stands out with its huge blue plaque, boasting a four-star accommodation experience and the girls let out a scream of delight. It looks the same as it did in the photo but I don't remember having it taken. My dad must have stood where I'm standing now when he took it.

'Let's get this holiday started.' Damien's enthusiasm is contagious. He and the girls step out of the car and run towards the beach to take in the sea. The child in my husband has come out and for a moment I remember him being like this all the time before we had the children. While they're occupied, I grab my phone and see that I have a notification. Will has accepted my friend request. I want to look at his profile and send a message telling him that I'm here, but Damien is already back and opening the boot. I throw my phone back into my bag. The girls run around the car, giggling and tagging each other.

'Are you staying in there all day?' He's already dragging a couple of bags out.

I step out of the car and take in the location. 'Sorry. I was just taking it all in.'

Over to the left, I see a pub I remember, the Admiral Boscarn. My dad got drunk in there a few times back then. My mum had tried to get him to slow down on the beers as Jessica cried in her pushchair. In front of the car park is a small bay of a beach that I remember being full of families when I was little. Today, the sand blows in the wind. The waves crash onto the shore throwing up white froth that look like little sprites being flung into the air. It's almost mystical and I find it both hypno-tising and terrifying. I stare into the distance and I don't see any boats, just a block of grey. The horizon is hidden by the sea tones matching those of the sky and it feels eerie. It's perilous and murderous. The sea will take and take.

'Millie, stop.' She's gone too far ahead and my heart is going.

'Mummy, we want to see the sea properly.' Millie grabs

Rosie's hand and they continue forward. I glance back. The key safe is open and Damien is already taking our bags in.

'Millie, come back now.' She doesn't hear me. Weaving in and out of the stationary cars, my girls are getting further away and they can't hear me so I run. Within seconds, I catch up with them and I spin Millie around. 'I told you to stop. When I say stop, you stop. Do you hear me?'

Her bottom lip begins to tremble and a tear runs down her cheek. Her damp hair is starting to frizz and her button nose is red. 'We wasn't going to go far, Mummy. We just wanted to see the beach more.'

I get down to her level, one knee in a puddle on the cold concrete. 'It's dangerous out there. Remember what I told you both about Jess.'

They nod.

'Right, let's go and see the cottage. I promise I'll show you both the sea later. Okay?'

We hurry back to the mid-terraced dwelling and enter through the pale-blue door. I feel the beckoning warmth of the cosy lounge with its cute fireplace. The walls are adorned with rattan hearts and inspiration quotes about love and family.

'In here,' Damien calls. The lounge takes my breath away. For a second, I see Jess in her pram in the middle of the living room but that image is skewered. I'm small and I'm looking up at her. It's like I'm back there.

'Mummy, can we have the craft box?' Millie grips my arm and I flinch.

'No, sweetie, we'll leave that in the car for a seriously rainy day.'

Rosie runs upstairs shouting about finding their bedroom. I hurry into the galley kitchen where Damien is already putting the groceries into the cupboard.

'Why don't we go out for lunch?' he says.

'I'm not that hungry. Shall we just make a snack?' My

stomach is doing somersaults and I feel sick. The journey did get a bit hilly.

'No way. Neither of us are cooking after that journey. I want to get this holiday started and I need a whopping big plate of something fatty and greasy.'

'Sorry.' Confusion runs rife through my body. I want to find out more but I don't. What if the truth is worse than I ever imagined? My hands are beginning to shake. I don't know why I'm feeling so het up. Will is probably some weirdo who saw the article and thinks it's funny to wind me up. 'I'll go and have a wash and change into a thicker jumper, then we'll go and get some food.' I wish I could believe that's all Will is but something is telling me otherwise. Do I trust my instincts on this? I have to.

I grab our clothes bag and haul it up the stairs. Peering around the door to the smaller back room, I see the girls fighting over who will sleep in the bed next to the window. The chintzy curtains and bed covers look old-fashioned but cute. Millie pulls out her blue flamingo stuffed toy and takes the least favourable bed. Rosie won that battle.

A moment flashes through my mind. I slept by the window and Jess slept in a travel cot next to me. The décor has changed but I remember staring up at the coving when I couldn't sleep in the strange house. I also remember pulling my pillow over my ears as my Mum and Dad shouted in their bedroom. I'd been shaking and Jess had been screaming, but no one had come to comfort us and I was too scared to get out of bed and comfort Jess.

Gently creeping across the landing, I find the main bedroom and I nudge the door open. I inhale its woody smell. The heavy bed frame and deep-grey walls are inviting, making me want to nestle down in the large bed and sleep. Then I spot the dink in the wall. I was there when my dad threw the ornamental paperweight. My mum had called him a useless drunk. Things were bad before we even got on that boat.

I grab my phone and click straight onto Will's profile but I see nothing. I thought that once I'd friended him, I'd see posts he'd made, friends that he had and all the things he liked. Instead, it's blank. Wait, I take another look at his likes and there is one page listed. I click into what looks like a photo of a Lobster Thermidor and my heart skips a beat. The page he likes is that of a pub called the Old Smuggler. He must go there. It has to be his local. Hastily, I send him a message.

I'm in Looe.

I grab the first jumper that I can find and I pull it over my head as I hurry down the stairs. Damien is packing the last of the food away.

'I've just been checking Tripadvisor.'

'And?' He closes the fridge door and turns to face me.

'There's a pub just behind the cottages, down one of the narrow streets. It's called the Old Smuggler.'

'Great, call the kids and let's go. Wait.'

He looks me up and down. I tilt my head and frown. Does he suspect that I have an ulterior motive? 'What's wrong?'

'Your jumper's inside out.'

'Damn.' I quickly take it off and as I do he holds me and strokes my bare back.

'I hope we'll find some time for us while we're here.'

I kiss him deeply. 'And me.'

He grabs his coat off the back of the kitchen stool. 'Let's go eat.'

Let's go explore and find out more about Jess. That's what I'm thinking. Will is leading me to the Old Smuggler and that's exactly where we need to go. We have seven precious days in this seaside town. Every minute is important if I'm to get to the truth.

As I zip my jacket up, I realise that Will knows what I look like but I have no idea what he looks like. He could be anyone. He could be the bar person; anyone who works on a boat; someone who works in a shop or... I glance out of the window and see a figure wearing a dark coat in the distance. Lifting up the net curtain, I hope for a clearer view but the person disappears behind a building.

Are you watching me, Will?

TWELVE

KATE

Rosie starts to hopscotch along the pavement and Millie skips beside her holding her flamingo. She never did give that stuffed toy a name, not like Rosie did with all her toys. Rosie yells as she lands straight in a puddle, splashing grimy water up her stripy leggings. 'Mummy, it's cold.'

'We're nearly there, sweetie. It'll be warm in the pub. You'll soon dry off.'

'Rosie trod in a puddle,' Millie sings as they both continue playing and it starts to rain.

I check the Maps app on my phone and it points down a path that is lined with tightly packed cottages and a few businesses, then I spot the sign creaking as it blows in the wind. A picture of a long-haired pirate fills it, one eye covered in a dark-grey patch. The menacing glare of his eye is backed up by his rugged bearded jawline. It's like he's looking directly into my thoughts.

'Kate.' Damien nudges me.

I realise that I've stopped in the middle of the pavement. A woman holding a baby in a sling almost crashes into me. I glance at the little white knitted cap that almost covers up the infant's closed eyes. Jess wasn't much older than that baby when she disappeared. The woman is soon at the door of the pub. It rings as she pushes it open and her straggly pink hair swings in its ponytail one more time before she's gone.

'Kate, hurry, we're getting wet.'

'Yes, sorry.' As we pass I catch my bedraggled reflection that is skewered in the bullseye glass panes of the main window. Beyond my reflection there is the shimmery orange glow of a fire.

Damien calls the girls and pushes the door open. Again, the bell pings and we enter into a pub that feels like a cave. Its white textured walls are covered in nautical memorabilia. Wheels, glass balls, netting and large wooden fish. I try to take in the mass of objects and the wall of photos.

'Mummy, it's Ariel.' Rosie touches the wooden mermaid figure that is stuck to the wall. 'I should have put my costume on.'

'Come on, little ladies, let's find a table.' Damien grabs their hands and leads them over to a free table. The open flames spit and crackle as a huge log is about to catch.

Damien pulls out two chairs and seats the girls. They look tiny in the adult chairs and I regret not bringing their booster seats so they can sit at our level. Rosie is too big for a high chair and the one I spot against the wall looks a bit greasy and splattered.

'Hey, do you need these?' The woman with the pink hair comes over with two firm thick seat pads. The girls slide off the chairs while she ties them to the seats. 'There you go.'

'Thank you,' I say.

'You're more than welcome, my lovelies. Enjoy your day.'

I glance ahead as she goes through the staff only door. Maybe she lives here and her baby is with another family member.

Flames begin to lick the log and spread further, and Millie is mesmerised by them.

'I think it's a charming place. It has a mermaid, lots of shiny glass and the friendly lady gave us some cushions for the girls.' I smile at Millie and Rosie. They nod in agreement.

'I like it here, Mummy,' Millie says.

After gathering the order up, I stand. 'I'll go order the food.' It's the only way I'm going to get a moment alone to look around properly. Maybe Will is trying to lead me to someone who works here or maybe he's here now, drinking. He might want to catch my eye but he won't feel comfortable if I don't leave this table, alone.

Squeezing through the sea of sweaty men, I finally place a hand on the bar. No one is waiting to be served, they're all just drinking.

'What can I get you?' A blonde-haired girl smiles, her lips thin but shiny pink with gloss.

I reel off all the food and drinks that we want. She puts the order through and goes to start the drinks at the other end of the bar. Several men laugh and cheer, I take them in first. Their accents are so thick I can barely make out what they're saying.

I glance around, hoping to make eye contact with Will but no one is taking any notice of me. In fact, I feel invisible.

'Here you go. Two Cokes and two lemonades.' The server holds out the payment machine and I tap my card.

'Hey, love, can you deal with Kyle's spillage when you're done here? Sorry about that, he won at golf. You know what he's like when he's had a victory.'

'Yes, 'course I will, Mary.'

'You're a gem.'

I weave through the people and the tables carrying the drinks, the music crackles into life. 'That's Amore' by Dean Martin comes on. I recognise that song as it was one of my Nan's favourites.

A man looks right at me. He then whispers into a woman's ear and she reaches across the table, covering her mouth while speaking to her friend. I turn to see another man with deep split veins on his bulbous nose. For a second, I think that he's going to come over and speak to me. I mouth the word Will and he stands as he stares at me.

He leaves his full pint on a table and pushes through everyone before running towards the door.

'Leaving already, Cody,' a woman shouts. 'Cody.'

He doesn't answer and darts out of the pub. The bell sounds over the music and all I see is him running past the front window as he pulls his dark coat on. He glances back and his stare meets mine.

'Kate, we're gasping for those drinks.' Damien shrugs.

My instinct is to dump the drinks and chase after the man but one look at Damien tells me I can't. How could I explain that one? If I leave, he will follow me with the girls and I don't want that. I glance around again and several people keep rudely looking at me and talking. I can't hear what any of them are saying over the music and the hum of voices.

'Food won't be long.' That's all I can murmur as I stare at the door, hoping that the man will come back. He owes me that much after getting me to come all the way here. It had to be him watching me earlier at the cottage. He wants to talk, I know he does, but I could see that something was holding him back and that something was fear.

Damien gets up to go to the toilet so I grab my phone and click on Will's messages and hit reply.

Why did you leave like that? I've come hundreds of miles to speak to you and one sighting, you run. I'm not giving up and I know what you look like now. I will find you, Cody!

The woman who called him as he left walks towards the

toilets so I stand in her way. 'Why did that man run when he saw me?'

She scrunches her brow as she takes me in. 'You're that woman who lost her baby sister, right? I thought I recognised you. I follow your page. That was a horrible article and it was all so long ago.'

I see Damien coming back. 'Can you message my page, please? I need to speak to you.' I hope my pleading look brings out the best in her.

'Okay. I don't know anything mind, but yes.'

'My husband's coming back. Message me.'

'Who was that, love?' Damien pats his damp hands on his jeans.

'Just a local. She said the girls looked cute, that was all.'

The woman comes back out of the toilet and winks at me as she heads back to her table. Immediately, her friends all start talking and glancing over at me. Without trying, I've become the talk of the town. I need to find Cody. That woman can help me, I know she can.

My phone buzzes. As Damien pours far too much ketchup onto his chips, I take a sneaky look at the message under the table.

It's Laura. I have a shop, Laura's Treasure Trove. You'll find me in there. Come tomorrow.

THIRTEEN

KATE

Sunday, 23 October

Running shoes on, I'm out of that door leaving Damien making pancakes for the girls and the last thing I did was promise not to be too long. The girls are eager to have some fun and I hope that I can let go of that message a little and join in with them.

The salty sea air hits me instantly. That's when I imagine being at sea. The whooshing waves sending the boat turning and plunging. My body slipping into the sea, unable to swim against nature's violent pull. An image of Millie and Rosie's deep brown and copper waves getting caught up in weed. I can't reach them and they plunge deeper and deeper. Glancing behind me at the sea, I shudder. Water splashes against the rocks and I turn away, trying to get all those horrible thoughts out of my head.

I can't waste any of this precious time. The clock is ticking. Laura knows something about Cody and I need to know what that is. Turning away from the seafront, I duck in towards the shops.

As I take the first left behind the cottages, I pull my phone from my pocket and see that I have no more messages from Will or Laura. Running through the tiny streets, I take in all the shops. Whatever you want, this little town has it. Art shops, jewellers, trinkets galore and cakes that look amazing. The waft of Cornish pasty comes from an open-doored shop, making my stomach grumble but I couldn't eat if I wanted to, not yet. Not until I've spoken to Laura.

A moment of my past fills my mind. I remember my dad giving me a pasty. I once sat on the path in front of that shop, screaming and crying on the floor because I couldn't have a cake as well. My fussing had started Jess off and my mother walked off, leaving my dad to deal with me. I shake that thought away. I'd been so upset that my mum was cuddling Jess. All I wanted was for her to hold me too.

I looked on my Maps app earlier and it said that Laura's shop was here. Maybe I'm missing something. Standing on the path, panting lightly, I gaze around. Staring at my phone, I continue walking. It's just a little further down.

Slam. I've crashed into a woman in her fifties carrying a shopping bag. 'Bleddy emmet.'

'So sorry. What?' I have no idea what she means or what an emmet is.

'Tourist. You lot, coming here and standing in the middle of the path with your noses buried in your phones. You're in the bleddy way as usual.' She shakes her head then scurries off past me.

'Sorry,' I shout.

I shrug my shoulders and continue, following the app's instructions and I see Laura's Treasure Trove on the opposite side of the road. It's tiny and could easily be missed with its lacklustre pale-grey sign that almost blends in with the white-painted wall. The window display is full of shells and boats in bottles. I gaze through the dusty window to see racks of games and toys. Shiny marbles catch the little ray of light coming through the window, creating a rainbow on the back wall. Cornwall playing cards and mugs fill another stand. What I don't see is her. I go to push the door open but it's locked.

The woman I recognise as Laura comes out of the back room and scurries towards the door. She slides a couple of locks and turns the closed sign around.

'Come in.' Her grey-streaked brown hair falls wildly over her shoulders and a pair of glasses almost drop into her ample cleavage as they hang on a cord around her neck.

The tiny shop is even more packed than I imagined. If Millie and Rosie were here, they'd probably tear around knocking everything over. As I turn, I almost knock a ship's wheel ornament off its stand.

'Your shop is lovely. I must bring the girls in for a stick of rock.' It doesn't hurt to be polite. I may actually risk bringing them in to buy a pack of cards or some sweets.

'You're not here to talk about rock.'

Straight to the point. 'No, I need to know where I can find the man who couldn't get out of the pub quick enough when he saw me. You called him Cody.'

'Yes. He said he had to go. His dad needed him, that's why he was in a rush.'

I know from the way he looked at me there was more to it so I shake my head and maintain eye contact with her. Maybe I need to blag this a bit more. Let her think that I know more than I do. 'He's been messaging me, about my sister, Jess.'

'Why would he do that? He knows about your sister, but he only knows what we all know; nothing more. It's no secret what happened to your sister. She drowned like the article said. Poor mite wasn't missing for that long. Such a shame. When we saw you, we couldn't quite believe you'd come back. Was it the article? I suppose it was a bit below the belt. Your poor dad made a mistake but the way they wrote about him. That was harsh.'

'Like I said, it was the messages from Cody, who's pretending to be Will. That's what brought me back.'

'Most of us have been on your page at some point. We've followed your story, your pleas for information. It's proper heartbreaking.' Her head tilts in sympathy.

I swallow. 'What do you all think you know?'

'You really want me to repeat the same story that has been said all these years?'

'Please tell me your version of what you know.'

She begins to unpack glass angels from a box. 'Look, I've got a busy day ahead.' She places them on the counter, one by one.

'It looks like it. Do you have children or siblings?'

'A daughter. She's in her mid-twenties called Bethany. No siblings.'

'Imagine your baby daughter all those years ago. One minute she's there, cooing away. Think of the bond and love you already have. She might drive you insane with her crying,' – I think of how annoyed I was that Jessica took so much of my mum's attention – 'but when you look at her closely, you see a little helpless human that you love deeply, that you'd do anything to protect. Imagine her little hands as she reaches to grip your hair. Jess used to do that to me. Always the hair. Do you remember your baby daughter's smell? I remember the way Jess used to smell. She was a little milky. Her bottle used to drip under her chin a little. Her gummy little smile, her warmth. Now imagine all that is there one minute and gone the next.'

The woman is grimacing and she doesn't quite know where to look. There is a creeping redness that has almost reached her chin. 'I can't imagine, really I can't.'

'That's what happened to us. I lost my sister. My mother

lost her baby and only now she's dead does someone message me to say they know what happened that day. Someone actually saw everything.'

Laura pulled her wild hair into a ponytail at the nape of her neck and her voice crackled as she said, 'I remember that day. My daughter was a baby then and it sent my blood cold. The search parties went into all the shops and businesses. Everyone who had CCTV passed it to the police but there was none on the harbour at the time. Or maybe there was but it wasn't working. There wasn't so much of it back then. Then, when the tide was going back out, there was no sign of her. It took what seemed like forever for the police dive team to come. The lifeboat went out, just in case, but we all knew by then that it was hopeless. Your sister had been swept out to sea. I had heard that your dad was drunk. I'm so, so, sorry for your loss, my love, but your mother left your paralytic father with a baby.'

The way she said that last sentence was more detached than the rest of her speech. I don't buy what she's saying. 'Yes, my father was drunk but my sister was in a portable car seat on the path next to him. She was asleep too.'

Laura shrugged. 'Babies wake up. They roll and crawl. She was close to the edge and could easily have toppled in.'

I thought I'd get more out of her but all I'm getting is that my parents are to blame and Jess's disappearance was an accident. 'Her body has never been found. Isn't that odd?'

Biting her bottom lip, Laura gives me that look of sympathy that I'm used to getting. 'No, my love. A small baby dragged out to sea. I don't like to say it—'

'Just say it, please.'

'I think she'd have been eaten. The sea is a big place and is full of danger as you well know.' Her eyes are glassing up with tears. 'Why did you make me say that?' A little sob comes out of her mouth.

I go to speak but she dismisses me with a hand. Right now, I can tell she's imagining her own daughter as a baby while we speak of Jess. Finally she is feeling a little bit of what I've felt for years. 'I'm sorry.' I place a hand over my mouth and shake my sadness away. 'I thought the same as you but I've been getting these messages from someone calling himself Will Wilcox and I'm confused.'

'Willy Wilcox is a pirate. There's a cave in Polperro where he supposedly left his stash. You should visit it while you're here. Polperro is amazing.'

'What?'

'Google him later. You'll find out lots of things. Whoever messaged you is joking around. Sick I know, but people can be like that. I'm sorry you came all this way because of a prankster.'

Sighing, I take a step back and stare out of the window. Will is using a pirate's name. Cody is pretending to be Will, he has to be, but why?

'When I saw that man, Cody, he ran out of that pub just after I mouthed the word Will to him. He says that he knows what happened to Jessica and that I had to come here as he'd only tell me in person.'

'No, that's not right. He said his father had taken a funny turn. That's why he needed to leave all of a sudden.'

I can tell I'm on my own here, even though I've disclosed what I know. She doesn't want to believe that Cody is hiding something. 'What does Cody do?'

'He has a trip boat. At the moment, he takes people out for mackerel fishing and pleasure trips.'

'He owns a boat?'

'Yes, well it used to belong to his father but what with his poor health since the accident and his dementia diagnosis not so long ago, it's all on Cody now.'

'Did Cody work on the boat twenty-five years ago?'

'Well, not often. He was a student back then. That poor

man wanted to escape the boats as a youngster. He studied biology, I think, but there's something about growing up in a town like this. It's a way of life. He didn't want to lose his roots or what his father had built up, so after university he came back. I know he was around that summer but I don't think he worked on the boat all the time.'

'You mentioned an accident.' I'm clenching my hands.

'Before your family came, his father, Archie, was involved in a huge car crash. Not his fault, mind, but the idiot didn't have his seat belt on. Took a nasty blow to the head, he did. Another car slid onto the wrong side of the road after a downpour. You've seen how narrow and windy the roads are. Then, a seven and half tonner came around the corner crashing into that car, shunting Archie's car too. It tipped over in a ditch. Somehow he managed to crawl out and help the people in the car. After that, he suffered with amnesia bouts and had a few blackouts. That's why Cody had to help him with the boat. The old man was okay most of the time, but, you know, he kept on having those turns. He never fully recovered. That's why Cody stayed. He'd also found out that he'd got a local girl pregnant when he came back the Christmas before. It ended well. They got married and he became a father. The usual story.'

'I'm sorry. It sounds like they've had it bad too.'

'They have. And then Cody's first wife died when their little girl, Daisy, was only two. Such a tragedy. It wasn't an accident, some heart defect is what I heard.'

I think I have what I came for. All I need is to head down to the trip boats and look for Cody. I remember roughly what he looks like so it shouldn't be too hard. My phone beeps. It's Damien wondering where I am. He and the girls are waiting for me so that we can go out.

I can't stop thinking about that cave in Polperro. Maybe the name, Will Wilcox, is a bigger clue than I thought. Maybe I'll find the answer in the cave. That's two leads. Cody and Willy Wilcox's cave. Laura isn't going to implicate Cody. I see it in her eyes when she mentions his name and I wonder if she has a soft spot for him.

'You know it's hard on us too. Please don't go upsetting folk. We don't know anything. We were devastated when it happened and when the media bring it up, it upsets everyone again. Cody is also going through a tough time at the minute.'

I don't know how to respond. It's not like I can let this go. 'Laura, may I call you Laura?'

'Please do.' Her phone rings. 'Sorry, I have to take this. It's my daughter.' I nod and wait for her to finish. 'No, Beth. Just bring the car here and we can load up the returns. You can take them back to Fowey.' She nods and ends the call. 'Sorry about that. I have to go soon. My daughter will be here and she can't park for long, which is a nuisance. She'll only be a couple of minutes. I don't know, we live up the hill and we have to do deliveries like this.'

I sense she's trying to get me out of the shop.

'Someone has brought me here because they know something. I'm not convinced it's a joke.' I don't tell her that when we arrived, a dark-clothed figure was watching me when I peered through the cottage window. 'Sooner or later, I'm going to find out who this someone is and I'm going to find out what they know. I will never give up on finding the truth of what happened to Jess, just like you wouldn't if it were your daughter.'

She awkwardly smiles and buttons her cardigan up. 'Okay, well have a good day and be careful.'

'What does that mean?' I can tell from her expression that I've snapped.

'Nothing, it's just, you know, these narrow roads and wonky paths. We get a lot of accidents. It's polite to say, that's all. Just be safe out there. You have a lovely family.' Her smile widens and she seems genuine but there's something behind her eyes that I can't quite fathom.

My phone rings so I hurry out, saying my goodbyes. I answer to Damien, being sure to puff and pant a little down the phone. 'I'm on my way. See you in five.'

Laura knows more than she's letting on.

FOURTEEN

NATALIE

As she cleared the lunchtime queue, Natalie took a deep breath and pulled another large container of chocolate ice cream from the freezer, ready to slot into the display. She glanced at Alan's phone, the keeper of all his secrets when he'd been alive. She should be mourning but all she could manage was more anger. She threw a few chocolate chips into her mouth and chomped on them as she scrolled down those messages again.

A teenage girl entered.

'What can I get you?'

'Double scoop, strawberry and chocolate in a waffle cone, please.'

She began to scoop the ice cream. As she looked up to smile, she caught a glimpse of a woman hanging around by the boats. Two little girls held onto the man's hands. The woman turned, catching the man's eye. In that moment, Natalie knew exactly who she was looking at. Laura had called her to say that the sister of the drowned baby was in town asking questions and everyone knew who Kate was. If they didn't before, they did after that article was published. So many talks had been run since on the dangers of not watching children by the pier and harbour. Jess was used as their prime example of what could go wrong but Natalie knew more.

Word had gone around that Kate was staying at the cottages on the front. Natalie thrust the ice cream at the girl, almost dabbing it on her T-shirt.

'That was close.' Her brows furrowed as she pulled out a handful of mixed coins and went to hand them over.

'It's on the house.' She needed the girl out of the shop and she certainly didn't have time to count out a handful of ten and twenty pence pieces.

'What?' The girl licked a bit of dripping ice cream from the back of her hand, clearly in no hurry to leave.

She hurried around to the front of the counter, ushering the girl out. 'It's free.' As she nudged the girl out of the door, she slammed it and turned the sign around to show that the shop was now closed. She couldn't talk to Kate, not yet. She'd barely got her head around what she'd heard, let alone found out if there was any substance to it. Now wasn't the right time.

Cody stepped off his boat and the man began chatting with him. Kate turns around and her gaze meets Natalie's. Without a moment's hesitation, Kate leaves her family and is running towards the shop. Her face is almost pressed on the glass of the door as Natalie ducked behind the counter.

'Can I come in? I just want to speak to you.'

'Sorry, we're closed,' Natalie shouted. She turned away, not wanting to see Kate's disappointment, then she scurried around the back, closing that door too. She clasped her trembling hands together. It was ridiculous. She should have spoken to the woman.

The constant knocking rang through her ears but she wouldn't go out there. She couldn't face her. First she needed to speak to Archie, if it was at all possible.

She glanced at her phone to check the booking. The visit

was booked for six that evening, after the residents had eaten their supper. The banging reverberated through her head.

'Just go away,' she whispered as she held her hands over her ears. After several minutes, she removed her hands and peered into the shop. Kate had gone back to her family. Cody glanced over, trying to look into the shop but Natalie stayed back.

She pressed Laura's number on her phone. 'Laura, I need to speak to you.' Natalie hoped that Laura could forgive her for the horrible accusations, after all, they used to be best friends and Natalie missed her. Maybe that shepherd's pie was her way of reaching out. Natalie hoped so.

'Has she been to your shop, too?' Laura's voice was shaky.

'She has. I closed it up and didn't speak to her. I don't know what to say.'

'That looks suspicious, doesn't it? You don't know any more than we do. You should have just told the truth.'

'But that's not the truth.'

Laura paused. 'What are you trying to say, Nat?'

'Exactly what it sounds like. I heard something, Laura, and I can't let it go. I can't prove anything so I can't help the woman, but I need to do something first.'

'Are you in trouble, Nat?'

'I don't know, maybe. What was the name of that copper or detective that came around, following up on a duff lead a couple of years ago?'

She heard Laura swallowing down the line. 'Err, Spokes, I think. I still have her card beside the till at the shop. Can't remember her title off hand. What's happened? You can talk to me, you know you can. We were good friends. At least I hope we are still friends, that is.'

'I'm surprised that you can forgive me. I didn't mean to go off like that. It's just—'

'Natalie, it's okay.'

'I know, I feel awful.' Exhaling, Natalie wondered if she

could share what she knew with Laura. She didn't want to be wrong about what she heard and saw on the night in question as she had been about Laura and Alan. 'I'm confused, so confused about it all. Can we meet up?'

'Of course. I'd love to. I've missed our friendship.'

'How do you fancy coming with me to visit Archie? I'm booked in to see him at six this evening.'

'Archie. I haven't heard how he's doing for years but, yes, of course I'll come. Are you going to give me a hint as to what this is all about?'

Natalie bit her bottom lip, pondering whether to say anything but she thought better of it. What she'd heard that night about the red hat on the pier all those years ago? That same red hat that was found floating in the harbour hours after the baby fell into the sea. Maybe Mary had been speaking to Laura. No, Natalie shook her head. Laura would never keep a secret like that for all these years. She was better than that.

'That baby didn't just fall into the harbour. There was someone involved. I can't say too much as I don't have proof yet.' She'd already said too much. A part of her felt that she should let it lie and forget everything. After all, the baby did go into the sea, just not where everyone thought she had. Natalie couldn't forget what she'd heard. She wasn't stone cold like Mary was, or some of the others she knew. Too sensitive for her own good – that's what her dear old dad used to say. 'We have to get proof.'

'Who said that, about the baby?'

'I can't say. Not yet.'

Laura cleared her throat. 'Was it Mary?'

'Why would it be Mary?'

'Look, Natalie. I know about Alan and Mary. She didn't love Alan and he didn't love her. Kyle didn't care because he's been as unfaithful as she has.'

'How did you know?'

Laura paused.

'Tell me, Laura.' Natalie clenched a fist.

'I'm really ashamed to say that I had a thing with Kyle. He knew about Alan and Mary and he didn't care. It's over now, only lasted a few weeks. That type of relationship isn't what I want. He isn't what I want. I was lonely and now I'm so ashamed.' She exhaled.

'Why didn't you tell me? I'm your closest friend.'

'Because I know how stupid it all was and if I told you about Alan and Mary, I'd have to have told you how I knew. I ended it with him and all I wanted to do was bury it. I really am sorry.' A sob came from Laura.

The truth had come too late. She'd never confronted Alan with it and now he was gone. She needed her friend right now even though she'd made mistakes. 'So you'll come and see Archie with me?'

'Of course I will. I want to be there. Whatever it is that you need to look into, I'll help. What do you know?'

'Like I said. Come with me to see Archie later. Meet me at The Brambles at six.'

'I'll be there. Should I bring anything for him, you know, some toffees or a bag of sweets?'

'I don't think so. See you later.'

Natalie hung up wondering if she'd done the right thing. There wasn't exactly an instruction book for these circumstances. What if she hadn't properly heard what she thought she had on that night? Perhaps Mary was talking about something entirely different and she'd totally got her wires crossed. Maybe she was making more of it because she was livid with Mary for what she'd done. The more it turned in her head, the more confused she got. Maybe this was her way of taking out some form of revenge on Mary for all that she'd done and her brain was twisting everything to suit her agenda. No, she knew what she heard and she owed it to Kate to follow it up.

She glanced through the shop again and watched as Cody stared out over the harbour, a cigarette dangling from his lips as he grimaced. He pulled it from his mouth and stamped on it, pressing out the smoulder, then he kicked the bench. Maybe Cody was the person talking to Mary that night. Looking at him kick the bench again showed that the man was none too pleased about seeing Kate.

The whole town was about to unravel and she had to find out if what she heard was true before the news was unleashed. Nothing would be the same again, her included. Why did that article have to come along and stir everyone up?

FIFTEEN

KATE

I enter Will Wilcox, Cornwall into the web browser on my phone. So many hits come up and I open the first one and stare open-mouthed. Laura was right.

I read through everything as I sit on a bench. Willy Wilcox is a Cornish pirate who supposedly drowned in a cave that had since been named after him in Polperro. I'm sure that's where we went on a boat the day my sister vanished. My father mentioned it many times, mostly when drunk. I click on an old article where someone has claimed to have seen his ghost in the cave. A shiver runs through me as I think of the person who sent the messages. They're literally a ghost too. I don't know who they are or what they want. I'm only assuming that Cody is Will.

So, my messenger has chosen this pseudonym and I wonder if there is a reason behind his choice. Is he giving me a clue by choosing to hide behind a pirate or was it some mindless choice? I place my other hand on the damp bench as I inhale the salty air.

I open another article and see a photo of people exploring the cave. It's tall and dark and I hate it so I turn my screen off.

I don't want to look at those harsh, pointy rocks any longer. I close my eyes and my mind wanders as I visualise taking a walk into the black hole, steadying myself on the cold rock as I go. I can hear the sea lapping on the shore. Echoing in the distance, a baby cries so I run. I keep running, searching for Jess but I'm lost and I can no longer hear the lapping of the sea.

A baby cries. I open my eyes and run up the pier to the little one and call, 'Jess.' As I lean in to pick her up a woman hurries back.

'What are you doing?'

I back off. 'I'm so sorry. I heard crying.'

She glares at me and walks off pushing her baby. I don't know what came over me a moment ago. Shaking it away, I hurry back down the pier.

Rarely do I get this overwhelmed by thoughts of Jess but the reality is, I think I'm going to learn what really happened and the truth might be far more sinister than my family have been led to believe. Is this Will saying that my baby sister was smuggled out of the harbour for a reason? Pirates smuggle things. They steal. The very thought of her being smuggled fills my mind with so many unwelcome thoughts.

Black market baby? Trafficking for all kind of perverts? Body parts? My mind is awhirl with all manner of evil possibilities. No, I'm being ridiculous. Her sun hat was found floating in the harbour. But is Jess dead?

Staring out at sea, I watch the fishing boats. I know the police had a list of all the boats that had been moored up but nothing out of order was found amongst them. My father was right, he was to blame and after that article, the whole of Cornwall knows that he fully accepts his guilt. He got drunk that day, he wasn't watching Jess and she died because of that. I swallow. If that was the whole story, why is this Will person messaging me? I check the time and realise that I have to get moving. I've wasted enough time sitting here and Damien will wonder where I am.

I finally reach the harbour and I hope that Cody is still there. How long is it okay to be out if all you went for is some fish and chips? There's a chippie along the harbour, we passed it earlier when we were window shopping. I can go there when I've spoken to him and when I get back to the cottage, I can blame the queue.

I zip up my hoodie. The breeze is picking up again and the bit of sun that had cast a lovely glow on the beach when we were playing earlier has long gone. The woman at the ice-cream shop was definitely trying to avoid me. Someone had to have alerted her to my presence in this town. It's not like I've made any announcements on Facebook. Maybe Cody or Laura have already spread the word, then there were all the people in the pub. I didn't imagine that everyone was muttering behind their hands and staring at me yesterday.

The scent of chips travels in a gust and my mouth salivates, not with hunger but with this low rumbling nausea that I've had since that first message came through. It's getting worse every time someone dodges me or tells me a lie. Shaking my head, I wonder if I've been too harsh. Laura seemed fairly nice and I imagine that in any other circumstances, I could be friendly with her but there was definitely something under the surface while we were speaking. I'm still not sure if her parting words to me were a threat or a warning.

'Hello.' I call down at the boat, impatient to see if Cody is there. The cabin door is closed so I carefully head down the stone steps and call again. Just as I lean over to peer through a porthole of the fishing boat, he steps out onto the deck. I didn't appreciate how weathered he looked earlier when the sun was bouncing off his sunglasses, but now I see the tired deep creases that surround his eyes and the large open pores in his nose. His hair is thin but covers his whole head.

He holds a calloused hand up, no doubt from tying ropes and being out in rough weather. 'Hello, err, sorry I forgot your name.'

He hasn't forgotten my name. He knows exactly who I am otherwise he wouldn't have scarpered out of the pub when he saw me. 'Kate.'

'You're booked in for a trip tomorrow. Everything okay?'

I'm sure that he'd love it if I just went away but I won't make it that easy for him, however much I don't want to go on that boat at eight in the morning. I checked and the weather is going to be drizzly with a breeze. What a surprise. I'm dreading it but the girls are beyond excited. 'I just need a word.'

'Oh, about?' He looks almost smug, like he's playing a game with me.

'Let's cut the crap. You know who I am.' I need him to think I can stand up for myself, that I won't leave until I have answers.

'I can't say that I do. We see many tourists around here. It's hard to remember everyone so if we've met in the past, I apologise for not recognising you.'

'In the pub yesterday, why did you run off when I was trying to get your attention?'

'Run off?' He scrunched his nose. 'I have no idea what you're talking about.'

I shake my head. 'I know that you're Will.' I let out a huff of a laugh. 'Will Wilcox. That's original. I guess all you're missing is the pirate hat. You got me here to tell me something, so please stop playing games with me. Do you know how much it hurts? I have a right to know what happened to Jess.'

He exhales and pulls a cigarette from his pocket. 'Want one?'

I haven't smoked for several years but I feel I should smoke with him, build some sort of a rapport. Maybe I've gone in a little heavy here. Actually, I know I have. 'Thanks.'

I take one. He lights his, then mine and he takes a long suck on the cigarette. I ingest the tiniest amount and let out a small cough. The nicotine instantly gives me a pleasurable hit and the tremble in my hands that I'm trying hard to hide is calming down.

'Can we start again?' I smile. 'Why did you run from the pub? Please, I need to know.'

He leans on the rail around his boat and puffs out some O shapes. 'Okay, I recognise you from your Facebook photo and that page. Now and again, a local story runs and it mentions the dangers of the sea and leaving children unaccompanied. Your little sister is always brought up and used as a lesson. Everyone here knows you. I'm sorry I pretended that I didn't recognise you. It's just, what happened hangs over this town and it's painful for us too.'

'Why did you leave the pub instead of speaking to me?'

He doesn't answer my question. I don't know whether he's trying to avoid lying by not answering at all, or whether he has a plausible excuse. I take another drag on the cigarette and this time I enjoy it a little more. My heart rate is more relaxed.

'It's my father. He's in a home and I got a call. He had a fall yesterday so I went to check that he was okay. He was fine when I got there. Not a scratch on him. He couldn't even remember falling but that's another story.'

'What do you know about, Jess?'

His stare pierces through me as he continues to smoke. 'That summer, I was back home after finishing uni so I helped my dad on the boat. He'd been in an accident so I picked up the slack. The day your sister went missing, he'd been with me on a trip but he wasn't himself, not since that accident. He'd get facts and all manner of things mixed up.'

'Would you mind telling me about it?'

'It has nothing to do with your sister.'

'Sorry.'

He blew out more smoke and sighed. 'It's okay. Everyone

around here knows what happened. It's not exactly a secret. He was in a crash with another vehicle and a large van. He ended up in a ditch, suffered terrible head trauma, which caused him a lot of confusion after. He saved a toddler from the other car and helped the parents out, just before their car slipped down a steep hill. He was a bit of a hero that day. Anyway, at first he seemed fine but very soon, he was suffering with an awful concussion, caused him amnesia too sometimes. That was about a month before your sister drowned. After that, I had to be on the boat with him all the time. He still loved it but he'd blank out here and there, which meant he wasn't safe alone.'

'Maybe he saw something that has never been said to the police.'

'I thought that when I first heard what had happened. I left him for awhile. I think I went to grab some food and when I got back he was asleep in the cabin. I don't for one moment believe he went out on deck and saw anything.'

'I remember a man in a pirate hat with a pixie necklace.'

'That would have been Dad. He used to wear that piskie around his neck all the time. He reckoned that Joan the Wad used to protect him when he was out at sea. All supernatural claptrap. But he did used to wear that pirate hat a lot. The kids loved it.'

'There was another man who wore a pirate hat.' I have this faint recall of another man in a hat.

Cody looks at me and grimaces. 'Oh yes, Kyle wore one now and again. When the mood took him.'

'Does Kyle still have a boat?'

'He and Mary do but they don't use it for trips any more. The family use it now and again to take friends out, things like that. I haven't seen them out on it for a long time. Him and his missus own the Old Smuggler now. They moved into the pub when they bought it. You can't miss Kyle, he's the one who's always a bit merry.'

'I remember him from yesterday.'

Cody laughed. 'Yes, most people remember him. Don't let his loud and drunken ways put you off. He's a great guy, does a lot of fundraising for local charities, things like that.'

'Where was he when my sister fell into the harbour?' He's loosening up so I need to get all I can out of him.

'I can't remember but I know he would have been with his wife, Mary. They have a daughter too. I remember them being devastated when the news broke about your sister. In fact, after that, I'd see everyone holding their little ones a bit closer when near the sea. I can't imagine how I'd feel if it had happened to my Daisy. She was born not long after the incident and I remember holding her like she was the most precious thing on earth. I still do. Not hold her like a baby, but treat her like she's the most precious thing. I can't fathom what your family has been through. I am really sorry, you know. But your little sister died in a drowning accident. I don't know who this Will is that you're after but it's probably some loser playing games with you. The internet is full of 'em.'

I shake my head. 'This one feels different.'

'Does it really?'

I'm not having this. He's trying to trivialise everything. I was so sure that he was Will but now, I can't tell. 'Which boat were we on that day?'

'Old Pritchard's or Mr P as we used to call him. Lovely fellow. He took your family on a pleasure trip. From what I remember, he went straight back out on his boat just after he dropped you off.'

'What if my sister was on that boat?'

He shrugged and stubbed out his cigarette between his fingers. 'The police checked everyone out, including us. There was no evidence that Mr P had taken your sister. He was the loveliest man, he just wouldn't do that.'

'The police were late checking the boats out. They spent all that time thinking she was snatched.'

'Didn't they find her hat in the water?'

I grimace as that red sun hat flashes through my mind. Mum had bought that for Jess while we were there and I cried so hard because I couldn't have one because they didn't have one in my size. 'Yes, but that was a long time after, from what my mum told me. The tide had gone out then come back in again. It was hours after.'

Cody presses his lips together like he has nothing more to say.

'It would really help if I could speak to your father. Does he live locally?'

'Like I said, he has dementia. He manages to recall some things but quite often he grasps for a memory and gets frustrated when it doesn't come. Sometimes he talks garbled rubbish, other times, it's like there's barely a thing wrong. He's in a home. His doing. I wanted him to stay with us for longer but he went on and on about how he didn't want to be a burden. I don't think upsetting him in any way would be a good idea. With his condition and the brain injury that he never recovered from, it all gets too much.'

'Please, I'll ask him gently. I just need to see if he can recall anything.'

'He can't.'

'But what if he can? He might just need his memory jogging.'

Cody steps forward and stares at me. I fight the urge to step back. 'No, leave my father out of this. If you want to go fishing tomorrow, see you at eight but that's all you're coming for. If your plan is to bother my dear old dad, stay away. You upset him, I'll upset you. From the look of how you were with your husband earlier, I gather you don't want him to know what you're up to. Is hubby fed up with you chasing false leads? I bet this could throw a spanner in your marriage.'

With that, the bulky man pushes past me and hurries up the steps, leaving me standing next to his tied-up boat. Darkness is falling fast and I know I have to hurry up and get back with those chips. I check my phone and see that Damien has tried to call me six times. Cody is right, I'll get on this boat in the morning and not say a word. Maybe I can find out a little more about Cody and his father, Archie. If I can find out where Archie is staying, I won't hesitate to visit without his permission. Maybe I'll be his niece who has come down from the Midlands just to see him. The truth is worth the lies.

SIXTEEN

NATALIE

'Do you want a bonbon?' Laura held out a bag of round strawberry sweets, her finger coated in pale dust as she popped another into her mouth. The scent of them rose up and made Natalie salivate with hunger.

'Maybe.'

'Go on, then. Help yourself.' Laura held the bag under Natalie's nose.

Natalie nervously smiled and popped one into her mouth. They'd been left in reception at The Brambles for ages. Darkness had now fallen over the car park, bringing with it an eerie look as the trees swayed in the breeze. 'Thanks for coming.'

Laura placed a hand over hers and smiled. 'I think we should forget everything and move on.'

A lump formed in Natalie's throat. She'd missed her friend. She laughed. 'You and Kyle, I can't get that out of my head.'

'Don't.' Laura playfully elbowed her.

A young man in a nurse's uniform entered the reception area. 'We're bringing him through to the conservatory in a couple of minutes. If you head through...' He held an arm up, pointing in the direction that he wanted them to walk in. The sound of a humming dishwasher came from the kitchen.

Soon they reached a large clifftop room with panoramic views of the sea where they both sat on the large window seat and waited.

'Great view.' Laura chewed what was left of her sweet. 'I hope we don't have to wait too long for him. Are you going to tell me more about why we're here or do I have to work it out as we go?'

'I'd rather speak to Archie first.'

'You do know how bad Archie is, don't you? I haven't seen him but Cody tells me all the time that his dad is getting worse.'

'Yes, of course I do. I also know that he has moments where he can remember. He's not completely lost yet.' Natalie had to have hope that Archie would give her something to work with.

Laura placed a hand on her shoulder. 'Just don't get your hopes up, that's all I'm saying.'

Maybe she'd pinned too much on speaking to Archie. Natalie swivelled slightly to get a full view of the sea under the light of the moon. She wondered where that child lay. Jess might end up embroiled in legend one day. The little baby mermaid, lost forever to the sea, haunting caves along with pirates of the past. She imagined her as a little sea urchin. Maybe that's what her memory would be in several hundred years' time.

An unsettling swirl in the sea tossed a small fishing boat about causing its lights to flicker. No one could survive falling into those waters when the sea was like that. With the swirling currents and the drag of exhaustion and hypothermia that would soon come, a mere human wouldn't have much of a chance.

'It's horrible to think of a little baby drowning in that, isn't it?' It's as if Laura sensed her thoughts.

She shivered. 'I wish I could stop thinking about it. It's literally haunting me.'

Laura gripped her hand. 'It's going to be okay.'

The trundling of wheels got louder as the young man pushed Archie into the room. He pressed the brakes on the wheelchair with his foot as they reached the other side of the table. 'Here you go, Archie. You've got visitors, how lovely. Can I get you all a cuppa?'

Natalie shook her head.

'No, thanks,' Laura replied.

'Just one for you then, Archie, my friend.'

'Y-y-yes. Cup of tea.' The old man nodded. The skin on his chin hung loose like it was dragging his lips downward, giving him a miserable look. The nurse left. 'I don't know.' Shaking his head, over and over again, Archie kept repeating those words.

'Do you remember me, Archie?' Natalie leaned forward a little.

The man ignored her, instead playing with some flakes of skin that had rested on his navy-blue cardigan.

'Archie?'

'Cody.' The man scrunched his eyes as he stared at Natalie.

'No, I'm Nat. I worked with my husband, Alan, at the ice-cream shop. You used to pick up tourists for your boat trips there.' The word husband had almost stuck in her throat. If he was still alive, a divorce would have been on the cards.

'I used to pick up tourists?'

'Yes, you took them on fishing trips and Cody helped you.'

'Where's Cody?'

'He was at the boat earlier. Cody is fine.'

The nurse came back in and placed a beaker of tea in front of Archie. 'If you could encourage him to drink it, that would be great.'

'I'm not an idiot.' Archie's tone had changed and the vein tensed in his forehead.

The man crouched down in front of the wheelchair. 'I never said that you were, Archie. We don't want your tea to go cold before you've drank it, do we?'

'No.' Archie gripped the beaker and sipped from the cup.

'I'll leave you to talk. Just come out and grab one of us when you're ready to leave.'

'Thank you.' Natalie turned her attention to Archie. 'How are you, Archie?'

'Very good. Who are you?'

'Natalie, from the ice-cream shop.' It was going to be a long chat.

'Ahh, I remember Alan. Handsome chap.'

He was handsome and Mary had thought that too. Natalie wanted to say something, to agree but the words stuck in her throat.

'How is he?'

'He passed away.'

Laura cleared her throat.

'Tell 'im I says hello.'

'Will do.' Natalie pressed her lips together in a forced smile.

'Is this your friend?'

'It's me, Laura, from the shop. You used to come in and say hello. You brought me that lovely spider plant when I opened it and you gave my Bethany a teddy bear when she was a baby. She used to coo at you.'

Archie looked blank and stared through the windows beyond them. 'Do you hear the crying? The water babies cry at night. It scares me. Can you hear?'

Slowly, Archie's expression changed. A stark look flashed in his eyes followed by the contortion of his mouth as he tried to say things that his brain was no longer wired to allow him to say.

'What babies, Archie?'

'Can you hear the baby?'

Natalie couldn't hear a thing but playing along might just

bring something out of Archie, something that would make
sense. 'I can. It's like a sadness. What do you think it is?'

'The little baby.' His chin began to shudder until a sob came
out of his mouth. Laura leaned over and took the beaker of tea
from his trembling hand. 'I want it to stop.'

Natalie leaned in a little closer. 'It's okay, Archie. It's going
quieter. The baby has stopped crying.'

'Yes, yes it has.' The man exhaled and wiped his crêpe-like
hand over his brow, sweeping his white hair back.

'Tell me about the baby.' Silence filled the air and Natalie's
heart beat so fast, she was sure that Laura could feel it booming
through their shared seat.

'I once saved a baby from a car.'

'You are such a hero. But do you remember the other baby?'

'What baby?'

'The baby you hear crying in the sea.'

'I don't hear a baby crying in the sea.'

'You just said...'

'Who are you? Go away.' This time Archie shouted so loud,
the nurse ran back in. 'Go away, tell them to go away. Go
away!'

The man crouched down, tending to the old man. 'It's okay,
Archie. You're safe.'

'I saved the baby.'

'I know you did.' The nurse was now humouring Archie.
Natalie could see that. 'Do you want to go into the lounge and
watch telly for awhile?'

Archie didn't reply. The nurse gave an apologetic smile and
wheeled Archie towards the door. 'I'll be back in a moment to
get you signed out.' With that, Archie was gone.

'Did any of that make sense?' Laura stood and stared out at
the sea.

The boat with the flickering light was now gone. The inky
blue was all-consuming if she stared at it for long enough. As

the clouds drew back, the moon was once again revealed; its reflection skewered on the choppy sea.

'I don't know. The baby crying in the sea. It could mean Jess. He knows something and he saw something that day. He was in the cabin of his boat, supposedly sleeping. He could easily have come out, taken the baby and headed up towards Banjo Pier and…' Natalie couldn't bring herself to say that she thought Archie had dropped Jess in the sea.

'That's a big accusation.'

'I know it is.'

'Why are you looking into this? It was a long time ago and all we've done is upset Archie.' Laura tucked her hair behind her ears.

'That young woman deserves the truth. Every day she and her family have to carry on, not fully knowing what happened to baby Jess. If I'm onto something, I have to find out more and tell her.'

'Nothing you do will bring that baby back. That woman, Kate, she'll poke around for a few days and then she'll go home.' Laura took another sweet from the bag. 'Why do you carry the weight of the world on your shoulders?'

She shrugged.

'Do you want to come back to mine for a bit of dinner? It must be quiet in that apartment of yours.'

Natalie glanced out at the sea one more time. Her apartment had been as cold as her ice cream since Alan died. She pulled her phone out of her pocket to see if Mary had messaged after that talk on the phone the other night, but there was nothing. A talk was in order about what Natalie had overheard, but that meant facing her husband's floozy and she didn't know whether she could do it without lashing out. There was another person there that night in the darkness and she needed to find out who it was. Who was Mary arguing with and how did that conversation end? She needed to go home and sleep on it all.

'About dinner?'

'Sounds good. We'll stop and get some wine on the way. I could use a drink.'

'I'm on board with that. We'll grab a takeaway too, can't be doing with cooking now.'

The nurse came back and gestured for them to follow him. Natalie took one glance back at the darkness through the windows and shivered.

'Are you coming?'

'Err, yes.'

Whatever Archie was hearing must be chilling him to the bone. In the back of her mind, she imagined the sound of a baby wailing, then worse. It stopped dead. Wailing meant life.

SEVENTEEN

KATE

I pull the quilt up a little higher so that it rests under my chin. I flinch as the wind howls against the window, causing the frame to judder and the loft to creak.

'They're both asleep. It's been a long day for them and we've got to be up early.'

Damien gets into bed and lies next to me, his nose almost touching mine. My conversation with Cody has been sending me into a confused spin and it would help if I was alone here and not creeping around.

'You never answered my question.' Damien's glare is fixed on me.

'Not this again. There was a queue, I told you.'

'For forty-five minutes? I called you several times to add the fishcake onto the order for Rosie.'

'My phone was on silent.' I can't look at him. He knows that I'm lying and it's not sitting well with me either. My stomach is grumbling. After pushing chips around my plate for twenty minutes, I had to say I wasn't feeling good.

'And you stank of smoke.'

'A couple were puffing like chimneys in the queue outside.'

'Look at me.' He places his fingers gently under my chin and lifts it so that I can see him fully. 'I don't feel like we're right at the moment and I understand that you must be feeling out of sorts with what happened here all those years ago.'

'I didn't go straight to the chip shop.'

'Okay.'

'I went to the harbour and took a few moments to think about Jess. I went to the bench where it happened.'

He still doesn't believe me. 'And that's all you did?'

'Yes. It's my way of getting through this. I'll be ready to say my goodbyes at the end of this week but I need a bit of space to work through everything.'

'And we can't be together as a family while you do this? The girls know about Jess now. They want to be a part of this. Don't shut us out, Kate.'

'I'm not.'

'I know you are.'

I should tell him where I was but he'll go off on one if he knows I'm chasing up leads on a Facebook message from someone who's using a pirate's name. I lean into him and kiss him. 'I'm sorry.' He kisses me back, then he reaches down and puts his hand inside my pyjama top, caressing my breasts. All I want is him close to me. I want to enjoy this but with my mind whirring, I can't.

'What's wrong?'

'I'm tired.'

He withdraws his hand before turning to place his phone on charge. 'I guess we should get an early night, then.'

My phone beeps and lights up. I grab it and turn away from Damien. With all that's been happening, I need to see what it is. My heart quickens. It's Will and there's also a message from Nadine but I open Will's.

It was lovely to see you at the harbour. X

Damien sits up and I close the message. 'You're not too tired for your phone.'

I reach over and turn my bedside lamp off. Damien does the same, and we turn away from each other.

My blood runs cold and all I want to do is wrap myself around Damien to steal his warmth but he's clearly not happy with me right now.

Will was at the harbour. He saw me and he didn't say a word. It has to be Cody. I can't think of anyone else who saw me. My mind wanders to the drunken man at the pub, Kyle, or the woman in the ice-cream shop. It creeps me out that someone is watching me. I wonder if Will is outside right now, looking up at the bedroom window.

The house clatters as a gust of wind passes and the creaks and cracks of the night feel sinister. Damien's gentle snores fill my ear. He's already asleep.

I think of the figure who was watching me on the day we arrived and I wonder why. When I was out, I should have been more vigilant. Gently, I step out of bed. The cold air hits me and I feel goosebumps rising on my arm. It's like a mild gale is blowing outside. Heading over to the window, I pull the heavy curtains back and stare into the darkness. The pub across the way has closed for the night. Raindrops bounce in the gutter and I notice that there's a dark figure in the same place as before. I press my nose onto the glass for a better look but the figure hurries out of sight. I know I didn't imagine it. There was someone there and they were looking my way. Whoever Will is, he's watching my every move. I need to be careful. My presence here has stirred up the hornet's nest and it's about to get dangerous.

EIGHTEEN

KATE

Monday, 24 October

The girls giggle and run towards the harbour for the fishing trip in their matching denim dungarees, wellies and sunny yellow raincoats. Thankfully, the stormy weather calmed down in the night and now golden rays reach through the morning cloud, bouncing off the puddle splattered paths ahead. A part of me hoped that the weather would cancel the boat trip but another part keeps telling me that I need to be on that boat so that I can snoop around. I also need to do my best to give the girls a happy memory of this holiday.

Damien waves to Cody and the man waves back as he prepares the fishing rods. His long rubber dungarees look like they'll keep him dry and for a second, I wonder if we're all underdressed for what's ahead. I don't think my skinny jeans and puffa jacket will offer much protection from the elements. A film of water sloshes in the boat and I swallow, wondering if it's safe to get into.

'Hop aboard.' Cody has laid out a metal plank that we can walk across.

The girls run ahead so I sprint over to them as they get closer and pull them back by their hoods. One step out of line, they will land in the sea, and for a moment all I see is Jess sinking beneath the boat. I can't believe I agreed to this. My heart pounds as I steady them along the plank. They merrily jump into the boat and squeal with delight.

'This is the first time we've been on a boat,' Millie tells Cody.

'Well, young lady, you're going to have a lovely time. My daughter is big now but she started coming on here when she was a baby and she loves the sea.'

I wince at that thought. He knew saying that would affect me but he said it anyway. Cody is good with kids, I'll give him that. He talks about the boat and how much he loves the sea. He goes on about what fun it is and they smile and laugh. Only I have seen the other side of that man. I swallow. If he or his father were responsible for what happened to Jess, we might be in danger. No one knows we've booked this trip today. I grab my phone, take a selfie and post it to Instagram with a caption.

Just about to go on a fishing trip with lovely host, Cody! Looe Harbour is splendid this morning. Wish me luck and fingers crossed that none of us get seasick.

I don't really make many posts like this, preferring to keep my personal life off social media but this has given me the reassurance I need. Cody won't hurt us if he knows the world is aware that we're on his boat. A lot of people know about Jess. There's a chance I'll get some caring emoji replies or a few comments of sympathy. That's a part of my life that I've plastered all over social media. The first flurry of replies come in. As predicted, the concerned emoji's are winning over the heart ones. A comment telling me that Jess will be watching over me pops up. It's Nadine. I click the like button.

Then someone with no profile photo in the name of Will Wilcox adds a comment.

The danger is real. Never trust the sea. Too many people don't come back alive.

My throat feels as though it's clogging up so I clear it and Cody glances at me. He places his phone on a shelf. Was it him? I click onto Facebook and check for more messages but there aren't any. Is Cody threatening me? We have to get off this boat before it's too late and we die in some tragic accident. I glance at Cody and his stare bores through me. We're not safe.

NINETEEN

KATE

I don't know how to convince Damien and the girls that we need to abandon our plans. 'It looks a bit choppy out there. Maybe we could go out another day. Girls, come over here, let me help you out. It's not safe to be here.' I'm trying not to show them how panicked I am inside.

'Mummy, we want to stay in the boat.' I go to reach for Millie to help her step back across the plank but she folds her arms and pouts.

'Kate, what on earth? It's okay. Stop doing this again. We're all going to be fine.' Damien's stern stare tells me that I've overstepped the mark again. He doesn't want me to ruin another thing for the girls. As he puts it, I'm so over the top sometimes and the girls don't have a life. 'Just get in the boat. This is going to be fun.' He can't look at me for long and he was cold over breakfast.

As I step towards Damien on the boat, I feel it bobbing underneath. The girls don't seem bothered but I am. Nausea swells inside me. We haven't even left the harbour and I already feel sick. The thought of being trapped with that man makes my knees tremble. I glance back at Cody but he's not looking at me.

He's busying himself with some rope. Maybe I've overblown the situation. My stomach churns away. I've never been boat sick before. I worried more that the kids could get ill but they seem fine. I walk over to the other side and look down into the water. I'm okay while we're moored up here. I can get off but once we leave the harbour and head into the open sea, I don't know how I'm going to be. *Never trust the sea.* Maybe it's less about the sea and more about who we're here with.

Damien puts life jackets on the girls, then passes one to me. Even though I can swim well, I know I couldn't win against the swell if it got choppy. The sea isn't a pool. I pop my life jacket on too.

'Right, ship ahoy,' Cody calls as he starts the engine. It rumbles beneath and I find the vibrations are making me unsteady so I grip the rail like my life depends on it. 'You can all sit on the back bench while we set sail.'

Set sail? It's a small boat with an engine and a tiny cabin. I peer into the cabin and spot a small bench that looks like it could double up as a single bed, and below that is a tiny closed door with a WC sign on it. As Cody navigates us out of the harbour, the girls wave and say goodbye to Banjo Pier. It soon gets smaller as we get farther away, that's when the sea feels choppier. Spray occasionally hits my face and the saltiness on my lips is adding to my nausea. I check my phone again and see that I have no signal. We're alone out here with only Cody to rely on. There's a radio that we can use for help if we need it. The boat falls and rises when he cuts the engine and I can't help but feel worse now. The sound was acting as a distraction.

'Are you both okay?' I ask the girls.

'Yes, this is brilliant, Mummy.' Rosie's cheeks are pink and her hair is already tangling up in the salty air as it falls from the ponytail I did for her before we left.

'Right, we have to catch a fish for dinner.' Damien stands and takes one of the rods out of the holder. He's been on one of these type of trips before and the girls look at him like he knows what he's doing. 'Kate, are you grabbing a rod.'

I shake my head. 'No. I don't feel good. Sorry. I'll be alright when I've got used to it in a minute.' Fishing isn't my thing. I don't like to see them flapping on the end of a line, fighting for life but Damien loves fishing.

Cody turns around. My husband and children are distracted. 'See, what a lovely day we're all having.' He grins and it's almost like he forgot that we bickered last night and this morning.

'Girls, stay behind your dad.'

'It's okay, Kate. I'm right here, with them. Let them have some fun. They're not going anywhere.' He rolls his eyes.

Cody's glare feels as though it's probing every corner of my mind and the fact that he doesn't blink is unnerving me.

I look away. I'm sure it was him who sent the message last night. I didn't see anyone else lurking around the harbour staring at me. He knew I was there. The more I think about it, the more I should focus on Cody. He was working on his boat on the day Jessica went missing. My focus has been on his father but I have to keep my mind open at this stage and my instinct tells me I should be scared of him.

'Kate, you're missing out on all the fun.' Damien roars as he nearly catches a fish.

Cody pushes past me and my gaze falls onto his phone. As he turns around, I go to grab it but he turns back. I almost slip over but I manage to grab the rail just in time.

'We've got a fish, Daddy.'

Cody reaches over Millie to help tackle the mackerel that is dangling on the shiny-ended rod. Swiftly I grab his phone and press a button. It's an older phone and it isn't locked. I quickly see if he has the Facebook app but I can't log in. As Cody comes back with a fish and throws it in the bucket, I pop his phone into my pocket and hope that he doesn't notice it missing.

My heart pounds as he rubs his head and looks at me. He turns back and sets Damien's rod up with a shiny lure. Without saying anything, he hurries through the door marked WC so I pull the phone out of my pocket and start scrolling. His contacts are filled with names of people I don't know but then I see one called The Brambles. That had to be a nursing home if ever there was one. There's no Instagram app on his phone. I pop the phone back on the shelf and push it out the way slightly to make it look like it had slid a bit.

I catch sight of an invoice for a fishing rod that is stuffed amongst other bits of paper and it's in the name of Cody Teague.

The girls yell while Damien jokes around with them. I should join in, be more fun, make some family memories but I can't, not right now.

Cody comes out of the WC and he's doing up his dungarees. He stares around his boat and grimaces as he spots his phone. 'Have you touched this?'

I shake my head. 'Of course not.'

He stares at me with a sour look on his face. He doesn't want me on his boat any more than I want to be on it but we're both stuck with each other for the next hour.

My stomach is all over the place and the boat starts to turn and sway. I hang over the side in the hope that I won't vomit. All this stress is playing with my innards.

'Mummy, are you boat sick?' Rosie grabs my hand.

'A little, sweetie. A little. Don't worry about me. You go and have fun with your dad. I'm alright.'

'Poor Mummy.' She gives me a clumsy hug from behind in her life jacket.

I'm sick of this boat. I'm sick of not knowing who is behind the messages and I'm sick of having to lie to find out the truth. I glance back at Damien and watch him being carefree with the girls. What I need is his level of simplicity in life. I glance directly down into the sea and I wonder how deep it is. In my mind, there is no bottom and I hold a tear back. Jess is down there somewhere. I have this weird feeling, like she's crying for me to find her. My tears drop into the sea and I stare at the same spot; scared that if I look up or across, I will be sick. I just want to get off this boat and call The Brambles.

Too many people don't come back alive. Those words hit me. I wipe my face. All I want right now is to get off this boat.

TWENTY

KATE

My heart pounds as the boat chugs into the harbour.

'Mummy, can we have ice cream?' Rosie looks up at me with pleading eyes and Millie turns to join in.

'It's nowhere near lunchtime yet. Maybe a little later, sweetie.' I glance across the water and I can see that the ice-cream shop is in darkness and the closed sign is showing. 'It's not open yet, see.' I point at it.

'Aww, I want it to be open. Daddy said we can have ice cream.'

'We can later.'

Rosie drops her hands and scowls.

Cody doesn't waste any time in hopping off the boat and tying it up. He gets back on and fixes the metal plank so that we can disembark and I can't wait to set foot on land. So much so, my legs are like jelly as I hurry off first, clattering across before taking the tiny jump to the ground. I grab the girls in turn and help them remove their life jackets. Then Damien comes off last, carrying their fish in a small bag.

The whizzing of wheels comes to a halt on the pavement above. Cody hurries off, nudging them aside. 'Hope you all have a lovely day.' With that he's climbed the few steps up and he stops to talk to the woman getting off a bike. She removes her helmet and a cascade of wispy brown locks fall over her shoulders. Her hair flows with the breeze and messily half sticks to her head. Her lithe figure looks like that of an athlete in cycling gear. I glance at Damien who I can see has clocked her. He looks away quickly and helps the girls to do their coats up properly.

From where we are, I can listen to what is being said.

'Daisy, my love.'

'Got you a greasy sandwich, Dad. Plenty of bacon, just the way you like it.'

'Just in time. I'm bleddy starving.' I listen as he unwraps the foil.

'Anyway, best get off. I have to meet Rachel at the café before I check in on Grandad. Got to give that baby a cuddle. See you later.'

'Send her my best.'

The woman rides off. As we climb the steps, Cody bites into his sandwich. His daughter looked to be about the age that Jess would be now. A shiver runs through me as I see the back of the girl I now know to be Daisy taking a left in the distance. Cody sees me looking and for a moment, I see something I haven't seen in him before – worry.

'Is that your daughter?'

He nods as he zips up his bag, then he checks his phone. Damien grips the girls' hands as they stand near the edge; too close to the sea for comfort. Behind him is Jess's bench but Damien wouldn't know that. He hasn't asked for the intricate details of what happened and I haven't told him. I know that my dad and my sister were on that bench the day she disappeared. When we came back, my dad was alone. Cody sees me and he too looks at the bench. He knows the story as he too was here on that day.

In an instant, I'm back there as a little girl. We've just stepped off the boat and I'm whinging already. I glance back and see that the man in the pirate hat that I now know was Mr P is telling me I should be good for my mother but that makes me scowl. There is another face, one in the next boat, peering out of the window and that man has a stark stare. He's about Cody's age now.

My heart begins to pound. I saw Cody's dad that day. He watched us getting off the boat. I have to see him.

'Kate.'

Damien shrugs as I stand there motionless.

'Sorry, I was in a world of my own.' Rosie is crying for ice cream, just like I was back then and I see what my mother was going through. She had a crying child and a baby. 'Rosie, that's enough. If you don't stop this, there will be no ice cream.'

My child is shaking and only now do I realise how loud I shouted that.

Damien shakes his head and grips her hand. 'Right, let's go and get a hot drink and maybe Mummy will snap out of her bad mood. Shall we try the café on the seafront by the lifeboat station?'

Rosie stops crying and nods her head. Millie has her knuckle in her mouth and a frown.

Cody clears his throat. 'I'd recommend the full English.' With that, he strides off in the direction of the ice-cream shop and down a narrow street.

'Nice bloke. Did we have a good day, girls?' Damien unzips his jacket as the sun begins to beam down. The further we move away from the harbour's edge, the warmer it feels. Now that Cody has gone, all I want to do is call The Brambles but it'll have to wait. Daisy was heading in this direction on her bike. I wonder if she'll be in the same café that we're going too.

'Yay,' the girls shout.

'Mummy looked sick though. Maybe that's why she's not happy,' Rosie said.

'I am happy and I shouldn't have shouted.' I force a smile. 'I felt a bit poorly. Sorry that I wasn't much fun.'

Damien places an arm around my shoulders and Rosie grabs my hand. I hope he's forgiven me. The walk to the café is pleasant and I'm thrilled that my nausea is subsiding now we're off the boat.

'Shall we sit out here?' I see Daisy and Rachel on the next table beside Daisy's bike.

'Yay, we can look at the beach,' Millie yells.

We sit and a teenage girl comes out to take our late break-fast orders and for the first time that morning, I'm ravenous. I lean back a little so that I can listen into the conversation going on behind me but I can barely hear a word. Daisy knows who I am. I can tell by the way she looks at me then whispers across at Rachel. They wave and another young woman runs across, apologising about being late.

'Ooh, Bethany. Got home late from a date.' Daisy points as she teases her friend.

'Oh, shut up. If you must know, yes.' The three young women huddle. 'How's the little angel.'

I glance around briefly and see that Rachel has her baby in a sling and a wash of sadness comes over me. I'd like to reach over and hold the little one just for a minute and pretend that I'd found Jess. Rachel's pink hair has fallen from her clip and dangles on the baby's face. I long to go over and move it so that Jess isn't aggravated. I stop and shiver. That baby isn't Jess. How could I even think that?

'Kate.' I glance up. Damien is waiting for an answer to a question I obviously didn't hear.

'Sorry, come again.'

He shakes his head. 'Girls, you can go and have a look

through the lifeboat shop window. Stay where I can see you both.'

Millie grins and is soon off her seat and Rosie grabs her hand. I can't take my eyes off them. 'I'll go with them.'

'No, they're barely five feet away, I can still hear everything they're saying. I'm capable of watching them while we talk.'

'Please don't be like this.' I don't need this right now. There's already too much on my mind.

'Like this. It's you that's the problem. I don't feel like you're here. I mean I can see you. You're there, but you might as well not be. The girls talk to you and you don't listen. I only asked if you wanted more sugar for your coffee and you ignored me. I know coming back here is hard but think of the kids. They need you to be present.'

'I am.'

'You're not. You're either glued to your phone or in a weird trance. It's too much.'

My muscles tense. 'What is too much is coming back here where my baby sister went missing and not having your support. You said you'd come with me so that I could finally say goodbye. I'm trying but burying the memory of my baby sister isn't easy when you take me on a boat trip that takes me back to that day. You don't understand.'

The three women turn to look at me and Rachel's baby starts to cry. They get up and go inside the café. I've lost them and it's Damien's fault.

'I do understand. I know that you're consumed, obsessed and it's driving us apart. You keep going off on your own gripping that phone like your life depends on it. I love you, Kate, more than anything but right now, I'm fed up. I wish we never came.'

My head is swimming. Millie looks back and waves, I wave back with a smile pretending that everything's okay. 'I'll put my phone away. I'm sorry. You're right. Maybe I need help, some more counselling. It's just hard, you know. I thought coming back here would help.'

'Let me see your phone.'

'Damien.' I tilt my head and my brows furrow. I can't let him have my phone, my browser is open. I need to deflect him. 'Back at the harbour you looked at Cody's daughter like a dog on heat. It's no surprise that I have a face like thunder.'

'How the hell can you say that? I thought it was sweet how the man's daughter brought him some breakfast. How can you even think I was leering? You're just saying that to detract from what's going on here. You know me better than that.'

He's right. He wasn't leering or being creepy. 'I was out of order. I didn't mean—'

'You know what they say about those who throw out the accusations. They're the ones who are lying. Right now, I don't trust you. Here, have my phone. Look at whatever you like.' He throws his phone on the table.

I don't reach for it as I trust Damien one hundred per cent. I give up and place my phone on the table. 'Please, Damien. I need you to trust me on this.'

He shakes his head and picks up my phone. He knows that my passcode is Rosie's birthday. Before he looks at what I have open he glances at the girls and they're both fine. 'I knew it.' He swallows and puts my phone back down. I know my Instagram was open and so was the internet and it was logged in and on my Facebook messages. 'Who were you seeing at the harbour yesterday?'

I go to answer but before I can say anything, he's up off the chair and he has the girls' hands. 'Right, girls. Mummy needs to rest because she's not feeling too good so we will go and get ice cream.'

They cheer and giggle as they're led away, leaving me holding my phone. I glance down and see the message he was reading.

It was lovely to see you at the harbour. X.

Sent from Will. I've royally messed up.

The server places a cooked breakfast, two slices of cake and a cheese sandwich in front of me. 'Hope you enjoy your food.'

She doesn't stick around or ask why I'm on my own. The smell of fried egg hits my nostrils and my stomach turns again. Pushing the food away, I hope that no one is judging me for the waste. I want to scream that I've been abandoned but no one will listen.

As I stand to leave, I glance back and see that Daisy is about to leave. She hurries to her bike and walks it over to me. 'Hi.'

I glance at her and smile. 'Hi, you're Cody's daughter.'

'That's right. Sorry if I'm out of order for saying this but we all know who you are and I read that article that was in the paper. Your poor dad, having to live with that on his mind. I just wanted to say, I'm sorry for your loss. I know it was a long time ago but you never forget. Coming back here must be hard.'

A tear drizzles down my cheek. 'Thank you. That's really kind of you to say.'

I glance into her bright hazel eyes and her peachy cheeks are well structured. For a moment, I wonder if Jess would have looked anything like her, then I mentally kick myself. All this second-guessing at what happened isn't helping. Jess is dead and a few moments ago, I thought Rachel's baby was Jess. I feel as though I'm cracking up. This place is doing that to me. Every street, every turn, I'm back there. I hear Jess, feel her presence and I'm angry that Will is messing around with me like this. What will help is if I find Will and have this out with him, in person. If her father is masquerading behind the identity of a pirate, maybe asking will trigger Daisy into speaking up.

'I don't suppose you know anyone who goes by the name Will Wilcox,' I ask her.

'Only the long-dead pirate. We all know about him over this

way. Have you been to Polperro and seen the cave?' There wasn't a glimmer of anything untoward in her reply or expression.

I shake my head. Maybe Will isn't prepared to give me another clue until I've cleared the ones that he's already sent me. I shake my head. What the hell am I thinking? This isn't a game. 'Maybe I should check it out.'

'You should. It's gorgeous over there. I'm a teacher and we sometimes take the kids there on a trip. They love it. I bet your family would have a great time. Go during low tide if you want to see the cave and take plenty of change. The car park costs a fortune. You can't drive into the town. You have to walk and it's a bit cobbly. Wear sensible shoes.'

'Thanks for the tip.'

She checks her smartwatch. 'Right, I need to give my grandad's home a call, see if he's running out of supplies. My list of jobs is getting longer as we speak. Enjoy the rest of your week.' She places her helmet on her head. 'Oh, and people will talk and it might look like they're staring. They're not being rude. They do care. They just don't know what to say.'

I wanted to tell that I thought her dad knew more than he was letting on, that he probably posted what could be perceived as a threatening comment on my Instagram, but I refrain. She's onside and friendly. I don't want to jeopardise that. 'Thank you, I know you're busy.'

'That's okay.' She throws a leg over her bike, one foot still on the floor for balance.

'Do you know the woman who runs the ice-cream shop by the harbour?'

'Oh, Natalie Thomas.'

'Yes. Was she working there back then, when Jess went missing?'

'Yeah. She and her husband would have been working with

his dad at the time. She's part of the furniture here. I don't even think she's ever left Looe before.'

'Thank you. I'm trying to gather a few thoughts and I'm hoping to say goodbye to Jess while I'm here. Finally allow her to rest.'

'That must be hard. Yes, you could have a chat with Natalie. She's lovely and always up for a chat. Have an ice cream while you're there. They're the best, especially the salted caramel.' Daisy looks at her watch again. 'I have to go. It was lovely speaking to you.'

Maybe I will have an ice cream before I call the home. The shop should be open now. I'll give Daisy a chance to get her call done. I stare at the lifeboat station with its little gift shop and I think of all the work they did when they thought Jess was out there. The volunteers had headed out into the sea, looking and searching to no avail.

I go to press Damien's number but then I place my phone in my pocket. He needs a little bit of time to himself, then I'll come completely clean tonight. Once he sees that he's made a mistake and that I'm not meeting up with some bloke, I'm sure we'll be okay. I gulp down the bit of acid that's climbing up my throat. It's not just about the message. I lied to him about why we're really here. It's not okay. We're not okay.

I leave the café and lifeboat station behind and head back towards the ice-cream shop. I'm going to wait as long as it takes to speak to Natalie. If she had nothing to hide, she'd have opened that door and welcomed me in. Maybe she and Cody are hiding something together. Whatever it is, I'm not going to let a mystery figure or a few social media messages freak me out.

I'm on the edge of finding something out and I can't let it go.

TWENTY-ONE

KATE

An hour has passed and the ice-cream shop is still in darkness. The sign on the door tells me it should be open. I haven't seen a peep out of anyone in there and that's not for the want of trying. In my desperation, I've knocked and peered through the window. I've stood back on the opposite side of the road, loitering outside the closed bag shop to see if I can get a glimpse through the upstairs windows, but the curtains remain closed. It's like the place has been abandoned. Post sits on the floor on the other side of the door, waiting to be picked up.

Other people have passed by and looked disappointed that it was closed. The sky is a little greyer than it was earlier so maybe the owner has decided not to open, but people are on holiday and having ice cream is what people on holiday do. I know when Damien left me earlier to go for ice cream, my own two children would have been disappointed if they'd come here. The pull in my heart makes it almost skip a beat. Again, I've let my family down and Damien doesn't trust me. I could find him now and say everything I have to say, but he needs time to simmer down. The best thing to do is to talk to him later after he's exhausted the girls and we can get some alone time.

It's lunchtime now and the smell of greasy chips and vinegar being carried on the breeze is almost making me salivate with hunger. My stomach makes an almighty gurgling sound. I give it a prod to try and calm it down but my nerves are getting the better of me.

Some of the boats are starting to sit on the sand in the harbour as the tide has almost lowered. They've gone from bobbing to stationary while I've been watching, the ebbed water leaving a carpet of sand, stone and tangled weed. It really smells like seaside now. Little rippled puddles reflect the midday sun although it's not like summer. The sun is up there but it seems like it's preparing to leave as it keeps ducking behind the rain clouds and there's a chill in the air that tells me winter is just around the corner. I zip up my jacket and consider realistically how much longer I can wait for Natalie to come back. I'm wasting precious time.

I wonder if Daisy has made her call to The Brambles. There's no time like now to find out. I do a search for the nursing home on my phone and Google soon comes up with the number. I press and wait for an answer. The longer it rings, the more my hands shake. This week, I've turned into a person I don't recognise. I'm a liar running scared. Not the best liar but I'm getting better. That's not something I'm proud of. I've ruined the essence of what was us and with all my heart, I wish Damien was more on my side and I didn't have to follow this up in such an underhand way. We've always trusted each other, but not any more and it was me who ruined that.

'Hello, Brambles Nursing Home. How may I help you?' Whoever was on the other end of the call hadn't a worry in the world given the upbeat tone of her voice.

'Err, hello.'

'Yes, what can we do for you?'

'I, err, wanted to know how Archie is, Archie Teague.' I can't help stumbling over my words.

'And you are?'

I didn't think this far ahead. I can't say Kate as the staff might mention me next time Cody or Daisy visit. I blurt out the first name that comes into my mind. 'Nadine. Archie's my great-uncle. I'm in the area. Is he okay since his fall? We were all concerned.' I remember Cody telling me about Archie's fall. That was his excuse for running out of the Old Smuggler when he saw me.

'Fall?'

'Yes, not long ago.'

'Oh yes. He's recovered now. He did have it bad last Christmas with his ankle. It's all better now, though.'

Now I know Cody lied about why he left the pub. What else has he lied about? He knows something about the day Jess died and other people know too. If he won't be straight with me, I will find someone who will be. I swallow down the hurt that is brewing within me. Am I sacrificing my marriage to follow duff leads and hoaxes? I can't be. There is something in all this. People don't watch and follow you, they don't send messages with a threatening edge, all because of a hoax.

'May I visit while I'm here?'

'Of course, my lovely. I'm sure old Archie would love a visit. He gets confused mind you, but that's all part of 'is condition. Just come along, chat away and have a cuppa with him. He'd love that.'

I exhale, a sense of calmness coming over me. 'Can I come later?'

'Let me check what he has on. Ah, this afternoon and evening aren't good. The chiropodist is coming today and we don't have a time for his appointment. I wouldn't want your visit to get cut short or for you to have to wait around. He's got nothing on tomorrow. Would that be okay?'

'Tomorrow morning, about ten?'

'After breakfast. Perfect. What did you say your name is again? I'll put it in the diary.'

'Nadine Turner.' I keep my own surname just in case I get forgetful.

'We'll see you tomorrow at ten, then?'

I end the call and hurry back to the cottage, my heart in my mouth, knowing that I'm going to have to tell Damien everything. As I approach, I knock. Damien took the key. All I have is a bunch of my own keys on me and not one of them will let me into the cottage. No one answers and the girls don't peer through the nets. They're not in. Pacing, I wonder if I can get in around the back so I hurry along the path, and when I get to our cottage, I try the back door, but it's locked. I stand and sigh. A shiver runs down my spine as I hear footsteps that stop just around the corner. I'm alone on this path around the back and I can't see who's loitering. Taking one step at a time, feeling as though my heart is stuck in my windpipe, I turn the corner but there is no one there. I scan the car park and the entrance to the pub but I don't see a soul. Then I hear an engine humming. There is a black, maybe navy-blue, car that is parked way back and all I see is a smeared peachy flesh colour where the driver's face is.

Swallowing, I know I have to get away from here for awhile. This place is making me paranoid. I can't even swear that I heard footsteps now. Will Wilcox could be anyone and he appears to know where I am all the time. A part of me wonders if I should walk right up to that car and see who's in it but my legs have turned to jelly. But I have to do this, I owe it to Jess. As I stomp between a couple of cars, the car revs up and pulls away before I have the chance to even see what make it was.

I grip the keys in my pocket and head towards our car. There's no time like the present to take a trip to Polperro and see Willy Wilcox's cave for myself. That is where he wants me to go, so I will.

TWENTY-TWO

NATALIE

Natalie blew on her hands in an attempt to warm them up, her car still cold. She'd wanted to go back into the shop and open up but Kate had been there again, so she'd remained well back. She pulled her phone from her pocket and checked the *Remembering Baby Jess* page but there had been no updates. Speaking to Archie had convinced her even more that what she had heard about Archie had been true, even though it pained her to admit that. Who else knew? She'd never look at anyone in the same way again. Her phone rang. She saw Laura's name flashing. 'You okay?'

'Yes, I thought I'd see how you were. How's the hangover?'

'I'm a bit delicate.' The curry and the two bottles of wine had gone down well, but this morning Natalie wished that she'd gone straight home to bed instead of drinking.

'Just thought I'd check. You were wasted.'

Having her best friend back had helped. Maybe it was worth it. She'd told Laura most of what she knew and Laura had done the same. They'd laughed into the evening and it was great to feel like her old self again. 'I'm fine, now. You know me. Just in my car about to go and get some shopping.'

'I'm heading out myself. Got to grab some stock from Fowey. You haven't seen Bethany around, have you? She's meant to mind the shop. I'm going to have to close it for a bit.'

'No, sorry. If I do see her, I'll let you know.'

'Thanks.'

'Laura, err... about last night. I'm sorry for—' She didn't know how to say it.

'It's okay, Natalie. You've just lost your husband. You're entitled to feel sad and you have a lot going on.'

As Natalie had walked along the streets in the dark to her home last night, her head had been whirring with thoughts of Mary and Alan. It had all become too much.

'What are you going to do about Archie and what he said? I haven't been able to stop thinking about it.'

'Me neither and I don't know. What can I do?' She was no nearer to knowing the answer to that question and she still didn't have proof of anything. She had a few partially heard words between two people and she only saw the one person. She also had an elderly man with dementia half-bleating on about hearing a baby crying at sea. Was it all the ramblings of a confused mind or was there more to it?

'The things you said, about what you think Archie did, gave me the creeps. I couldn't sleep for ages when you left. Listening to him talk about the crying baby at sea, it was weird. Why won't you tell me who you saw that night, saying all those things? I feel like you've drawn me into something only to push me away. All I want to do is help.'

'I will soon but I can't yet.'

That was the truth. Lives would be blown apart but what would it achieve? She had to be sure before she let it all out. Nothing would bring Jessica back, therefore nothing could be gained by opening old wounds with very little evidence. Then there was the fact that Cody was her friend and he'd been a wonderful friend to Alan. Archie wasn't a bad person. The poor old man had suffered enough. It was a tragedy, nothing more, but she also knew that Kate wouldn't see it like that. The family had lived with this lie for too long.

'Got to go or I'll miss my collection slot.' With that Laura hung up on her.

Natalie turned the engine on. There would be no ice creams sold today. She wasn't going to open the shop. Maybe she'd keep the shop closed all week.

Kate kept coming back and she'd keep coming back. Something had to be done and it couldn't wait. She grabbed her phone and pressed Cody's number. ''Right, Cody.'

'What's up?'

'What's up is that I went to visit your dad last night.'

'I told you he were getting bad.'

'I'm sorry. I hope me and Laura managed to cheer him up for a bit. He said something a bit odd.'

'He says a lot that's odd these days.'

'But this, Cody, it sent shivers down me. I need to talk to you in person. Maybe I can come by your place later. Or, maybe we could meet at the Smuggler for a pint.'

'What is it, Natalie? Just say it.'

Natalie swallowed. 'It's about the baby. Jessica.'

Cody went quiet. 'It's Kate, isn't it? She's got to you and she thinks that we had something to do with her sister's drowning. When will she accept it was an accident?'

Natalie had to flush out more. 'Was it though?'

'What are you trying to say?'

'Nothing. I'm not trying to upset you. You know I think a lot of Archie. He's a good man but since his accident, he had those problems, dissociation something.'

'Yes, and he saved that kiddy in the other car. That's what he gets mixed up with. He pulled a baby from a car and he didn't have anything to do with a baby that drowned. Look, if you think my dad had something to do with all that, you can stick your drink at the pub and stay away. Oh, and Kyle knows about your Alan having his end away with his wife, so it's best you don't go in the Smuggler for a bit. It's all too raw. That man was absolutely gutted when I saw him.'

Laura had told her that Kyle knew about the affair, so why was he so upset now? She wondered if Mary had finally confessed all to her husband. Natalie had read the messages where Alan was begging Mary to leave Kyle and Alan was going to leave her. She swallowed down her upset. If Kyle had seen those, it would have been a shock. An affair that went on that long was more than a fling. Alan and Mary had lived another life.

'Stay away from my dad.'

'Cody, I didn't mean—'

It was too late. Cody had hung up on her. Today couldn't get any worse. Cody wasn't happy with her, Laura was upset that Natalie wouldn't tell her who she'd seen that night and Kyle was upset. If only she could leave Looe and never come back.

She whacked the steering wheel over and over until her wrists ached. None of this was her doing. It was everyone else.

Why did it still feel as though she knew so little? She shook her head. She did know one thing for certain and maybe it was time for everything to come out. Then there was that one message, the one that sent Natalie's head in a spin. Did Kyle know about Rachel?

As she checked her rear-view mirror before backing out, she saw Kate's car trundling through the narrow roads. The woman stopped to let a group of tourists cross the road. Did Natalie want to help Kate or did she want to protect the people she knew and loved? She thought about that question for a few seconds and she had her answer. The whole town had probably known about Mary and Alan and no one had thought to tell her. Humiliation burned her face as she let the handbrake off.

TWENTY-THREE

KATE

The sun has been replaced by some miserable-looking clouds that threatened to turn angry at any moment. I pull into the half-packed Crumplehorn car park and hurry over to the machine. Several cars follow me in, all trying to find a decent space to park in. After grimacing at the price, I fish for all the coins I have in my purse and bag and push them into the slot, buying myself the afternoon to explore Polperro. A tinge of sadness comes over me as I think of the girls and how much I wish they were here. They would love to walk around a quaint historical seaside town with me. I miss Damien and the reassurance he gives me. I'm alone and it feels like it.

With thoughts of him running through my mind, I have to call him. I know I thought some space would help but I've pushed him too far. I can't let him go on thinking that I met up with some man. I press his number and he answers. 'Damien?'

'What?' I hear Millie playfully screaming in the background.

'It's not what you think.'

'Really? I saw that message. Don't treat me like I'm stupid.'

'I would never do that.'

'Where are you?'

I glance around, wondering if I should tell him. I can't lie, not again. No more lies. 'Polperro.'

'I thought we were going to go there as a family.'

'Yes. Trust me on this. I need to find out what happened to Jessica. That's why I'm here. That message you saw—'

'Kate, I need some time to think. I don't know if I can do this, us, any more.'

I almost choke as I gasp. 'What are you saying?'

'None of this is right. You lie to me, you're obsessed with chasing Jessica's ghost and I'm fed up. It's not good for the girls. When we get home, they're going to spend Sunday with my mother and we are going to have a talk. I've already arranged it and she's delighted at the thought of finally having them over for a few hours.'

'But—'

'I can't do this now.'

He ends the call, leaving me standing outside the car park, hands shaking. With a red face, I'm on the cusp of bursting into tears. I've finally pushed him over the edge and he gave me no time at all to explain. Fanning my tears away, I try to stay focused. A part of me wants to get right back into the car and drive to him, beg him to listen. He'll see where I'm coming from, he has to. I can't lose him. But I have to see this through.

As I walk past a row of houses, most of them converted into bed and breakfasts, I catch up with a couple of people and I hope that I'm following them in the right direction. I see shops in the distance and very soon, I'm there, passing a café, then an art shop. My mind keeps flitting back to Damien. I've hurt him and it feels horrible. The lies I've told are because he's stopped supporting me.

Tiny, packed in cottages line the paths as I enter the maze of Polperro. White cottages, blue cottages, vacant signs, fully booked signs. Some have little balconies jutting out and others have large picture windows featuring model ships and cosy dining rooms. I'm transfixed. A terrier sniffs at my feet and its owner pulls it away and continues walking. For a dreary Monday in October, this place is packed. For once, I feel safe. Being in a crowd gives me company and no one will hurt me in front of all these people. My phone beeps. I snatch it out of my pocket, hoping that it's Damien but it's Will.

You need to leave, now.

Will has got me to come all the way here, I trust him when he says that he has information about Jess and now he wants me to leave. No way. I've invested too much and jeopardised my marriage in the process. I reply.

No, you should keep your promise and meet me. I'm fed up with waiting. Was it you watching me at the cottage earlier? You seem to know where I am all the time. Why are you doing this to me?

My hands shake. A man carrying several bags of shopping nudges past me on the narrow path. I wait for a few seconds but there is no reply. As I'm about to continue exploring, I see another message flash up.

You're in danger. Go home, Kate, before it's too late!

As I go to click on it to see if there's more, I find that it's gone. Will Wilcox has gone. His whole profile has been deleted leaving me with the earlier messages but not the last one; the one that tells me I'm in danger is nowhere to be seen. He must have deleted it before I had the chance to open it properly and read it.

I keep repeating that last message in my head, over and over as I don't want to forget it. Before it's too late – too late for what? It's definitely threatening. I should call Damien. Maybe the girls are in danger. I press his number but all I get is his voicemail. I'll try again in a bit. I think of whoever was in that car, watching me, and a tingle runs through my body. Maybe he's back in Looe, watching my family. No, I shake that thought away. This person wants to scare me, that's all. Damien won't let the girls out of his sight and he can look after himself; he's strong in that way. They're safe with him.

Whoever has been sending these messages, playing with my mind, knows how close I'm getting to the truth and, for some reason, they're trying to stop me by telling me that there's danger ahead. I think of that car and the person who's been watching me and I feel that if they wanted to confront me, they would have. They're cowards, hiding in darkness or driving off. My head is full of conflicting thoughts. One minute I believe I'm in danger, the next I feel that someone is playing a sick joke and I'm nothing more than entertainment to them.

Seagulls squawk from above and I get nudged out of the way again by a huge family trying to pass. The children seem to range from toddler to teenager and there are at least eight kids and three adults. Before I know it, I'm swept up in the crowd. I hear them talking of Willy Wilcox's haunted cave so I follow them in the hope that they will lead me to where I need to be. Will wanted me to see it so I'm going to see it. He may have ghosted me but I'm going to follow this ghost until I find out if Archie hurt Jessica and if Cody has been keeping it a secret all these years.

TWENTY-FOUR

KATE

After weaving around more tiny paths, I follow the family to a square with a restaurant on one side and a café on another. The restaurant is Nelson-themed but all I can think of is pirates and Will. The image in my head of an eye patch and grisly beard sends me a little dizzy. I haven't eaten today and my stomach spasms. The café is in a tiny courtyard and there are a few tables, chairs and umbrellas by the door. The waft of frying onions and something cheesy makes me hungry. The restaurants are all open and each one gives off an appetising aroma. I gaze at the square and wonder what fun things have happened here in the past. It looks to be the hub of the community with its posters advertising the entertainment to come.

I feel sick with hunger now and I know I must eat. Following the family into the café, I order a small Danish pastry then I wait and watch, hypervigilant of everyone who is around, each one of them possibly watching me. There's a man in a dark anorak and a woman wearing a navy headscarf. Both make me shiver. The worst thing is not knowing who is following me and sending the messages. Maybe the person watching me is Will, maybe he isn't. Maybe the messenger and my stalker are two different people. Or maybe they are Cody. My mind is still on him. I don't trust him at all.

The large family with its line-up of children all take dough-nuts out of a paper bag, then they continue walking. I glance at another man sitting on a wall and a woman catches my eye as she talks on her phone. I don't recognise either of them but maybe they recognise me. Word is well and truly out about my being here, and maybe it's spread to the next town. That article had spread far and wide.

One of the children shouts about the cave again and I hear their mother telling them that they can go there now. The little girl's lips are covered in sugar and she giggles with delight as she follows her mother. An older woman leads the way, at a guess I would say she's the grandmother. The large man, walks behind them, huffing and puffing as he uses his inhaler.

Within minutes of walking past more shops and restaurants, I'm gaping at the most beautiful harbour. Surrounding it are houses that reach heights that make me a little giddy. I imagine the views from up there to be amazing. The thought of not sharing this with my little family wrenches at my heart.

I wobble slightly as I'm transported back to that day on the boat with Jess and my parents. We came here. I remember mooring up and walking along that huge wall. It was the same back then, except the people now all have mobile phones. Some snap away with their cameras, others sit on the benches. Fishing nets are hung up everywhere, drying out on boats and on the path, just like back then. I take a moment to appreciate what's in front of me as I take a bite of the pastry, enjoying its buttery flakiness. Despite my emotional state, it's going down well. If only we'd known what would happen next when we got back to Looe Harbour. A bit of pastry catches the back of my throat and I cough violently as I try to dislodge the crumbs. There was no point in toiling over the what ifs. Jess died and nothing will bring her back.

The family keep chatting as they pass a pub and a jewellery shop. Polperro is a town that a person could get lost in for hours, taking in the coffee shops and having long lunches but I haven't come here for that. I'm here to find out why Will Wilcox wants me here and how that relates to my sister. Something about this place draws me in deeper. It's a puzzle waiting to be solved and only Will knows how it will all pan out. The family stall, but I hear them saying that the beach is ahead and I know that's where I need to be. They stop at another café. That's where I leave them.

I swallow the last of my pastry then I follow Quay Road until I see a sign for the beach. My churning gut has settled for now. I carefully hurry down the steps and my feet crunch on a bit of shingle on the beach. Small flecks of rain dampen my cheeks as I take a look. The lapping of the tide feels as though it's closing in on me, then I realise that the tide is coming in. That's when I see the cave. It's nothing more than a dark gap in the landscape.

A gust blows my hair in my face. It's as if Willy Wilcox himself knows I'm here and he's conjuring up a storm to welcome me. A baby begins to cry, then I see that one of the family I followed down is holding a newborn in a sling. One of the adults moans about how bad the weather is getting so they turn back. Suddenly, I'm on my own and the heavens open up. I glance back at the roaring sea, the surface of the water rippling with every turn of the breeze. Seagulls make the strangest of sounds and to me, if I close my eyes, I imagine it's Jess. *I'm here*, I want to tell her. Never have I been one to believe in spiritual things but a part of me needs to close my eyes and imagine that she's guiding me through this next step.

I've arrived but I don't know what I'm meant to do next. Through the rain that slides over my forehead and down my face, I glance up at the house above. I read about that house. It belonged to Willy Wilcox – the pirate himself. I'm sure I saw a shadow in one of the windows, but when I glance up again and squint a little so that I can focus better, there's no one there.

I think of Wilcox's pirating days. Smugglers brought in tobacco and spirits and maybe many other things I don't know of. My heart palpitates as I think of Jess. Was she smuggled out of Looe, out of Polperro, out of Cornwall, or even out of the country? Everyone wants me to believe she drowned. The police neatly tied up the case and in my heart, I believe they were slack when investigating, or maybe one big cover-up is going on. The sea can't tell me what happened, I wish it could. Only I can search for the answers.

I don't want to be here when the tide comes in. The sea is giddying to look at and while I stare, it almost sends me to the ground as I half lose my balance. The atmosphere is intoxicating. A gasp slips from my lips as I imagine the sea dragging me out into the bottomless abyss. I place my shaking hands in my pockets and turn to face the cave. I'm not going anywhere near the sea and the less I see of it, the better.

I'm going to have to go into the cave. My messenger may have left something in there for me. I take a deep breath and before I know it, I've escaped the elements and my rapid breaths echo in an unsettling way.

Why have you brought me here, Will? I step further in holding my phone torch out. Glancing back, I feel reassured that I can still see the beach. From where I'm standing, the houses on the opposite side of the bay seem almost misty with spray from the rain. Jagged stone frames the entrance, and layer upon layer of cold rock has formed in sheets of reddish colours and greys that blend into a bluish tone. Reaching out, I press my palm onto the cold dead stone. The brutality of it is terrifying. Hostility stares back at me. As I step further in, the cave gets narrower and I can't hear much outside. All I keep focusing on is my short, sharp, breaths that threaten to make me light-headed again.

As I tremble, the light from my phone flits everywhere. I'm unable to focus on one spot. I deserted my family for this. Kicking the rock, I flinch as my toe cracks. I peer ahead. From what I can see, I think I can go in further. Slowly, I creep forward, trepidation in every step. I read about the ghost that people claim to have seen in this cave and I feel a shiver work its way up my spine, then my neck. My hairline tingles in a way that says, *get out, while you still can*, then my torch begins to fade. That message rings through my mind. *You're in danger. Go home, Kate.* My battery is going. Damn! I grab my hair and pull it in frustration before wrapping it in a bun at the nape of my neck.

I can't see the beach but I know those waves are lapping ever closer to me. It's getting late in the afternoon. Is Will trying to say that my sister ended up here? I imagine a helpless baby being cold in this cave as the tide came in to take her. A seagull squawks making me shudder. I can't go much further. With the last bit of light I have, I crouch and stare at the rock ahead. In it I see faces that I know can't exist but my mind is enjoying taunting me. My phone beeps, telling me that it's about to go and I feel my stomach drop.

'Why did you bring me here?' I yell as tears roll down my cheeks. No one answers because there's no one there. Will was never giving me a clue, he was playing games with a desperate woman. I've embarrassed myself and I've hurt my husband, all for this. I won't visit Archie tomorrow; I'm chasing fool's gold. People are watching me because no one wants me here. The loitering person was probably trying to take a photo of me to send to the paper. All I am is next week's news. Whoever was in that dark-coloured car drove off and was probably no one. I'm seeing what I want to see. It all means nothing.

I'm going back to the cottage. I'm going to tell Damien how he was right all along and how much I love him and how sorry I am. Then I will hold the girls with all I have and read them a story. My phone dies and I'm staring into darkness as I listen to my sobs echoing.

I flinch as I catch a noise so slight, I might have been mistaken. Then I hear it again. A slight shuffle of a shoe.

As I go to turn, a heavy blow hits my head and I fall onto a pile of stones. Darkness pulls at me and in an instant all I can see before me are Millie and Rosie. My gorgeous little girls, and I wonder if I'll ever see them again. My vision prickles to black nothingness.

TWENTY-FIVE

KATE

I'm sinking deeper and deeper. At first the sea was blue and I could see the sky above. Now, it's as if the lights have been turned off. I hear Jess's cries but my eyes aren't working. I can't see through the murky water that froths with every stroke I take. As I swim deeper in search of my sister, the icy fingers of the sea pull at me, dragging me deeper still. I know I'm getting closer to the truth.

I reach through the pea soup water and a shimmer twinkles ahead. One of my hands grapples with strings, long grey and black hair. As I try to move my arms, it tangles around and around until I'm bound up so tight, I can't move my arms. My heart revs up and I'm desperate to inhale. The crying is piercing. Jess needs me. I poke my fingers into anything and everything, that's when I feel a nose and an eye. It's Willy Wilcox. Deep eyes stare at me but he has no irises, only large opaque pupils. I fight with all I have, until I feel his bones crack as I push through. It's all so surreal. That's when I see the seabed. The crying lures me over and when I get there, I scream and bubbles fizzle out of my mouth. It's not Jess, it's Millie. Her reddish-brown hair splays out in the water and her glassy eyes don't respond to my presence.

The dream has gone as quick as it came.

Can't breathe, can't breathe. I'm shivering so violently, it sends my body jerking. I cough the salty water out of my throat and sit up.

I'm in the cave, lying face down with water lapping around my face. Coughing again, I expel more water out of my lungs and croak as I go to yell. My head throbs. I feel for my phone and pull it out of my pocket and I remember that the battery had gone. I reach in my top and pop it into my bra in the hope that it won't get drenched.

I can't see. Darkness has fallen and disorientation is smothering me. Trying to get up, I wobble and fall as a wave crashes through, propelling a bundle of weed forward that slaps against the rock. The tide, it's coming in and if I don't get out I'm going to die. A sharp pain runs through my head and reaches my eyes like a lightning strike.

I feel along the walls but which way? The sea has now reached my shins. It's coming in fast. I have minutes, or is it seconds? Did my messenger do this to me? Someone hurt me. My heart sinks and my throat feels as though it's going to close up. I keep coughing hard and all I can taste is saltwater. 'Which way?' I croak.

A seagull squawks behind me. That has to be the way. Another joins in and I feel as though Jess is there, leading me out with the seagulls. Her cries; their cries, are calling me, urging me to move. I wade through the water, unable to feel my legs for cold as I push through. Shaking the string of weed that has caught in my arm and fingers, I finally feel free. A vision of the pirate's hair of my dream flashes before me.

Keep following the seagulls. As I reach the entrance, I know I have to wade and swim like never before. It's dusky and across the bay, cosy houses in the rock face have their fires lit and I crave that warmth. I've never trained for waves and extreme cold. My mind flashes back to all the nice warm pools I've taught others to swim in and how the sea terrifies me.

'Are you okay?' A man calls from midway down the steps. His dog begins to yap at me.

'Help,' I croak. That's all I can manage as I crawl on the wavy surface, water crashing over my head as I slip and lose my pace. My strength is dwindling which is why I can't seem to stand without falling. It's as if my legs don't belong to me. Through chattering teeth, I try to call him again but I can't. My arms are deadening too. Cold, so cold. I wonder if I'll make it to the man. All I have to do is push further and harder. A clash of thunder fills the air and rain begins to pelt down. I can't do this. I'm not going to make it. The sea keeps trying to drag me out. Is this how it ends? The sea taking both sisters?

The man might only be a short distance away but the sea kills and I know it's trying to kill me right now. Another crashing wave sends me falling and hurtling under the surface and I feel my arm crunch against a rock. As hard as I try to hold my breath, it's no good. I let that water in and I'm suffocating.

I'm going to die. Will killed me. Bringing me here was his parting shot.

TWENTY-SIX

KATE

Where am I? The shouting hurts my head. As I open my stinging eyes, I'm at the top of the steps covered in a foil blanket. I've been saved. The man's terrier begins to lick the salt from my face and I welcome its warmth.

'You're okay,' he says, as he places a warm hand on my arm.

I glance at the angel above me and gasp. There's no way I can answer him right now but I'm safe.

'We're going to get you in the pub, warm you up a bit, okay? Paramedics are on the way but it could take awhile.'

All I can do is cry, grateful that this man put himself at risk to help me. Two men and a woman head over and they all help me up, and part carry me into a cosy pub. Flames lick the hearth as a huge chunk of wood catches. The customers are asked to retreat to the lounge, leaving me alone with my rescuer and the woman. As I violently shiver, the man hauls my limp body onto a couch by the window and the woman hurries over with a pile of towels and a huge fluffy hoodie. My teeth won't stop chattering, making it impossible for me to create coherent words. I want to thank them, tell them that I owe them my life, but I can't.

'Hello, my lovely. There's help on the way. We going to get you checked out, just hang in there. Was there anyone else out there with you?' The woman dabs and rubs at me with the towel, then she removes my jacket and replaces it with a dry hoodie.

I nod.

'Jeff, we need to get rescue out there, now.'

'N-n-no,' I stammer. 'Someone attacked me.'

'Forget that, Jeff. Don't call rescue, call the police.'

With stiff fingers, I pull my phone from my bra and pass it to the woman. She takes it but it's not coming to life, then I remember that it died. I wonder if too much water got in it. If I can't get my phone going, I have no idea how I'm going to contact Damien. He doesn't have any idea I'm here and that someone left me in that cave to die. Tears fall down my face and the woman wedges in beside me and gives me a hug, transferring her much-needed body heat.

'It's okay. Let's get you properly warmed up. Jeff, throw some more logs on that fire.'

I want to tell her it's not going to be okay.

'You're safe now.'

I'm not safe. Now that I know someone wants me dead, the game has changed. Will brought me here to kill me, to kill me along with Jess. Reaching deeply into my jeans pockets, I pull out my keys. I have to get to the car and get back to the cottage. Damien has to know what's going on. Nudging the woman, I try to get up.

'You're not going anywhere in this state.'

I snivel and choke on my tears as I try again, this time succeeding. 'I can't stay here. My family might be in danger.'

At first I walk with a stagger, then I manage a few steps in a straight line. With the feeling coming back to my body, I'm good to go. All I want to do is get back to the cottage, be with my family and have a hot shower.

'But the police are on their way,' the man with the terrier says.

'Thank you, all of you. I'm sorry.' With that I open the door and allow it to slam behind me. I'm shivering so hard, I ache and tiredness enshrouds me. I want to get back to the cottage, then I'll go to the police with Damien. First, I need him to know how much I love him. Then, I need to sort my phone out. I'm going to find out who did this to me, if it's the last thing I do.

After what feels like an eternity of stepping into puddles and listening to the low rumbling of thunder above, I reach the car park just before the heavens open. Hopping and staggering, I hold my keys out. It's a far cry from earlier. I'm the only person in the car park and there aren't many cars. I instinctively gaze around for the dark car that was by the cottage but I can't see it.

It takes me several attempts to press the open button. It doesn't work. The seawater must have killed that too, along with my phone. I prod the key at the lock but scrape the paint instead. 'Damn it.' All I want to do is curl up and cry. Taking a deep breath, I try again. This time the key enters the lock and I open the door. Without wasting a second, I turn the ignition on and pop the heating on its highest setting. Cold air comes from every vent. As I go to start the wipers, I see a bit of folded paper on my windscreen. It's a parking ticket.

I ran out of time. Great. I read on, looking for the number to call in order to sort this out when I get back. The paper mulches in my wet hands and I can barely read what's on it. That's when I see the message in the dirt on the passenger window, then rain starts to pepper the glass, washing it away. This can't be real! I plug my phone in, hoping that it will spark to life, but it doesn't. I don't even know the way home without Maps.

My gaze flits to every corner of the car park. I see a figure walking along the back of the car park through the rain-smeared windows, but it vanishes into the darkness. Struggling to control the sobs that are forcing themselves up my throat, I lock the doors. I lie back as the warm air floods me, my senses getting sharper. That message tells me everything I need to know. I feel sick to the stomach knowing that someone tried to kill me. The scrawl is barely readable now as the message drips away down the window. Slamming my hands on the steering wheel, I yell as tears fill my face. I can't even take a photo of it. The message is lost, forever, but I'll never forget what it said.

YOU'VE ALREADY STAYED TOO LONG!

A face appears at the window and I scream. He's trying to open the door. The man in the dark coat stares at me with pleading eyes as I grip the handle. All this time, my father was here, following me. Was it not enough that he allowed Jess to die that day? Did he have to come back and finish me off too?

'Katie, open up.'

I shake my head. There's no way I'm letting him in. Tears drip down my face as I rev up the engine. I have to get out of here, now.

'I can explain.'

No he can't. How did he know I was here? He had to be following me. It's only now, I wonder if he is Will. Why would my father do this to me? He hasn't changed at all.

TWENTY-SEVEN

NATALIE

Natalie gazed through the window, close enough to see through the distortion on the curved glass. She could see Kyle propping the bar up, nursing one of what looked like many drinks, judging from the empties and shorts lined up next to him. No, she couldn't walk in there while Kyle was with all his friends and show him the message about Rachel. But, then again, the man deserved the full truth. What kind of relationship did Kyle and Mary have? Kyle had a fling with Laura, and Mary had... Natalie shook her head as she imagined her husband naked with Mary. A tear slipped down her cheek. Alan hadn't touched her like that for years now and that hurt. Where had they had sex? On Mary's boat, in their cars, in their marital beds? She pulled a sour face as she imagined them grunting away on her bed. She was going to get a new one as soon as possible.

She pulled the hood up on her raincoat and waited, weighing up what to do. Selecting Mary's number on her phone, she sent a WhatsApp message.

I'm outside the pub. If you don't come out I'm coming in and I'm going to tell Kyle about Rachel. I will tell him everything.

Natalie watched as the two ticks turned green. Mary had read the message. A rumble of thunder sent a shiver running down her spine. Soon, another shower began to fall.

Within moments she heard bottles spilling into the bin around the back. Mary appeared through the alleyway that led to the pub's beer garden that was currently closed for refurbishment. Mary had told the whole community enthusiastically about the new play area, but Natalie didn't care then and she didn't care now. Mary's umbrella opened out with a whoosh. First she checked behind her, then she checked down both sides of the path before she beckoned Natalie over.

'Can we go somewhere else?' Mary didn't stop to hear the answer that Natalie was about to give. Instead, she hurried through the streets.

Running to keep up, Natalie followed her to the end of the path. They turned a corner and she kept walking, all the way past the Admiral Boscarn pub and onto the seafront. As they passed the beach café, the woman finally slowed down.

'Nat, I'm so sorry. We didn't mean to hurt you, we really didn't and I didn't want you to find out the way you did.'

'You didn't want me to find out at all.' Natalie shrugged. 'Kyle knows too. How could you do that to him?'

'I'm not the only one who cheated in our marriage.'

'But you're the only one who cheated with my husband.' Tears rolled down Natalie's cheeks. She could see what Alan had seen in her. The woman looked amazing. She glanced down at her dowdy flat boots and the old jeans that were tucked in.

Mary stepped closer and placed a hand on Natalie's arm. 'I didn't mean to hurt anyone. You lost Alan and he thought the world of you. We were stupid and it became a habit, it meant nothing. I know you want to burst into the pub and upset Kyle more than he already is, but it wouldn't help.'

'It would help me and don't try to tell me that an affair that lasted decades meant nothing.' She shook the woman's hand away.

'I'm begging you. I love Kyle. We've both made mistakes and I want to work things out with him for the sake of Rachel and our granddaughter. Please believe that I've changed. If I could go back and do everything differently, I would.'

For the first time ever, Natalie could see that the woman in front of her – her husband's lover – was feeling the pain too. 'Where did you both meet up?'

'You don't want to do this to yourself.'

'You don't get to say what I want? You owe me the truth.'

Mary swallowed and wiped her eyes. 'At my boat.'

Exhaling, Natalie clenched her fists. All that time they were having sex in that boat and she hadn't suspected a thing. How stupid had she been? Cody knew. Kyle even found out somehow. Everyone probably knew.

'And Rachel? Does Kyle know that he isn't her father?'

'What! We had an affair but that doesn't make Alan her father.' Mary turned away and shook her head. 'I had a paternity test done. Rachel is not Alan's daughter. She's Kyle's.'

'That's not what Alan thought. I saw the messages. All these years he wanted to see the results of the paternity test and you wouldn't show him. He said the timings added up. Just tell the truth, Mary. Show me the results. I don't want to have to ask Kyle.'

Her gaze met Natalie's. 'Kyle is Rachel's father. She loves him.' Mary began to sob loudly. 'I've made so many mistakes and I hurt you too. You have to leave Rachel out of this. It will destroy her.'

'Like you destroyed me. We were friends, not just friends, close friends and I thought the world of you.'

The rain began to pelt and Mary kept back. 'And I ruined it and for that, I can't forgive myself. I miss you, Nat.'

'You don't miss our friendship at all. You're still the selfish little bitch you always were and you'll never change.'

Mary's umbrella blew inside out as a gust caught it. She whipped it on the floor in a temper before depositing the crunched up metal and material into the bin.

'Mary, what's come over you? Things not going as planned? You thought I'd forgive you and we could all move on and play nicely in the playground again.'

'No, I know I'm in the wrong. I love my daughter more than you can imagine—'

'More than I can imagine.' That touched a nerve. All Natalie had ever wanted was her own child and she could imagine the love she'd have given. 'If you loved your daughter like you say, you wouldn't lie to her.'

'And if you told her all this, you'd destroy her. Kyle is her father. You have to let this go.'

'I have to, do I? Why? Because you said so?'

'I didn't mean—'

'I know what you meant.'

'Okay, let's put all our lies on the table. Your friend, Laura, had a fling with Kyle, did you know?'

Natalie's stomach dropped as she brushed the raindrops into her hair. 'Yes.'

'So why didn't you tell me?'

'Because you deserve it.'

'Right. There's a fair bit you don't know about Kyle or me. Kyle and I have had a patchy relationship but we always forgive each other.'

'But he wouldn't forgive you if he found out Rachel wasn't his.'

'I'm sorry. How many more times do I have to say it? I'll do anything. I'm a shitty person, a disgusting excuse of a friend, but I'm a mother, one who loves her child so much, it hurts. Kyle is her father.'

'I'll reserve judgement on that. Show me those DNA results.'

Mary pulled her phone out of her bag and it rang. Kyle's name on the screen lit up the darkness. 'I've got to go.'

As the woman turned to walk away, Natalie called out. 'I heard you one night in the beer garden. About a month ago. You were telling someone what you saw on the day baby Jessica disappeared. I know everything.'

Mary stopped under a lamplight, keeping her back to Natalie. 'If you know what's good for you, you won't say a word.'

Natalie sloshed in the puddles until she reached her. Grabbing Mary by the arm, she spun her around. 'Is that a threat?'

A worried look appeared across Mary's face and she swallowed. 'No, you can't say anything. Promise me, you won't. Too many people will get hurt. Let that poor baby's memory rest in peace.'

Peace? Natalie had seen the hurt etched on Kate's face as she watched her from the shop. The family weren't at peace and with journalists bringing the story up over and over again, they never would find peace. She went to speak but she couldn't get her words out. Why would Mary want to keep the secret about Archie? It was like a light bulb moment. 'Have you been sleeping with Cody, too? Are you trying to protect him?'

Mary's eyebrows furrowed and her bottom lip trembled. With a shake of her head, she walked away in the rain, leaving Natalie alone. Cody had told her to keep away from Kyle and the Smuggler, but that was a lie. Cody only wanted her to stay away from Mary, nothing more. That woman had him wrapped around her little finger, just like she had with Alan. Natalie thought of Cody's second wife; a lovely woman who'd brought his daughter up as her own for all these years. How she'd have killed for their life. Cody had everything, a lovely daughter and an all-round great life. Did Cody know what Mary saw and was she helping him to contain the secret? After all, if it was his dad's fault, keeping a secret that big would turn the whole town against him. It was so easy to blame the baby's drunken father and leave it at that.

Natalie stared at the sea and roared in frustration. No longer was she going to allow Mary to keep her secrets and she wasn't going to take threats from her either.

She'd made her decision and she knew what to do next. Doing what was right came with a price and she was ready to pay it.

TWENTY-EIGHT

KATE

Eventually, I find my way back to Looe. After a wrong turn, my phone finally warmed up and came on. I thought about pulling over and calling Damien but what I have to tell him would be better said in person. All this time my dad has been here watching me. A part of me wonders if he's been drinking again. Why else would he do this?

I carefully drive along the treacherous little roads as rain pelts on the windscreen. Several delayed messages begin to ping up. I keep seeing Damien's name. A woman steps straight into the road and I brake hard, skidding right up to her. She holds her hands up and shakes her head before continuing.

Stepping out of the car, I shout that I'm sorry but she continues. 'Hey, you work at the ice-cream shop.' I snatch the keys from the ignition as I chase after her. 'Wait, I just want to talk to you.'

She turns and glares at me with watery eyes as she lets out a sob. 'Kate?'

'You know who I am? I knew you did when you hid in your shop while I knocked. You know something, don't you?'

Swiping the tears from her face, she shakes her head. 'I

don't know what I know. What I think I know might be nothing. I can't talk right now.'

She turns and hurries away.

'You can't say that and walk away from me,' I shout after her.

'And I can't talk right now. Come and find me tomorrow.' She's clenching her jaw and fists. I don't know whether it's because of me or something else. I suppose me nearly running her over might not have helped.

I chase after her and grab her shoulder. 'Stop.'

I realise there's no one around. It's just her and me in a dark alley, in the now pouring rain. There's a solid strength about her and that scares me. I'm also weak from being cold and damp, the shakes that have plagued me since I came out of the sea are still there. A streak of lightning reaches across the sky, allowing me to see more of her features. Her stare is stark and the crinkles around the edge of her eyes are deep.

'You have to tell me what you know. I can't wait until tomorrow. This is my little sister we're talking about.'

She takes a step towards me. 'It's all about you, isn't it? You're just like the rest of them. No one cares about what will happen to me. You, you, you.' She jabs the air with her index finger. 'Just leave me alone.' She turns and walks away.

'No,' I yell as I catch up with her again. I go to grab her arm but she spins around and grips my wrist so hard I can feel her nails digging into my skin. There is a sadness etched into her face. With trembling hands, she loosens her grip and sighs. For all I know, she could have been trying to kill me at the cave earlier. She could be the one watching me and sending those messages, and here I am on a dark rainy night, at her mercy. But it was my dad, it had to be. No, however much I try to picture him in that cave, I can't picture him hitting me over the head and leaving me to die. Maybe he is following me, but he wouldn't kill me, would he? Damn, my thoughts run rife. I don't know what to think any more. 'Were you at Polperro earlier today?'

Her brow furrows. 'No.' She pauses. 'I'm sorry, I shouldn't have grabbed your wrist like that.' Shaking her head, she stops dead.

'That's okay. Please tell me what you know. I've spent years not knowing the details of Jess's accident. You don't know how it feels to be left in the dark for so long.'

Thunder clashes and she flinches. 'I know exactly how it feels to be lied to, deceived and treated like an idiot.'

A tooting horn makes me gasp. 'Damn!'

'I think your car's blocking the road.' She hurries away, seizing her opportunity to escape my questions.

'Wait.'

'Tomorrow.' With that final word, she's gone.

I dart back to the car and see three cars lined up. I'm parked badly, blocking the whole road. I hold up a hand and shout my apologies. The shaking heads and angry groans tell me that I need to move out of the way, so I pull over on the kerb.

Two cars pass and my father pulls up behind me and gets out of his old red car.

'Katie, I need to explain.' He's at the window again. If I don't face him now, he'll follow me back to the cottage and I don't want to take whatever argument we're about to have back for the girls to see.

I get out of the car. 'What? Actually, tell me why you've been following me?'

'I got here today and when I saw your car parked up opposite the cottage, I knew you'd come back. When I came around the back and heard you, I bottled it. I'm so sorry, Kate.'

'So you followed me to Polperro?'

He shook his head. 'Not quite.'

'But you knew I was there?' He's starting to creep me out. 'How did you even know I was here right now?'

He pulled his phone from his pocket. 'I was worried about you so I put a tracker on your phone when you came to see me. That's how I knew where you were staying and that's how I knew you went to Polperro. I couldn't lose you too, Katie. Not after losing Jessica. I have been a terrible father but I beg of you, please give me a chance to do the right thing.'

I pace up and down, pressing buttons on my phone but I can't see the tracker.

'I'm sorry.'

'What did you think you'd achieve? Did you think I'd say it was okay and we could all play happy families and continue with the holiday?'

He shook his head. 'No, I wanted to be here, to help you.'

'Well, that backfired.'

'Your signal went off at Polperro Harbour. When I saw you crawling out of that cave, I grabbed the man with the dog and begged him to help you. I didn't want you to see me because I knew you'd be angry.'

'But I saw you in the car park.'

'I know.' He shrugged.

My father was there, at the beach. 'Did you hurt me when I was in that cave?' I stare into his eyes, determined to spot the lie but all I can see is fear and loss. The memories of Jess are haunting him to.

'You have no reason to believe me, Katie, but I would never intentionally hurt you. I came to help you and I want to stay and do everything I can.' He takes his long black coat off and wraps it around my shoulders.

'How about the scrawl on my car window? Did you do that?'

He looks confused. 'I don't know anything about any scrawl on any window.'

I can't think. This is all too much.

'Can I stay with you?'

'No,' I shout. 'My children barely know who you are. Where are you staying?'

'In my car.' I glance over and see the quilt folded up on the back seat.

'Jeez. Just go home, Dad.'

'No, I lost Jess. I won't lose you. I'm sorry I wasn't there for you. I'm sorry for all the mistakes I've made. This time, I'm going to be right here. Call me if you need me.'

'I won't need you. Go home and lose the tracker. I don't need you spying on me.'

He bows his head and gets back into his car. I watch as he drives past me and takes a bend.

Less than a minute later, I park up in our allocated space and get out of the car. Damien is already at the door, shrugging with his arms folded in front of his chest.

'I've had it. You don't answer your phone, you vanish for hours. Do you know how worried I've been? No you don't because you don't answer your phone.'

I lock the car and run across the road. My straggly sea-crisped hair sticks to my face and I know I'm a little beaten, I can feel the sores on my lips and face. My damp jeans cling to my legs and I can't stop shivering. It's like the danger I was in has finally hit me. Someone tried to kill me. The strength I had is all gone and my stomach churns like I'm going to be sick with fear. My mum bracelet escapes from my sleeve and I touch it and cry knowing how close I was to never seeing my babies again.

Damien helps me into the house and dumps me onto the settee. I grab the snuggle blanket and pull it over myself, taking a moment to think. Damien has moved to the doorway and picked up a bag. 'I've called a taxi.'

'Damien, stop.' I'm up off the settee trying to grab his arm as he opens the door.

He bats my hands away. 'Be a mother. Spend some time

with the girls. We'll tie up loose ends when you get back. Enjoy your holiday without me in the way. Whoever this man is, he can have you all to himself now.' With that, he's gone, slamming the door in my face.

I open it but he's already striding around the corner. A car pulls up and he gets in. I've gone and done it. I've blown it with the person I love and he's gone. I grab my phone and call him but it goes straight to voicemail. Sobs begin to escape as I close the door.

The last thing I want to do is call my dad, but I can't be alone right now so I touch his number and hold my phone against my ear.

'Katie?'

I cry like never before.

TWENTY-NINE

KATE

I tell my dad everything from start to end as I sip the sweet tea he made me. He's worried sick that I put my life in danger by running off to Polperro, alone, when someone is clearly targeting me. I sit on the settee, enjoying the comfort of the blankets and my fluffy bathrobe.

He runs his hand over the grey stubble on his chin. 'You know, Katie, whoever is sending these messages, they don't want to help you. They've seen that article and now they've made you a target, and what's worse is you've played into their hands. They're like catfishing you or stalking you. I don't know what it's called but we have to call the police.'

'The police never do anything. I'm sick of them taking my statements and never doing anything.'

'I've had this too, over the years.'

'Messages.'

He nods. I hadn't thought for one minute what my dad had gone through. 'I started reporting them to the police, like you. They all turned out to be nothing and eventually they stopped listening. This is different, someone tried to kill you today.'

'I'll think about it.' I don't need him telling me what to do.

'Do you want me to go?'

I shake my head. 'I can't do this alone, Dad.' I pass him the blanket. 'I'll get you a pillow.' I don't know how I'm going to explain all this to the girls.

'Thanks.' He goes to hug me but I move back.

'Sorry.'

Embracing my dad would be weird. I feel as though I don't know him. Shame burns through me.

'The people who helped me back at the pub in Polperro called the police, but I left them so that I could hurry home to Damien and now he's left me. My phone was dead and damp and I thought he'd be worried.' I begin to rub the sore bump on my head.

'He'll come round. Give him a bit of space.'

'It was all over that message.' I pat my seeping head with a tissue.

My dad gives me a sympathetic look. 'Let me take a look at that.' He gently walks around me and pulls my hair apart. 'It's red and a little scabbed. You should really have it looked at.'

'No.' There's no way I'm leaving the girls to wake up and find him in the house without me at least explaining what has happened and I don't want to spend all night in a queue at A&E. 'It's just a bit of a lump. It'll go down. I'm okay.'

I think my dad is right though. My head is banging and I'm still nauseous, but then again, I did swallow a lot of seawater and then there's the stress of it all.

'You're not okay. You're going through a lot.'

One of the girls starts walking down the stairs.

'Who's there?' I call.

I pull my hair back over my sore head and smile. The last thing I want to do is alarm my children.

'Come here, Rosie.' I give her a huge hug, enjoying her warmth and the smell of shampoo in her hair as she clutches Millie's flamingo toy.

'Where have you been, Mummy?'

'I've been on a bit of an adventure and a big wave went over my head but I'm okay now.'

'We missed you today, Mummy.' She pouts and waits for me to answer, looking cute in her Little Mermaid costume.

'I missed you too, sweetie. Mummy had a few things to do, that's all.'

'Like what?'

'I had to spend a bit of time on my own, thinking about Jess.'

'Poor Mummy.' My sensitive little girl hugs me again. I close my eyes, trying hard to contain my tears. She rubs her eyes and stares at my dad. 'Who's that?'

'That's your grandad. He's come to spend some time with us.'

'Hello, Rosie. It's lovely to meet you.' He holds a hand out for her but she hides her head behind my arm.

'I love your mermaid costume. Are you a mermaid?'

Rosie smiles and nods. 'Where's Daddy?'

I exhale. 'He had to go home, sweetie. An urgent job came in but we're staying here for the rest of the holiday. I tell you what, you get into bed and I'll be up soon to read you and Millie a story. Okay?'

'Okay. Is Grandad staying?'

I nod. 'Yes, he'll be sleeping on the settee.'

She nods her head in an animated way and shrieks before running off. I hear her shouting with Millie as she closes their bedroom door.

There is a loud bang at the front door and I can't help but jerk in alarm. My dad gets up and pulls the curtains apart slightly. 'It's the police.' Slowly, he opens the door.

'Hello, we're investigating an incident that was reported earlier. Do you mind if we step in? I'm PC Barnes, this is PC Bickerford.'

The tall, uniformed PC wipes his feet on the mat and the

younger female officer takes her raincoat off, so she doesn't trail water into the living room.

'I'm Kate.' I know they've come to speak to me, I just don't know how they found out where I was staying. 'How did you find me?'

The woman with the bobbed brown hair gripped away from her face smiles. 'An incident was reported out in Polperro this afternoon and while we were speaking to everyone, we were given the coat you left behind. You had a water-damaged work ID in it and a soggy receipt for a chip shop in Looe. We just about managed to work out the name of the place from the mulched up paper. After asking around the pubs and restaurants, the landlord of this property recognised you and told us where you were staying. It's a small town thing.'

'Do you have my coat?'

The woman nods. 'Given the nature of what's been reported, we'd like to keep it for forensic analysis. We don't anticipate getting much from it given that it got pretty wet but you never quite know.'

I nod in agreement before sitting on the couch. Millie runs down, her auburn hair crazily up in several ponytails in only the way that Rosie does it when they play. 'Mummy, are you coming to read us a story?' She's holding her oversized party dress up so that she doesn't trip.

'Yes, sweetie. You go back up, I'll be there soon.'

'Who are these people?' Millie puts a finger in her mouth and begins to bite her nail.

'They are from the police. They just want to talk to us about something.'

'Are we in trouble?'

The male officer takes off his hat and bends down to Millie's level. 'I'm PC Barnes and it's lovely to meet you. Your mummy is helping us, that's all. No one is in any trouble.'

Millie giggles and runs back upstairs.

'Can I get anyone a drink?' Dad leans against the kitchen door frame.

'I think we could both do with a cuppa,' PC Barnes says as he manoeuvres his gangly frame further into the room. He places his hat on the coffee table and PC Bickerford pulls out a notebook from her top pocket. 'May we sit down?'

'Yes, of course.' I step ahead of them, grabbing all the toys and books, then I throw them in a pile on the carpet.

PC Barnes continues to speak. 'From what we were told, you were found trying to crawl off the beach as the tide was coming in. You then told our witness that someone attacked you. Can you tell us what happened today?'

I take a deep breath. All I want to do is sleep and try Damien's phone again. Everything is going to have to come out now. I bite my ragged bottom lip and I wonder if I'll ever find out who Will is and why he's playing with me.

THIRTY

KATE

Clearing my throat, I begin. 'I was in the cave.'

'In Polperro?' PC Barnes seems to be the one doing the talking while PC Bickerford writes.

'Yes, Willy Wilcox's cave.'

'Do you know what time that was?'

As much as I try to recall even an estimate of the time, my mind is blank. It's like the whole afternoon and evening have mingled into one.

'Sorry. I got to Polperro after lunchtime. I had a pastry at a café and walked around for awhile before heading to the beach.'

The sound of PC Bickerford's pen scraping on paper is setting my teeth on edge. My head is sensitive and everything throbs. Even the light in the room is starting to hurt my eyes.

PC Barnes breaks the silence. 'Tell us what happened after you reached the beach.'

'I remember that it was getting cold and rainy. There was quite a breeze picking up. The beach was empty. I guess everyone had more sense than me.' I let out a nervous laugh. 'I went into the cave. It was dark so I used my phone torch to light the way. Then I remember my battery ran out and the light did too. That's when I felt a blow to my head and I think I was in and out of consciousness for awhile. The next thing I remember was the sea lapping into the cave. That soon brought me round. I hurried out but the tide was coming in fast. I fought through it and at one point, I thought the sea was going to sweep me away. That's when I saw the man with the dog. I think his name was Jeff.'

'Yes, he called the incident in. The people at the pub were concerned about you.' PC Bickerford flicks through a few pages in her notebook.

'I'm sorry I left like that, especially as they helped me, but I wanted to get home.'

PC Barnes clears his throat. 'So what happened after that?'

'There were a few people, three I think. I was wet and cold. They sort of half carried me into the pub. The woman gave me a hoodie and helped dry me off in front of the fire. That's when I realised that my phone had died. I knew my husband, Damien, would be worried and I don't know his number by heart so I left them.'

'Going back to the incident, do you remember hearing or seeing anyone in the cave?' PC Barnes's radio crackles. He speaks through it, explaining where he is.

I continue after he stops talking. 'No. All I felt was the bang to my head. I thought I heard something, like a shoe scraping on the ground.' I think back, trying to grasp at anything that might help but I don't have a thing.

Then my heart quickens as I think of the message scrawled on the car window. 'Someone followed me there. Before I left Looe, there was a dark-coloured car parked outside the cottages. Either black or blue. I came back while my husband was out with the girls. Realising that he had the cottage keys, I decided to head off to Polperro. The driver must have waited for me to leave and followed me. Then there was the message. Whoever was in that car must have left a message on the passenger's side window while I was in Polperro. I found it when I went back to the car park.'

'Do you know the make and model of the car?'

'I wish I'd taken more notice. I don't know what make it was. It was a normal-sized car, not a four-wheel drive or an SUV.'

He leaned forward slightly. 'We can see if there is any CCTV covering the car park. Do you have a photo of the message?'

My dad walks in and places two mugs of coffee on the table.

'No, as I said my phone had died but there was a parking fine on my windscreen but it wasn't in a plastic bag, which I know they normally are. That was odd. I'll have the car park ticket too, the one I paid for from the machine. That should say on it when I arrived.'

'I'll get them for you,' my dad says.

'Wait, I'll come with you. The parking fine might be evidence if someone took it out of the bag and touched it.' PC Barnes stands. My dad grabs the keys from the table and pops the door on the latch as they both head out.

PC Bickerford takes a swig of the coffee. 'Your dad makes a grand coffee.'

As I wait for them to come back, I listen to the girls running around above us, yelling and laughing. If only my life was as fun and simple as theirs.

'How old are they?'

'Four and five.'

'I have a five-year-old. Lovely age.' The PC smiles.

The officer and my dad wipe their feet as they come back in out of the cold. PC Barnes grips the small plastic evidence bags that now contain the ticket and my fine. He then spends a couple of minutes standing under the main light scrutinising the paperwork. 'Where did you say the message was?'

'On the passenger window but the rain washed it away.'

He scrunches his brow. 'There's something half written along the bottom of the parking fine. I can make out smudged ink and the words *stayed* and *long*.'

It's a good job that I made myself remember exactly what was written. 'It said on the window, you've already stayed too long. They must have written in the dirt on the window first. Realising that it would probably rain, maybe they wrote it on the fine too.'

'Normally, when parking fines are issued they come in a little plastic bag. You're right about that.' PC Bickerford scrunches her brow.

'There was definitely no bag.' My attacker must have removed it to write the note then forgotten to put it back.

PC Barnes sits again. 'Why did you go to Polperro alone today?'

I pull my phone out and pass it to the officer with the message chain open showing them Will's closed account. When they click on his profile, nothing comes up and in the message chain he's also nameless.

Barnes scrolls around a little, taking in my profile too. 'You're the Kate whose baby sister drowned, aren't you? I follow your page. I'm guessing that article has brought the cranks out.'

'I follow it too. Such a sad thing to happen.' PC Bickerford tilts her head.

Everything floods out. It's as if I can't stop talking. This is what I came for and while I have the police here, I want them to do more. I tell him about how I felt the messages were more than just a hoax, how I'd been watched since we'd arrived in Looe.

'See, he even sent me a message stating that he saw me at the harbour. He was watching me then. My husband saw this and now he's left me.' Tears trickle down my face. I didn't even get the chance to tell Damien that I'm not having an affair. That doesn't excuse all my lies though, but I hope that he'll be able to trust me again.

PC Barnes nods. 'We take threats like this very seriously. If you see anyone hanging around again, call us straight away. When you received these messages, why didn't you call us?' PC Barnes presses his lips together.

'I've called so many times with these type of messages and so has my dad.' He nods. 'They always lead to nothing. I thought I should dig a little more before contacting you. I didn't want to waste your time again.'

He drank down the coffee and stood. 'You will never be wasting our time. If anything else happens or you remember something that might help us later, call straight away. We'll head to Polperro tomorrow and ask a few more questions, see if anyone saw anyone acting suspiciously. We're already trying to locate where all the CCTV is and someone will go through it all, but that could take awhile and there's definitely not any by the beach.'

'I was there too.' My dad speaks up.

'At Polperro?'

'Yes.' He glances in my direction. 'I came to see Katie and when I got there, I could see that she was in trouble so I signalled for help.'

PC Barnes scribbled down a few notes.

I exhale with relief. At last, I'm not alone. The police believe me and that's all I could have hoped for.

For a moment, I wonder if I should say anything about the woman who owns the ice-cream shop but I can't. If I tell the police, she might clam up and say nothing to them. She seemed reluctant to speak to me when I chased her down. No, I can't afford to lose her trust. I will see her tomorrow and I will visit Cody's father in the morning like I'd planned to do. The police have enough on their plates with going through CCTV and interviewing people. I'm not allowing Jess's case to take a back seat, besides I'm only here for a few more days. I have to know what happened and I know the ice-cream seller is going to tell me what she knows.

I have to hang on a little longer.

Right now, I wish Damien were here. I want someone to hold me and comfort me in only the way that he does. If only I could turn back the clock on today and start again.

It's as if my dad can sense my sadness. He places an arm over my shoulder. 'It's all going to be okay, Katie. The police will get to the bottom of all this.'

I wish I had as much faith in them as he does, but I don't. Right now, I've never felt so abandoned and alone.

THIRTY-ONE

NATALIE

Tuesday, 25 October

Four in the morning.

Four ten – gust of wind rattles bedroom window.

Four thirty-five – seagull squawks.

Four thirty-eight – joists expanding as heating kicks in.

It's no good. Natalie had barely slept all night and trying for a minute longer was tantamount to torture. That and the racing stress dreams that seemed to merge her encounter with Mary and bumping into Kate. She stepped into her slippers and headed to the kitchen. She didn't intend for things to get that heated with Mary and when Kate nearly ran her over, it was like a sign that this all had to end. No more lies. She wasn't going to be the one who prolonged this heartache any longer.

Mary, Kate, Cody, Laura, Archie – each one in turn flashed through her mind. She flicked the kettle on and gazed out over the harbour. Still the rain came down, although it was more of a misty drizzle now.

She tossed a tea bag into the same cup she'd used all day yesterday. Stained around the rim and bitty at the bottom, she didn't care. Reaching into the fridge, she pulled out the last of the milk and gave it a sniff. Recoiling, she poured it down the sink. The sour milk perfectly reflected the sour mood that cast a shadow on the beautiful seaside town that she'd spent all her life in.

Grabbing her phone from the side, she took a seat at her little table and sipped the black tea. A tinge of bitterness hit her. The seat still had the awful seat pad on it that Alan used to like sitting on. For years, she'd tried to get rid of it. Now she could, it was proving hard. As scruffy as it was, it would stay for now. She glanced at the blue lint that had come off his jumper, still stuck to the rough material.

She swallowed as she thought of Rachel, the girl who had no idea who her father really was. She glanced at the photo of her in-laws that was hung on the wall. Rachel definitely had Alan's mother's eyes, she was certain of that. As Natalie hit the table, her phone bounced. There was so much she wanted to scream at Alan right now but that opportunity had never been an option. Her suspicions had been there but only in death had they been confirmed.

She grimaced as she drank her tea, the bitterness and strength almost drying her tongue out. All she could think of were Mary's pleas for forgiveness. Maybe it would be better to drop everything. Drop Kate, drop Rachel and the truth. Drop it all and concentrate on the future.

Glancing out of the window she saw Cody sitting at the back of his boat, drinking from his flask as rain trickled down his face. Natalie wondered if he had been up all night too, similar things churning through his mind. It's hard to sleep when you're lying to everyone.

Hurrying to her bedroom, Natalie put on the same jumper that she'd worn yesterday and a pair of old jeans. She needed to speak to Cody again. Once upon a time, she'd have done what she could to protect the man and Archie, but not now. She owed them nothing now that Alan had died. Grabbing her coat, she almost slipped on the threadbare hall carpet as she hastily left out the side door. She jogged over to Cody.

'You bleddy liar!' She knew that he'd had something going on with Mary and that they were all in this together.

'Go back to bed, Natalie. Go and sleep whatever it is off.' Cody put his cup down and stepped off his boat.

Natalie hurried down the concrete steps and pushed Cody.

The man stepped back and placed a hand on his chin, his brows furrowed. 'What the hell? I know you're grieving, Nat, but you're acting like a crazy.'

She'd give him crazy. 'Are you sleeping with Mary? Is that why she's protecting you?'

Natalie tried to picture Cody and Mary in the cabin. Her legs wrapped around him as she screamed with ecstasy and the thought turned her stomach. All of a sudden she saw Alan instead. A shiver ran down her spine. Everything about her life felt cheap now. Her memories erased and replaced with the truth of Alan and Mary. She felt like a pound shop bargain that had still ended up in the reduced pile. Had they laughed about her when they were together? Humiliation burned her cheeks.

Pacing back and forth, Natalie roared and leaned against the wall. 'Answer me.'

Cody stared at her, not saying a word.

'You probably need to stay on her good side so she doesn't blab about your dad. Is that why you'd risk everything?'

Before Natalie could take a deep breath to continue, Cody darted over towards her and slammed her against the wall. 'You leave my dad out of this. I am not sleeping with Mary. Never have done, never will. You go about spreading those rumours, I'll spread your remains on the seabed and not lose a single night's sleep. You will not upset my wife or daughter. Do you hear me?'

She didn't believe a word that came out of the man's mouth. If he could keep the secret of his father for that long, what else was he keeping in that head of his?

'What happened, Cody?' She had to push him harder. Speckles of saliva hit her cheek as the man seethed, breathing in and out through the thin gaps between his teeth.

'Nothing. Absolutely nothing.' Cody let go of Natalie and stepped back.

'Dad.' Daisy stepped down, a cool box gripped between her fingers. 'Is everything okay? What's going on?'

'Nothing, my love. We were just saying how dull it looks today, weren't we?'

The last thing Natalie wanted was to upset Daisy. The girl had nothing to do with any of this. 'Yes, awful-looking day.'

'Natalie, are you okay? You look as pale as a sheet.' She knew Daisy could sense all was not right.

'Just a hangover, love.'

'Natalie was just saying that she has a lot on so she was just leaving.'

'Yes, got to go.' Natalie exhaled as she tried to hide her shaking hands but the tremor in her voice was harder to disguise.

'By the way, Dad, I can only help you out this morning. I'm meeting Bethany and Rachel for brunch. Making the most of half-term. So, you taking me out fishing or are we staying here talking all day?' Daisy stepped onto the boat, placing the cool box on the back seat. She slipped her hood off as she reached the cabin and allowed her long caramel-brown hair to fall over her shoulders.

'Yes. We best get going.' As Daisy headed deeper into the cabin, Cody moved close to Natalie until their noses nearly touched.

'I'm going to find out exactly what it is that you're covering up.' Natalie stepped back not wanting to ingest any more of Cody's coffee breath.

'I won't repeat myself. If you know what's good for you, you'll keep out of it and mind your own business.' Cody turned away and got onto his boat.

That was the second threat she'd received after having Mary say almost the same thing. Cody was definitely sleeping with Mary and they were both hiding what Archie did together. God knows why. It's not like Archie was even in a position to be questioned by the police given how ill he was. She watched as Daisy passed a sandwich to her father and took one for herself.

When the truth came out, it was going to rip through the town like a tornado, leaving destruction in its wake.

As Cody's boat chugged out of the harbour, she watched on. She was sick of putting everyone else's feelings first while they all laughed at her. 'Let the truth commence,' she whispered.

THIRTY-TWO

KATE

The satnav is telling me to turn left but I can't see how unless I head straight into woodland. Then I spot the tiny single-track road that is almost overgrown at either side. I turn into what must be The Brambles, clattering over the bumps. After seeing two passing places, I'm wowed by the most amazing view as I pull up. One wrong move in the car could see me tumbling into the sea below from this dizzying height with death being the only possible outcome.

My stomach clenches as I think of Damien. I told him that I was coming to Looe for closure and I haven't deviated from that plan. Only closure doesn't only involve spreading a few flower petals off the harbour, it involves delving as deeply as possible into what happened that day. I wished he'd answer his phone. I've left messages, lots of them, but he hasn't replied and that hurts.

Now, I feel awful about leaving my children with my father. His only instruction was not to leave the house under any circumstances and no drinking. Not a drop. At first the girls were shy but when I left, he'd made them breakfast and was playing board games with them. I have no option but to trust him. He was worried, I could tell. Not about looking after the girls, about me coming here today, alone.

I told him that not much harm could come to me while visiting a nursing home. He pulled a bit of a frown but he understood. I'm doing this for both of us. We need to bury this chapter of our lives to move on. I now realise that my father needs that as much as me.

Swallowing, I wonder if the lie I told to get my visit here will catch up with me and if the police will find out and wonder why I didn't tell them that I was coming here. I know they'll only slow me down by saying that they'll do it, then they won't get around to it like the times before. They take leads and they never follow up on them properly. They care that I was attacked but my long dead sister isn't a priority for them.

I glance up at the huge white building that looks to be about ten rooms across and three floors high. Some of the rooms have balconies, others have full-length windows. It must have been a grand family home in the past. Time waits for no one and I have to get in there, do what I came to do and get out. I also have to remember that I'm Nadine Turner, a relative who is visiting the area. *Don't say your name is Kate*, I remind myself.

My phone rings and what a coincidence, it's Nadine, the very person whose name I'm using. I remember that I didn't message her back. 'Hi, Nadine.'

'Hi, lovely. How's your holiday going?' She pauses. 'I know you mentioned that you were going to Looe and I was thinking about you and your sister. It must be so hard being back there. Thought I'd just see how you were.'

I almost want to cry at her concern. She speaks so warmly to me and we've become really good friends in such a short time. She's my lunch and cake buddy and I've spoken to her a few times about Jess. She's one of the only people who's listened to me go on and on about what happened. 'So much has happened.'

I fill her in and end on the events of last night and a lump sticks in my throat as I tell her that Damien has left me.

'Shit. Are you okay?'

'The sore head and nausea hurt less than Damien leaving.'

'That's awful. I hope they catch the bastard that attacked you and Damien will come round when he's had a chance to calm down. What are the police doing?'

'The usual, checking CCTV. They took my coat for forensics. I doubt they'll search the cave given that the tide comes in on it but you never know.'

'Don't go putting yourself in any more danger, lovely. You've got to take care of yourself for those little girls and I need my friend back.' I swallow. So much of me wanted to never go back to work so that I could wrap my precious daughters up in cotton wool, but I have to admit, I miss Nadine, Brett, and the pool now. I miss being me and not just Mum, but I'm not increasing my hours. No way. 'So no more expeditions into creepy caves on your own. Promise?'

'Yes, sir. Promise. I have no intention of going into a cave ever again.' I let out a slight chuckle.

'Are you doing anything today?'

'As it happens, I'm just about to visit someone in a nursing home.' It sounds stupid telling her that.

'What? I didn't know you knew anyone who lived there.'

'I don't. I'm playing detective. The chap I'm visiting was close by when Jess went missing all those years ago. I need to speak to him.' I don't mention that Archie is a man with memory issues; that the only thing that might result from this visit is a man who is even more distressed and confused than usual. But, now that I remember seeing him peering out of his cabin just before Jess drowned, I can't get the man out of my mind.

'So you're doing the job the police are meant to be doing?'

'Something like that. I must be mad, I know, but how much

danger can come of me visiting a nursing home? Someone wants me out of the way and they left me for dead in a cave. That's how close I'm getting. The police don't have the resources to do what I'm doing and my days here are limited.'

I hear a click down the phone when Nadine swallows. 'Please take care of yourself. I need my partner in cake to come back in one piece. Promise me you'll play it safe?'

'I will. Look, I have to go. Lots to do and plenty of leads to follow. I'll stay in a crowd and make sure I'm seen at all times.'

'Call me if you want to talk. Okay?'

'Okay. Got to go. Bye.'

I end the call before Nadine starts talking about something else. There will be plenty of time for catch-ups when I'm back at work on Monday. Time here is too precious for me to stay on the phone. It's Tuesday and the only thing I hear in my head is the ticking of the clock telling me that I only have three whole days left then it's back home.

Glancing back, I catch sight of the bonnet of a navy-blue car sticking out of the nearest passing place to the house, almost tucked in the hedge. It's the same car, it has to be. I start to follow the steep path down and as I follow the bend in the path, I lose sight of the car. The car door slams and skids as it turns with a revving engine. I barely catch sight of it before it speeds off. When I reach the passing place, it's as if the car was never here. A gust of wind causes the trees to shake and branches to sway. I shiver. It's like I'm not alone, ever. I stare in each direction, wondering if I'll catch a moving person but I see nothing but dense woodland.

From now on, I'm going to check my rear-view mirror all the time. I need something, anything. A registration number. The make of the car.

I glance down and see a few fresh drips of oil where the car had been parked. I'm looking for a car with an oil leak. When I get back to Looe, I'll check the parking space that the car was parked in. If there's leaked oil there, it will tell me if it's the same car.

I grip my phone and consider if I should call the police, then I place it in my pocket. I'm on the cusp of solving their case for them, which means I need to keep going. Talking to them might prevent me from investigating and that can't happen.

THIRTY-THREE

KATE

As I enter The Brambles, the woman who buzzed me in has arrived to greet me at the door. 'Sign in the book. Name, time and registration.' I catch her name badge – Sylvie. There's a smell in the air, a little like disinfectant mixed with scrambled eggs. Swallowing, I fight the nausea that sits in my throat. Now is not the time to get sick. I have too much to do and I daren't mention how rough I feel to my dad as he'll go on about me going to the hospital for a check-up.

I go to write Kate but scribble out the K and write Nadine. Sylvie looks at me with furrowed brows. 'Sorry, people normally call me by my middle name. I don't like Nadine.' I nervously laugh off my mistake. Today, I look less dishevelled. I'm wearing my smart jeans and a fitted jumper, my hair is twisted into a topknot and I've left a clump down to frame my face and hide a tiny scratch on my forehead. I feel as though I look the part of visiting a relative. 'I'm here to see Archie.'

'Oh, yes. He has been popular this week.'

'Popular?'

'Yes, his son has been, his granddaughter and a couple of friends. We all love him here.'

I smile. 'Yes, he was always quite the charmer. It's been awhile since I saw Great-Uncle Archie.'

What do I know? I know that he was there the day my sister went missing. I feel as though his son is hiding something and I only hope that the man has a spurt of lucidity while I'm here. I know his granddaughter, Daisy, uncannily has hair like mine and my figure. He may mistake me for her if his memory is playing up. I also know that Cody lied about his father having an accident at the home the other day. Why? The man I'm about to see is the key to solving the mystery. The answers are now mine to lose.

'He's probably worse than when you saw him last. When was it?'

'Erm, I can't remember. When he was still living at home. It's my first time visiting here. I'm staying for a few days so thought I'd pop by.'

'So you haven't seen him for at least a couple of years?'

I shake my head. 'Should have come sooner.'

'Follow me. Let's hope it's a good day for him. He's had his breakfast and we've put him in the visitor room overlooking the sea. It's got a charming view. Would you like a drink while you're here?'

Shaking my head, I follow the woman. 'No, thank you for offering.'

What I want is some private time to speak to Archie. I hope there are no other visits or even worse, I hope Sylvie doesn't stay in the room.

'Okay, here we are. Archie, love. You have a visitor. It's Nadine.'

'Hi, Uncle Archie.' I sit in the window seat, opposite him. Thankfully, he doesn't call me out on my lie. There's a streak of what looks like egg down the front of his jumper and he stares at me with his mouth open, exposing several gaps in his teeth.

'I'll pop by in a few minutes, see how you're both getting

on.' The woman leaves and the room is silent except for the humming of a heater.

'Lovely view.'

'View?' He sniffs and huffs out a lungful of air.

'Archie, my name is Kate.' I don't have long and there's no point beating about the bush. 'Do you remember baby Jessica.'

He scrunches up his forehead and runs his tongue over his cracked lips. 'Baby in the car.'

'No, the baby who drowned in the harbour many years ago. She was my sister. You were in your boat at the time, with Cody.'

He keeps shaking his head, over and over again. 'Crash. The car crashed.' His brows furrow and he begins fiddling with the edge of his cardigan. 'Red hat.'

My heart bangs. Jess's red hat was found floating in the harbour later that day. 'Tell me about the red sun hat.'

'No, no, no!' He begins to yell so loud I keep well away from him as his foot kicks out at the table, nudging it in my direction. Then he grabs his beaker of tea and begins to bang it hard on the chair's arm and the lid flies off, sending tea spraying all over the coffee table and floor. 'No, no!' He keeps repeating the same word over and over again.

The woman runs back in. 'Archie, stop it, my love. You're okay.' She pats him down with a towel and takes the beaker off him. 'We'll need to get you changed out of this damp jumper in a minute.'

Tea drips from my hand and there's a wet streak across my jeans.

'Sorry about that. This happens sometimes when he's not having a good day.'

But he mentioned the red hat. I need to know more. 'Archie, tell me about the red hat.'

The woman glances at me as she continues to clean him up. Archie looks up. 'The red hat?'

'You know about the red hat?'

'Oh, he goes on about that sometimes. Cody told me about the toddler he rescued from the car. Apparently he was wearing a red sun hat and sometimes that's all Archie can remember. Silly isn't it, what the brain chooses to keep. You were a hero, weren't you, darling.'

'Wasn't a red hat found in the harbour when the baby drowned a few weeks after?'

She stops and bites her bottom lip. 'Who are you?'

'Nadine.'

'No, no, no, no!' Archie shouts. 'Jessica.'

'What do you know about Jess?' I can't help but push him a little more. The last thing I want to do is see him like this but I need to know.

The man yells so loud, my ears almost pop.

'I'm sorry, Ms Turner, or whoever you are, but you best leave. As you can see, Archie is distressed. Please wait in reception and I'll get you signed out in a minute.'

I've blown it. She's suspicious of me and Archie's in a bad way. They'll tell Cody and he'll put two and two together. If it is Cody who tried to kill me, he'll want to do it even more now, especially if the woman tells him what happened or describes me. Cody is trying to hide what Archie did and I know the lengths he'll go to. My life means nothing to him.

'I said, can you wait in reception? Now.'

I've seriously blown it.

THIRTY-FOUR

KATE

'Okay.' I back out from the chaos, knowing that Sylvie's not happy with me. My mouth dries up and my shaking fingers won't keep still. She's going to call the police, I know it. What happens to a person who pretends to be someone else to visit a resident of a nursing home? Am I in trouble for this?

Just as I'm about the leave the room, he calls out. 'Stop the noise. The baby in the sea is crying. No, no, no.' Tears stream down his face and I feel my own eyes welling up. *The baby in the sea*. I know he's taking about Jess.

I hurry out to reception, trembling with teary eyes. The heat surrounds me like it's thick in the air. So hot. My vision wobbles a little and a wave of dizziness passes through me, then I dry heave slightly. I have this sick headache over my temples.

'Are you okay?'

Sylvie passes me a box of tissues and I realise I've made a mess of my face as I rub mascara onto the tissue. Now I've started crying, I can't stop.

'You're not related to Archie, are you?'

'I'm sorry. I just need the truth and everyone around here is lying to me.'

She takes my hand and leads me to a chair. 'What's going on?'

'I've been here investigating the death of my baby sister, twenty-five years ago. Her name was Jess. Everyone said that it was an accident, that she drowned in Looe Harbour. I know there's more to the story. The investigation was shoddy and I think the police just wanted it off their pile. Archie was there that day and the red hat he was shouting about, that was my sister's sun hat. He mentioned the baby in the sea. He's not talking about the car accident. He's got both mixed up in his mind and he can't tell me what he knows.'

'I know something.' Sylvie checks the corridor.

'About my sister?'

'Not exactly.' She shakes her head. 'I could lose my job, everything. It's not my place to say.'

'Please. I swear I won't bring your name up at all.'

She bites her lip and takes a deep breath. 'If you do, I'll deny everything.' Letting out a huge sigh, she continues, 'I don't mean to pry but sometimes I hear Archie's son talking to him. Normally, it's when I want to check to see if they're okay and I'm waiting for a gap in their conversation, that's all.'

My heart bangs that hard, it feels as though it's about to burst through my ribcage. 'Please, I won't tell anyone that you said anything. Not knowing the truth is eating me up.'

'I heard Cody having quite a go at his old man, telling him to stop mentioning the baby. Of course, Archie still keeps shouting about the baby in the sea. It's normally when the seagulls are sounding away. He seems to think they're crying like babies. I heard him say that he wanted to keep the hat but he threw it into the sea. Cody was quite mean to him. Just as he looked up at the door, I ducked out of the way. That was one incident, they've had this conversation a few times. I've no doubt that Archie knows what happened that day but I also know without a doubt that all you'll get is red hat and a baby crying in the sea.'

By now, my face is sodden with tears. For the first time since coming here someone has told me the truth. Everyone else has made me feel like I'm going crazy with their denial. Cody knows everything and he won't tell me. I only hope that the ice-cream seller will be more open. At least I can tell her what Archie said to me today. I won't mention Sylvie. The last thing I want is for this wonderful human being to lose her job and looking at Cody and the way he is, he'd insist that she went.

'Thank you. I was beginning to think I was losing my mind.' I'm going to call it murder now. I believe that Archie killed her, reason unknown, and Cody either helped him or covered it up. All I need to do is prove it.

Reason unknown. What could those reasons be? Did they try to smuggle her away and it all went wrong? I still can't forget the pirate clue that Will was dangling my way before he went offline. Was it something to do with the man who took us out that day? Mr Pritchard. Were they all into something bad together? Is that why no one is talking? If I'm on the cusp of unravelling everything, my life is seriously in danger. I can't ask Mr Pritchard now as he's dead.

'Come here.' The woman places an arm around my shoulder.

'Thank you for everything.' I splutter and blow my nose. 'Can I just ask another question?'

''Course, lovely.'

'What colour car does his son drive?'

'It's a silvery grey saloon.'

That's not the car that has been following me but then again, he could have used his daughter's car or maybe his wife has a car. 'Thank you again for everything.'

'That's okay. You take care of yourself, do you hear me?'

I nod and smile as she buzzes me out. Blue sky pierces through the clouds. Running to the car, I open the door and throw my bag onto the passenger seat. My phone rings and I answer immediately. 'Dad, is everything okay? The girls.' My heart revs up as I imagine allsorts. 'Are they hurt?'

'No, they're fine. We've been playing Buckaroo. They're hungry and they mentioned that you went out for a pub lunch. They want to go to the mermaid pub for food.'

'I don't think that's a good idea.' He lost Jess. I remind myself that he can't be trusted with a responsibility so huge.

'I promise you, Katie. I will guard them with my life. I know you hate me—'

'I don't hate you.'

He pauses and clears his throat. 'I always thought you hated me.'

A tear slips from my eye. 'I did, I thought I did and I want to believe that you've changed.'

'I have. I'm not the same person. Please give me a chance to make it up to you.'

I sigh. It's less than a five-minute walk. 'We went to the Old Smuggler. Go straight there and hold both of their hands. If a hair on their head is damaged, I will never forgive you. Don't let go of them. Promise me.' I feel like I might throw up. The thought of them all going out. People will look at my dad and they'll point but we can't hide away.

'I promise.'

'Okay,' I croak. I feel so sickly yet I'm starving. The lack of food in me is probably making things worse. I need to eat before I faint. That churning is there again and it reminds me of a feeling I'm familiar with. I reach in through my coat and cup one of my breasts, searching for the sensitivity I'm all too familiar with in this potential situation. 'I'll be with you in about half an hour. Order me something with chips, curry maybe.'

'Will do. See you there.' With that he hangs up.

My mind casts back over the past few weeks. I was late with some of my pills and I forgot one or two. The stress of everything, of leaving the girls to go to start my new job kept my mind on other things. It's not concussion, I'm pregnant. This nausea has been going on for days, maybe even a couple of weeks. It just so happens to have got worse since yesterday.

I gaze at the sea and several steps forward would see me plunging down the cliff to my death. I creep closer and gaze down, the swells and swirls making me giddy. Taking a step back, I almost gasp with relief. That's when I hear the seagulls. I close my eyes, one hand on my tummy, the other in my pocket as I think of Jess. The gulls really do sound like crying babies and I don't want to open my eyes. I fear I might see the ghost of her being taken by a wave.

I need to buy a pregnancy test when I get back to Looe. If I am carrying a new life, I feel a duty to protect it with all that I have. From now on, I'm not taking any risks. One thing I love more than anything is my children and I know I have enough love in my heart for another. I choke up as I think of Damien and the fact that he's not here.

The squawks send a tingle down my spine and with eyes still closed, I feel a presence behind me, like the whoosh of a breeze. The seagulls get louder as do the cries. Whoever did this to my baby sister will come for me and my baby. I should message Damien but this isn't something that should be revealed in a message and I haven't confirmed it yet. No, the secret is mine, for now. A crunch in the leaves behind me has me opening my eyes and too scared to turn. Just a slight nudge forward and I'd be over the edge; dead.

Shaking, I eventually turn but there is nothing but a crow feeding on what looks like a dead mouse lying on a patch of earth. The shiny innards spill out. Holding my hand over my mouth, I run to the car and lock it as soon as I get in. A few moments pass and I get the image of the mouse out of my head. A gull crashes into my windscreen and I flinch. I have to get away from here. The landscape is open but all I feel is overwhelming suffocation. I double-check that I'm in reverse and drive out of that car park as fast as I can. Away from the crow, the seagulls and the ill feelings that the place is giving me.

THIRTY-FIVE

KATE

As soon as I enter the Smuggler, several people turn their heads but I ignore them. My dad has ordered me curry and chips. The girls have already eaten and he is just tucking into what looks like a wedge of chocolate fudge cake.

'How did you get on?' Rosie and Millie are sitting a little away from us in the window seat where they have a pack of colourful cards spread out on the table. 'I haven't let them out of my sight.'

'I spoke to Archie. All he kept saying was red hat and he went on about a baby crying in the sea. I'm a few years too late. He can't tell me what he knows.' Tears drizzle down my face as I shove a curry-covered chip into my mouth. My emotions were all over the place when I was pregnant with both of the girls, that's how I know for sure. On a normal day, I'd be able to have this conversation without snivelling in the pub while still ramming food into my mouth.

'I'm sorry, love. You do know that the chances of finding out exactly what happened are slim. It was such a long time ago.'

I nod. He's right but in my heart I refuse to believe that. In fact, I believe more than ever that I'm on the brink of revealing everything. Cody will have to give up his secrets and the ice-cream seller is going to tell me what she knows. I check my watch. As soon as my dad and the girls are settled after lunch, I'll head over there. At least I don't need to lie to my dad, not like I did to Damien. I swallow the food in my mouth and take a long swig of lemonade.

'Thank you.'

He awkwardly presses his lips together to smile.

With that, I wolf down the rest of my food and enjoy it like it's the best thing I've ever eaten. When we leave here, I'll need to pop back to the cottage. Not wanting to waste any time after returning from The Brambles, I rushed straight over to the pub. What I need to do is check the parking space where I saw the car. If there's a patch of fairly fresh oil, I'll know that the same car was following me today.

The man who was falling over drunk the last time I was here enters the pub with a baby in a pushchair.

'Kyle, want a drink?' a man asks.

'No, I'm on babysitting duty. Looking after this little dot. The wife and daughter have not long gone to Plymouth on a shopping expedition so I'm on grandad duty.'

'She's a sweetheart that little baby is and so are Mary and Rachel. You're a lucky man.'

'I know I am. Family is everything, aren't they, chick?' He strokes the baby's cheek and she gurgles, then he offers up a dummy to her mouth. As the man rubs his hands in front of the fire, I can't help gazing at the baby. If I'm right, I'll have another baby in several months' time. Her pinched little face with red scratch marks is all that I see as the rest of her body is wrapped in a hood and a blanket. My two often scratched their faces and they kept pulling their scratch mitts off. I wish I didn't see Jess every time I saw a baby.

Placing my cutlery on my empty plate, I take a deep breath and feel heartburn brewing up inside me. The dummy in the baby's mouth bobs up and down as she drifts off to sleep. Jess used to do that. Guilt washes over me again. I swallow down the guilt of that day. It's easy to blame my dad but I need to face up to what I did. Shaking that thought away, I wonder what Jess would be like now, if she'd been alive. We might all be on holiday together. Jess might be married or she might have children and my dad would never have had a twenty-five-year battle with alcohol addiction. That in turn made my mum unhappy, it ruined my childhood. We have all suffered. Rosie and Millie have been robbed of an aunty and it's my fault. I started it.

'I see Jess every time I look at a baby. It never gets easier.'

'Mummy, will you play pairs with us. Grandad got us some cards with fruits on them.' Millie looks up at me, doe-like. How can I refuse her simple request?

'We popped into one shop. I held their hands the whole time.'

'Of course I will, sweetie.' I shuffle my chair a bit closer to them and join in for ten minutes. The least I can give them is a bit of my time after being so vacant.

'Is Daddy coming back when he's done his work?' Millie places a card down.

'I don't know. We'll see.'

'Are the police coming back?' Rosie asks as she picks up all the cards, ready to lay them all out, face down again.

I shake my head and smile. 'I don't think so but if they do, it's okay.'

'Why did they come?'

'Someone had an accident on the beach yesterday and I was there. They're just asking what people saw.'

'What kind of accident? Did they die?' Rosie won't stop questioning me and I feel a little guilty about lying but I don't want her to worry about me. My girls are too young to process the truth; that someone attacked me and left me for dead.

'No, they're okay now.'

'Did you help them, like when you saved that baby at work?'

A twinge of guilt washes through me. I haven't put them right about that as I was hoping they'd forget. 'Something like that. Some nice people from the pub carried her from the beach and warmed her up.'

'They must be kind people, Mummy.'

I smile and begin playing their game. They were kind people. I must go back and thank them but I don't know if I'll have time. Half an hour soon passes and the place is filling up. 'Right, I think we should head back in a minute.'

As soon as they finish a game, the girls pack the cards away and we start walking back towards the cottage. When we reach it, my dad ushers them towards the door and I check the car park. The parking space I need to look at is free.

'I just need to check something, I'll be in in a minute,' I tell him.

He nods. 'Are we ready for some more Buckaroo?'

The girls yell with delight as they go in.

I run across the car park, the huge meal I ate now gurgling away in my stomach. When I pop out later, I need to find a chemist and take a test to see if I really am pregnant.

A few more steps and I'm there. A shiny patch of black sits in that very space. I was right. I'm being constantly followed. I look in all directions frantically, then I squint as I try to gaze through windows and into the distance. Cottages dot the hills and the beach is quiet apart from a few people walking in coats. All I want to do is scream in frustration.

Who are you?

THIRTY-SIX

KATE

As I approach the ice-cream shop, I peer around the corner. If Cody is there, I don't want him to see me entering. Whatever this woman has to tell me, I get the feeling it would be best if I were to see her alone and not under the scrutiny of Cody, who is likely to be involved.

On the harbour Cody gazes about, hands on hips like he's the king of his castle. By the bench, I see a bike and two young women sitting on it. I instantly recognise Daisy. She's leaning back and eating while talking to the other girl she was with at the café. It's not Rachel, the young woman with the baby. Damn. I need them all to go.

The tide is low and the boats look off-kilter, stranded in the sand and weed. They're like me, stuck in the moment and unable to move.

Cody says something to his daughter and strides off with his bag. Now I can make my move. After jogging to the ice-cream shop, I join the queue and hope that no one else comes in after me. First she serves a woman, then some teenagers. I place my hands palm down on the glass counter. 'Hi, we need to talk.'

She steps out and closes the door, turning the closed sign

around. 'Come through.' She heads through the door at the back and it's like my feet are glued to the ground. Someone attacked me yesterday and for all I know, it could be her. This could be nothing more than a lure to get me alone again. 'Are you coming? I can't keep the shop closed for too long.'

'I, err, can we talk here?'

She peers out of the shop window. Cody has just come back. 'You need to get through here now. He can't see you. No one can see you here. They all talk, you know.'

I glance back and realise that my knees are knocking and I feel like I'm turning to jelly, but I follow. My desire to get answers is so strong there's no way I'm going to turn around and walk out. I follow her through what looks like a storeroom. There's a large walk-in freezer and I shiver, not because it's cold, because I don't want to end up in it while she tries to work out where to dump my body.

Following her up the narrow dark stairway, I take in the old black-and-white photos of people standing outside the shop, all taken at different times. The stairs creak and crack, like they might fall from beneath us and there's a damp patch on the ceiling. A musty smell makes me recoil. This feels like a place a person would come to die. As I reach the top, she leads me into the kitchen. I wonder if she's hiding any secrets behind the other doors.

A chopping board and a chunk of cheese is all that sits on the worktop. A hard crust has formed in the corners and the slightly stale smell teases my nostrils, making me want to cover my face. I swallow as my gaze falls upon the bread knife, a beam of sunshine glinting from its blade. I inhale, then I exhale slowly. I've gone and done it, I've put myself in danger again.

The woman grabs the knife and sweat prickles at the nape of my neck. She throws it into the water filled washing-up bowl, then wraps up the cheese. 'Sorry about the mess. I don't get many visitors. Okay, Kate, take a seat.'

I sit on one of the two chairs that are neatly positioned at each side of a small drop-leaf table that is pushed up against the wall. The view outside takes me away for a few seconds. The boats, people walking and laughing do nothing to calm my nerves. I try to focus on the outside for a second, to calm my heart rate down.

'You want to know what I know, and I'm prepared to tell you.'

'Thank you. I really appreciate what you're doing.' I don't want her to stop talking.

'Coffee or tea?'

I shake my head. My stomach is still feeling yucky after wolfing down that huge lunch. The spicy curry is repeating on me too, leaving a bitter taste at the back of my throat. I wish I hadn't eaten it. She leans forward and I flinch but I soon realise that she's not reaching for me. She grabs a photo of one of the fishing boats and it looks like it was taken many years ago.

'I apologise for scaring you last night. That's not me. I'd just had some really bad news and when you stopped me, my mind was still on it.'

I breathe a sigh of relief. 'I'm sorry too. It must have been a bit weird, me chasing you around the streets after nearly running you over. Is your name Natalie? Have I got that right?'

'Yes. They call me Nat the ice-cream lady, well the kids do.' She chuckles. 'This shop was my in-laws and my father-in-law's parents before that. I guess it's mine now that my husband has also passed away. I have no one to leave it to.' Natalie's eyes glass over and she rubs them. 'I was thinking of packing up and starting afresh. I'll probably need to do that once the truth comes out. I won't be welcome here any more.'

Swallowing, I'm ready for the truth.

'See that photo.' She nods at it and I look as closely as I can. 'That's Mr Pritchard. Your family went out on his boat. He used to always wear that pirate hat to entertain the kids. The one next to Mr P belonged to Kyle and Mary Penrose, they now own the Old Smuggler. They sold the boat, bought the pub, and they keep a small boat instead. The other boat you see is Cody's boat. I saw your family going out with him the other day. He used to work with his father, Archie.'

'I went to see Archie earlier today.'

'And?' Natalie scrunches her brows and sits opposite me.

No longer worried about being in this room with her, I feel myself relaxing slightly. 'He knew who Jessica was. He kept repeating himself, talking about the baby crying in the sea and Jess's red hat.'

'I went to see him the other night, with Laura. She said that you've been in her shop.'

'Yes. Why did you both visit Archie?'

'The same reason you went. We wanted to find out more. This town has lived under a shadow since that day and the article brought it all back. With you turning up, everyone has that day on their minds. But I didn't give it much thought for years until I overheard something being said one night and I'm trusting you with this.'

'Who said it?' I swallow the lump in my throat, not daring to blink in case I miss a sign.

'I didn't see who.' She looks away. I don't know if Natalie can't stand the intensity I'm projecting or she's hiding something. 'I couldn't hear well enough to recognise the voice as it was so low. I heard what I heard then I hurried away, not wanting them to know I was there. I was somewhere I shouldn't have been, let's put it that way. Don't ask me any more on that as you won't get anything. My reasons for being there were personal.'

That's not what's important to me. Her spying on someone was none of my business. What is my business is what was said and how it will help me find out what happened to Jess. 'Okay, what did you hear?'

She stands and walks over to the worktop, placing both hands down as she stares out of the window. Shaking her head, she stares into the washing-up bowl. 'Archie dropped your sister's sun hat into the sea at Banjo Pier. It must have washed up in the harbour when the tide came back in. I'm saying that Archie was involved but he may not have fully known what he was doing. He was having these episodes, these funny amnesia attacks after his car accident. Anyway, that's what happened. I've read the posts on your page for ages, not knowing what to do. I wanted to tell you before but this is my home. These people are my community. This place is all I've ever known.'

I'm trembling. There will be no justice for Jess if I don't get the truth. Maybe someone else was in on it and Archie was covering up for them? Maybe it was Cody? Could he have sent his father on a mission to get rid of evidence?

'Did this person say that they saw Cody with Jess?'

She shook his head. 'No, just the hat.'

'So he might have killed Jess, or maybe someone else did and he was covering up for them? Maybe he was covering for his son.' This is all too neat for me. Why would someone attack me over this? As Archie couldn't stand trial now given his mental capacity, even if it was intentional, why would someone attack me and leave me to drown. I don't believe it was all on Archie. He's an easy target to lay all the blame on given his situation.

'I don't know, but what I do want to do is help you in any way I can. I've decided that this place doesn't matter to me now. I have nothing to stay for. In fact, I want the truth to come out, wherever that might lead. I tell you what, I'll do a bit of digging and let you know what I find out in a day or two.' She turns around and tucks a straggly piece of hair behind her ear.

'You don't know how grateful I am, thank you. I only have three more days here.'

She blows out, her puffed red cheeks reducing in size as she exhales. 'I best get a move on then.'

'Someone has been messaging me, well not any more. They've gone offline. They've been using the name Will Wilcox. The pirate.'

'Laura mentioned that. She told me what you said.'

'Do you have any idea who this person might be?'

'No, not a jot.'

'They tried to kill me yesterday. I went to the cave at Polperro and this person followed me. They knocked me out and the tide came in. Another ten minutes, I'd have been swept out to sea.'

She shook her head and pressed her lips together. 'That's awful to hear.'

'They've also been following me in a navy-blue car. Do you know anyone with a car of that colour?'

'There are probably loads of people in this town with a navy-coloured car.'

'It has an oil leak.'

'I'll keep an eye out. Anyway, I best get back to the shop. Here, take my number.' She grabs a curled up old notebook and pulls a sheet of paper out before noting down her number and passing it to me.

'Thank you again for helping me.'

'Are the police involved?'

'They're looking into my attack but they don't know I went to Archie's nursing home or that I was coming here.' I realise that I've just made myself vulnerable with that statement so I add to my sentence. 'I told my dad I was coming here, though.'

'Okay. Give me a day or two.' She ushers me up and back down the stairs.

'Thank you. I'll text you in a short while so that you have my number.' She nods and opens the door to an angry-looking man with three children and an elderly lady holding his arm.

I shuffle past them and back out onto the pavement. That's when I see a navy-blue car pulling up. It stops on double yellows with the engine running. I stand behind the wall and peer out. Daisy and Cody have gone but the one remaining girl gets off Jess's bench and runs over to the car shouting, 'Mum, unlock the doors.'

I can just about see through the sky reflected in the windscreen. It's Laura from the shop, smiling. Her daughter jumps in and she reverses out. As soon as they're gone, I run over to where the car was parked, heart banging away as I check for an oil patch. There's nothing on the road but then again, she'd only been parked there for a few seconds. There was only one thing to do. She must be going back to her shop in awhile.

I'm going to wait for her at closing time and I'm going to follow her home. She must be popping out to get supplies. I know she lives close by and parking isn't good in this town and there's none by her shop. She said so herself. I hope that she takes her car back home after her little trip, then she or her daughter go back to the shop. I will follow either of them home. When I get there, I'll find her car and I'll check out her parking space. If there is an oil patch, I will know who's been following me. That person is probably the same person who tried to kill me in the cave.

In the meantime, I have to get to a chemist. I need a pregnancy test.

THIRTY-SEVEN

KATE

I hurry back to the cottage, after a stop at the chemist, and Dad opens the door before I even reach it. 'How did it go?'

I scurry through to the kitchen, passing the girls who are colouring. He's as invested in getting to the truth as I am.

'Natalie, the woman who owns the ice-cream shop, told me that she heard someone saying that Archie, the man in the nursing home, was standing on Banjo Pier with Jess's hat on the day that she went missing.'

'Did they see Jess?'

I shake my head. 'But he had her hat.'

'Who said this?'

'She said she doesn't know.'

My dad raises his grey eyebrows. 'Really? She heard someone say all that. She probably knows everyone and she doesn't recognise a voice.'

I sit at the table. 'I know, I don't believe her either. I think there's a reason she's holding back on me. She said she's going to do a bit of digging, see if she can find out more.'

'I always knew there was more to it.' My dad hyperventi-lates a little so I place a hand on his back. Only now do I see how fragile he is and for the first time ever, I know we're on the same team and that fuels my determination.

'We're going to get the full truth, Dad. I won't stop until we do. It's clear this town is hiding so much from us.'

My dad fights back his tears and grabs two glasses and a carton of juice. He pours me one. 'Do you trust this woman? She could've been the one sending you the messages.'

'It wasn't her.' I sip the juice but this only aggravates my heartburn.

He plants his palm on his forehead. 'I hope not.'

'Archie kept yelling about Jess's red hat. It all makes sense to me. When I went into Natalie's shop and up her stairs then into her kitchen, alone, I didn't feel at all worried. She's trying to help us.'

'I thought you were just going to the shop. Be careful what you do. You don't know these people.'

'But she didn't want Cody to see me there talking to her. We had to get away from the window as Cody was sitting on the bench, Jess's bench.' My cheeks are burning hot.

'Look in there, Katie. Those children need their mother. Please promise me that you won't put yourself in danger. If something were to happen to you after Jess, I—'

I wipe my eyes. 'I'm sorry.'

'Those little girls have missed you. They've been happy playing with stranger grandad but they need you too.'

'I'm sorry for leaving you with them for so long. There's one more thing I need to do, then that's it.' I um and err as to whether I should tell him about the navy-blue car and the oil leak, then I decide not to say anything. He's already nervously tapping his fingers on the table. I will know for definite as soon as I find out where Laura lives.

'Is it dangerous?'

'No, I promise. All I have to do is go to Laura's shop. She's definitely not dangerous.'

'Should we all go?'

'No, I don't want to drag the girls along for this conversation. It's not right.' I can't tell him that I'm planning to follow the woman.

He looks at me like he doesn't believe a word I say. 'Why don't you call the police now and tell them what you've found out. They can talk to Laura instead. It's their job, not yours.'

'I will, later. I promise.' As soon as I've said that, my phone rings. I snatch it immediately and place it to my ear. 'It's the police,' I mouthed. 'Have you found anything?'

I listen for a few seconds and add the odd yes and okay, then the call ends.

'What did they say?' My dad leans forward, waiting for answers.

'A witness said they saw a woman on the beach about the same time that I was there. At the moment, they're treating her as a witness. They're putting an appeal out on social media later today with the help of the local press. They said she was wearing a black coat, a hood and walking boots. There's no useful CCTV. What they have is grainy and I'm only caught on two cameras.'

'A person, dressed in black, following you. That sounds like the description you gave of the person watching the cottage.'

The more I think of Laura, the more convinced I am that she's the person who has been following me but I can't say that to Dad right now. She has to be Will Wilcox and I want to know why. She doesn't scare me one bit. In the cave, she caught me off guard but not now. I'm on to her. As soon as I've checked her car out, I'm passing what I know over to the police.

'What are you thinking?'

'I don't know.' I'm confused. The answers have to be there, all tangled up in what I know but I can't unravel them. I think back to that day, twenty-five years ago. My mother dragging me towards the ice-cream shop. Now I know that Natalie was in there, serving. It couldn't have been her. Her husband, who died, maybe it was him? It's like my memory is clicking into place. I didn't spend long looking at my dad and sister, all I saw was Archie's face pressed against the window of his boat. If only I had. My mother has said many times that she doesn't remember any more.

I check the time and it's nearly four. I have to get ready to go to the shop.

'It's getting on a bit. I said to Laura that I'd meet her at her shop and I don't want to miss her. I promise I'll stay around people. I won't go in anyone's house, car, boat or anywhere else, I promise. I won't be long. Maybe when I get back, we could take the girls for an evening walk on the beach.'

'I'd love that. I found some mackerel in the fridge by the way so I put it in the freezer.'

'The girls caught it with Damien.' I swallow my sadness down. He's still refusing to engage with me. 'I'll be back before you know it.'

My dad grabs a tissue and wipes his eyes.

'Are you okay?' I ask him.

He shakes his head. 'I sat in this kitchen with your mother. You and Jess were in front of the television with some loud cartoons blaring out. She hadn't talked to me for hours, which is how things often went when we'd been bickering. I can't even remember what we argued about now. Anyway, that's all I remember. It's nothing. If I could go back to that day and do everything differently.'

Right now, I know my dad is the only person on earth who understands how I feel.

'It's hard. I'm reminded of the life I never had with Jess. I'm hoping that we can move on after this. We have to be able to.'

Grabbing my bag, I leave my dad in the kitchen. I need to hurry upstairs, do this test and head out before I miss my opportunity. I'm running out of minutes, hours and days.

I lock myself in the bathroom and pee on the stick, then I stare at it willing time to go faster. The results show up. I throw the stick in the bin under a batch of used make-up wipes and I sit on the loo, head leaning back against the wall.

I really don't know where my life is going right now. A part of me wants to run down the stairs, pretend that all this isn't happening. On a normal day, I'd be happy and Damien would be thrilled but now, he won't even communicate with me. We've talked about another baby before but he'd been hesitant. He thought I would be even more stifling if we had three and he said it was too much work because I'd never let anyone help with the children. I think I've proved otherwise with Dad being here. Gulping down the ball of emotion in my throat, I take a deep breath and decide to mull it over for awhile before I try to call him again.

For now, the knowledge that I'm pregnant is mine and mine alone. Right now, I have a woman to follow.

THIRTY-EIGHT

KATE

What little sunshine there has been today has been replaced by a collection of storm clouds. The weather is as changeable as I am at the moment. One minute I feel I know nothing and that I should stay safe with my family, the next I'm like a rabid dog, chasing the tiniest of leads like I'm on a mission. Jess is worth every risk I've taken. If something happened to Millie or Rosie, I'd do everything I could.

I stand in the doorway of a vacant shop, my grey hood covering my brow line. Before leaving the cottage, I stared out of the bedroom window, checking everywhere for the navy-blue car or any sign of a person loitering. Even though I couldn't see anyone, I still went out of the back door with the feeling that my heart was in my throat.

As I wait for Laura to close the shop and leave, I bite my thumbnail to the skin and flinch as I draw blood. I grimace at the metallic taste in my mouth, wishing that I had a bottle of water. When I arrived about fifteen minutes ago, I'd casually walked amongst a crowd and peered in. Laura had been tidying up and she was alone. There was no sign of her daughter.

Rain begins to trickle so I keep my back against the door to avoid the heavily plopping raindrops. Right now, I wish I'd worn my waterproof coat but it is what it is. I listen as a door creaks open, then I peer around the recess to see that Laura is leaving. My phone is on silent and I'm ready to follow her. My fingers tingle until they shake and my head begins to throb

She steps off the path and crosses the road. As she passes a couple of takeaways, she heads inwards through a narrow street. I follow at a safe distance. She turns again up a steep hill. I let her go ahead until she takes a bend. On my right is a cutesy little bookshop. I carry on and take the bend that leads to some steep steps. By now, my calves burn like hell and I just want this upward trek to be over. I spot her ahead, through a cut in the foliage but she's fast disappearing. Panting, I realise that I'm almost striding vertically as I manage the last bit of the hill. I'm losing her. She's heading to her right alongside a row of houses.

Church bells ring, telling me it's now five in the evening. I don't know why but right now, I feel vulnerable. There doesn't seem to be anyone around and darkness has come over the skies with the rain, making it feel like night has fallen. Something snaps behind me, like a branch. I turn and stand there feeling almost light-headed as I glance at how high up I am. A boy appears from the steps I came up, holding a skateboard. I exhale and hurry towards the houses that Laura went into.

A light flashes on and I see her walking around her white-painted house, then she closes the curtains. I glance up and down the road, searching for her car but I can't see it. I run down a little but it's not there either. Maybe it's further up the hill. While darting back and forth, I spot a large building buried behind trees and then I see her car. Bingo.

I swallow, hesitant to walk into the darkness, alone. However much I try to control my short sharp breaths, the more I feel out of control. The boy with the skateboard is long gone. If I was meant to go missing anywhere, it would be here. Taking a deep breath, I force my shaking legs to proceed forward. The road below narrows and potholes and piles of grit below tell me that I need to step carefully. One wrong move and I could twist an ankle.

As I near her car, I peer in. The seats are devoid of any clutter, not like our car. There are no used parking tickets in the centre console, no toys or bags of snack food. It's creepy back here so I need to hurry up and get this over with.

Lying on the gravelly tarmac, I shine my phone under the car but I can't quite see where I need to. I shuffle under a little, that's when I hear clacking heels getting nearer. Rolling from under the car, I keep low and head to the rear of the car.

My heart bangs so loud I'm convinced that if she gets any closer she'll hear it. How do I explain that I'm lying in the road behind her car? She will know that I followed her. My heart is telling me to get up now and run. I'm fit, far fitter than Laura probably is. She can't see me. Light bounces off the floor and her phone rings. I stay still, waiting for her to answer.

'Hi, I'm on my way.' She pauses for a moment. 'No, whatever you do, don't do that and don't say anything.' She walks around to the driver's door. 'Sit tight.' She ends the call. As the car beeps, I flinch, kicking a bit of gravel as I do. Instead of getting into the car, Laura stands there, listening as if she's waiting for another noise. Hand on heart, I watch as a cat darts into a bush. She gets into her car and starts the ignition. I only hope that as she pulls away, she doesn't check her rear-view mirror and see me lying in the road. Within seconds, she's pulling away. Lights fade as she turns out of the road. I lie back and the rain soaks me through.

I get to my feet and examine the ground for any evidence of oil but I can't see anything. Reaching for an overhanging branch, I snap it and begin whipping the floor with it. Frustration boiling over, I want to scream. I'm no closer to knowing anything. I can't even follow Laura and I get a feeling that wherever she was heading would have told me all I need to know.

Don't do that. Don't say anything. Sit tight. What was that about?

'Kate?'

I didn't hear her creeping up on me. My mouth opens and closes like a goldfish out of water as I toil with what to say.

THIRTY-NINE

KATE

Daisy holds an umbrella, her brows furrowed like she's trying to work out what I'm doing. I'm soaking wet and gripping a branch with so much strength, I must look deranged.

'Hi.' I drop the branch and brush the grit and bits of twig from my leggings.

She steps closer to me and smiles. 'Here, get under the umbrella. You're soaking.'

'Thank you.' I shuffle up close to her to stay dry from the pelting rain.

'It's set to pass in a minute. What are you doing all the way up here?'

'Oh, I just came for a run and fell over. I must have tripped in a pothole in the road. How about you? Do you live up in this part?' I have no idea where she and Cody live, maybe they live close to Laura.

'No. We live over the other side of the bridge, up another big hill. It's all hills around here. I'd normally come on my bike but I fancied a walk. You get solid legs living in these parts.' She lets out a little laugh. 'I'm just heading to my friend's house for a couple of beers and a bit of TV.'

As we stride towards Laura's house, Daisy stops. 'Right, this is me. Good thing you only have to run downhill to get back to your beach cottage. Just follow this slope and it will take you back into the village.'

'Thanks again for keeping me dry.'

'You're welcome.'

As she walks up the steps towards the house, I call her. 'Daisy, how did you know we were staying in a cottage down that way?' I hadn't told her where we were staying and as far as I knew, only my stalker would know.

She steps back towards me. 'I shouldn't have said that. Sorry.'

'But how did you know?' Has she been following me? She is a woman and her jacket is dark. It has a hood too.

'Everyone knows. You're the talk of this town.'

'Has everyone known where I'm staying from the start?'

She presses her lips together and nods. 'The landlord of your cottage is Kyle Penrose, he owns the Smuggler with his wife. He recognised your name from the *Remembering Baby Jess* page when you booked and on the day you arrived, he saw you pulling in and after a few too many drinks, he told everyone it was you. He's such an asshat. I'm sorry he did that to you. You and your family deserve your privacy.'

'Where were you, yesterday afternoon?'

She stares at me for a moment longer than comfortable. 'Why?'

'I just need to know. Please?'

The front door opens. 'Daisy, what's taking you so long? The beers are getting warm.' Both Daisy and Bethany stare at me. Stepping back, I look up and down. We're alone on this road.

'On my way. Don't want to be out here on a night like this.' She turns to me. 'I was with Bethany yesterday afternoon, wasn't I?'

Bethany nods and grimaces. 'Yes. Why are you asking me that?'

'No reason, Beth.' Daisy smiles at me. 'Sorry I can't be of any more help. Watch your step down that hill. It's steep.'

'Yes, take care,' Bethany calls as Daisy joins her at the doorstep.

I glance back and they're still watching as I hurry down the hill. The weight of their stares are so heavy, it feels as though they are pushing me with their eyes. A lone seagull squawks making me jump as it lands on a doorstep ahead and glares deep within me. No longer does it sound like a crying baby, it sounds like an alert. For a moment, I think that everyone's curtains will open and they'll stare at me.

I gather pace and run until I reach the shops. Within a few seconds, I'm passing the Old Smuggler. The orange glow from within makes me shiver out here in the rain. The fire flickers and the man I know to be Kyle is sitting at the bar. It's his fault that everyone knows where I am and why I'm here. I hate him, I really do. His wife totters around, smiling at him and leaning in for a kiss. Her blonde hair falls over her shoulders and as she leaves him to collect a glass from a vacant table, her gaze catches mine. She smiles and waves, then her smile turns into a look of sympathy.

Hurrying away, I stop at the corner before going into the back of the cottage and take my phone from my pocket. Damien still hasn't messaged me back.

I run along the front, past the lifeboat shop and I step onto the pier. Waves gently crash against the concrete structure and I look out to sea. In the distance, lights come and go as the boats turn and bob on the choppy sea. The vacuous blackness gives me a chill and like yesterday, I'm once again soaked through. Another shower begins to fall. Hugging myself, I stand there wondering where Archie stood on that fateful day with my sister's sun hat. Was he here, or was he all the way at the end? I have no way of knowing exactly.

For a moment, I wonder if I want it badly enough, that I will feel her presence. Stupid, yes, but I need to believe that she is guiding me. I close my eyes and take a deep breath hoping for some sort of miracle, but as expected nothing comes and I feel silly for even thinking it might. All I hear is the rain and sea crashing against rock, but all I crave is the warmth of a cosy fire and a cuddle with the girls while we watch junk on TV with a huge bag of sweets. I want to be with Damien, too, but he's left me.

My hand reaches for my stomach. If Jess was alive she'd be happy at my news. As I open my eyes I see two people sitting over at the other end of the beach. One woman is looking at her phone and I can see that it's Laura. Then I glance at the other woman. It's Natalie. Laura had to be on the phone to Natalie when she left her house. Natalie wants to tell me more, Laura wants her to keep quiet. Daisy and Bethany know something too. Everyone does. They're all in it together, trying to conceal the truth and sending me on fools' errands. I mean, all they have to do is waste the next few days then I leave and they get to carry on like they always have done.

I feel threatened, stupid, played with and laughed at, all at the same time. My neck and cheeks burn with rage. A part of me wants to run over and confront them both but I remain still, staring. Laura's umbrella keeps both of them shielded from the light rain that has replaced the downpour and it looks as though they are sitting on a sheet of plastic. Laura's playing with her phone and Natalie looks like she's carrying the worries of the world on her shoulders. I'm hidden in the darkness. There are no lights on me. Laura prods another button on her phone.

I feel a buzz in my pocket. Grabbing my phone, I can see that I have a message. It's a text from an unknown number. I open it and my knees wobble.

This is your last warning. Go home!

I believed Natalie. I trusted her and I thought Laura was genuine up until tonight. It seems that everyone is in on my torture. Bethany and Daisy – they knew. They must have messaged Laura as soon as I started running down that hill. Natalie – she's been stringing me along. Kyle and Mary – they exposed me by telling everyone I was here. Laura – liar. Cody – another liar. All of them – liars.

My fists are clenched so tight, I press through the skin of my palms with my fingernail. There's no way I'm going back to the cottage without confronting them. It's time they were called out for what they're doing to me.

FORTY

KATE

I hurry away from the pier and across the beach, the sand firm underfoot.

'I thought you were helping me but all this time,' – I point to Natalie – 'you and her have been in this together, playing games with me. You know what happened and you send me these pathetic messages. No, I won't go home. I don't scare that easily and I don't give a stuff about your warnings. Do you hear me?'

They both look up. Laura's brows furrow. 'Kate, what are you talking about?'

'Like you need to ask.' I wipe my soaking wet forehead and I know they can see that I'm trembling with anger.

'Kate, I don't know what you're on about. Nat has filled me in on your conversation earlier. We were just talking about it.'

'Here, on the beach in the rain? Really?'

'I'm not welcome in the pub and too many people gossip around here.' Natalie shakes her head and looks down. 'We wanted some privacy, that's all.'

Ignoring her, I keep my focus on Laura. She was the one sending the message and all I need to do is prove it, then I can finally put a face to Will Wilcox.

'Let me see your phone.' I hold my hand out. She had her phone in her hand when I received that message and even though there was no oil under where her car was parked, I still think she did it. Maybe the rain had washed the oil away or maybe it was too dark to see properly.

'What?' She brushes her damp curly hair off her face.

'Your phone. At the moment I don't believe a word you say.'

She unlocks the screen and holds her phone towards me. I snatch it from her and head straight to her text messages. The last one she sent was to her daughter saying she'd be home late. I tap my number in her phone but it doesn't come up as a contact. She didn't send the message. Natalie didn't have a phone in her hand so it couldn't have been her.

'Sorry.' I hand it back to her.

'What's happened, Kate?' Natalie stands and brushes damp sand off her jeans as Laura stands. Her long mac billows as a gust of wind catches it and her umbrella creaks as it fights to stay the right way.

'I was standing on the pier, thinking of Jess when this came through.' I show them the message. 'Then I saw you with your phone in your hand.'

'I can see how you might think that but I promise you, we're not playing any games at all.' Laura places an arm over my shoulders.

I can't help but sob. It's been an emotional day and my hormones are all over the place. The woman envelops me in her warmness. I allow her to guide me off the beach and both of them walk me back to the cottage. As we stop, Natalie steps a little closer. 'We're trying to help you, Kate, and we will help you. Go home and I'll call you tomorrow. Okay.'

My dad sees me through the window and he hurries to open the door. He waves and smiles politely but I can tell he's worried about the state I'm in.

Once again I trust Natalie and Laura. I also wonder if I'm being a fool. Everyone in this town is one step ahead of me. They have been all along. Maybe the police will tell me more in the morning.

FORTY-ONE

NATALIE

Laura linked her arm in Natalie's as they passed one of the cosy harbour restaurants where they watched on as people dined. She imagined how simple their lives were. Safe relationships, homes, marriages, children, stability. She wondered if any one of the patrons were hiding a secret lover, hidden away from the front window for all to see.

'Laura, will you come up with me. I don't want to be alone.'

'Of course I will. Are you okay?'

Natalie shook her head. 'Every part of that flat reminds me of him and when I think of him, all I see is her. I can't sleep in my bed because he might have brought her here. I can't think, I can't eat properly, I can't breathe.' She began to fight for breath.

'Nat, Nat.'

She held up a hand and bent over as she tried to catch her breath and then the tears followed. 'It hurts.'

'Your chest?'

'No, Alan hurt me and I can't forgive him. I can't heal, I'm stuck.' The sobs came fast and hard.

Laura pulled Natalie close and hugged her tightly. 'There, there. It's all going to be okay. I promise. Let's get you inside.'

She nodded and held on to Laura. The path ahead swayed as Natalie fought her anxiety. Eventually she would get Mary out of her mind but not until the truth came out. Rachel needed to know. 'About what we spoke about.' Natalie placed the key in the door of the ice-cream shop.

'What's that?'

'Rachel. I have to know for sure if she's Alan's. I can't get her out of my mind.'

'She's always believed that Kyle is her father. News like that would kill him. He dotes on that girl. Some things are better left as they are.' Laura paused. 'I've never told Bethany who her father is.'

'Why?'

'Because she doesn't need to know. I brought her up. She's mine. Before Bethany came into my life, I was married. I didn't live here back then. I was with a brute of a man who threw me about like a rag doll.'

'I didn't know, I'm sorry.' That's the first time Laura had ever mentioned her life before Looe to Natalie.

'It's okay. It was a long time ago.'

It wasn't okay. People didn't just move on from being abused like that. 'Was he Bethany's father? Is that why you didn't tell her?'

With a downturned mouth, she shook her head. 'No, he wasn't and no again. I wanted Bethany to be all mine. I told her that I had a one-night stand after a drunken night at a club in Plymouth. Besides, when she was born, I knew I couldn't share her with anyone and we're so close. She could have left this town for good but she loves it here as much as I do and she keeps coming back. It's like the sea is calling her. She was bright at school but we run the business together. I made the business for her and for me. We live together so that I can keep her close and I'd never rock that boat by putting someone who has had no part in our lives into the mix. What I'm trying to say to you, about your situation, is that some things are best left the way they are. Bethany is so happy. Rachel is happy. Kyle loves her and she loves him. She will hate you for upsetting that bond.'

'Who is Bethany's father?'

She turned to face Natalie. 'You haven't listened to a word I said. That has never mattered. Sorry, I have to go.' With that, Laura pushed past Natalie and stomped away.

'Laura, wait.' Puddle water sloshed into her boots as she chased after her friend. 'Wait. I'm sorry. That was none of my business but I'm not going to let it drop with Mary and Rachel.' Natalie couldn't spend the whole night in her own head again, fighting off the constant rotation of internal arguments with everyone. 'Please don't leave me alone. Come up. Let's have a drink.'

'Okay, but no more having a go at me.'

'I promise and I'm sorry.'

Tomorrow was going to be explosive. She'd not only tell Rachel everything, it was time everyone knew about Mary's conversation and about Rachel being her deceased husband's daughter. There was more to the mad method that she'd chosen. When people run on their nerves, they slip up. Once a cat escaped the bag, the rest would follow.

She would flush the truth out. Kate could finally have her answers and so could she. No longer was she going to be told to shut up. Cody and Mary could both go to hell.

FORTY-TWO

KATE

Wednesday, 26 October

'Mummy, I don't want toast.' Millie looks at me with a frown.

'Come on, Millie. Just eat your breakfast.'

'I don't want toast either.' Rosie throws hers back onto her plate. 'We want to go out to play.'

Impossible, not until the police had been. Not knowing what time that would be, we have to stay in all morning. 'We're going out later. You know Mummy has to stay in until the police have been.'

Millie gives up on getting anything better for breakfast and bites into the toast. 'Why are the police coming?'

'They just want to show me something.'

'What?' A puff of crumbs escape her open mouth as she chomps.

I don't know what to tell them. Maybe the police are going to tell me who attacked me, who knows? Millie is staring at me, awaiting my answer. 'I don't know until they've been. It's just about what happened the other day. Nothing for you to worry about. I tell you what, do you want to watch telly while you eat?'

Rosie claps her hands together. I knew that would cheer them up. I normally forbid meals in front of the TV, preferring to have some family time. They grab their plates and I follow them through to the lounge and put some cartoons on. Within seconds, they're pacified so that I can mull over what the police might have to say.

Creaking comes from the floorboards above. My dad is emerging from the shower. He was worried sick about me being brought home in a state last night. He thinks I'm not well from the blow to the head and maybe he's right. Instead of allowing him to help me, I pushed him away. I only have three days to get to the truth. I'm going to trust that Natalie will have something for me soon and in the meantime I will keep my ears and eyes open, while spending some time with the girls. I've promised them a fun day and I need to deliver. I can't have their lasting memory of this holiday being about police and me never being here. We will plan our good-byes to Jess for Saturday morning before we leave. The girls still want to scatter petals in the sea and I want to do that for her too.

I call Damien again and still he ignores me. A message pings up.

I need some time, Kate. X

That kiss at the end of the message gives me hope so I reply with a simple kiss.

Dad is coming downstairs so I hurry to the kitchen and pour him a large coffee. It's the least I can do after leaving the girls with him all day yesterday. He looks worn out this morning as he walks in, T-shirt creased and the hem of his pyjama bottoms half tucked into his socks.

'Bacon sandwich?' I ask.

As he sits, he smiles. 'Thanks, Katie. I'd love one.'

I grab the pan and fork a couple of rashers into it before turning on the gas. Within seconds, sizzles and aromas fill the air and my stomach begins to churn. The only thing I fancy is chips, again. I can't tell my dad about the baby, not before I've spoken to Damien.

'As soon as the police have been, we're going out to have some real family time. There's also a box of craft stuff in the boot that I packed just in case it rains. We'll get it out later, do some fun things. The girls really like you.'

'I really like them. When we all go home, can we keep in touch?'

I nod. 'We'd love that.' He's proven himself and I've decided, I want my dad back. We can heal from this together. Damien's mum can have the girls too. Life is going to be different from now on. A shaft of sunshine reaches through the window and casts light across the kitchen. 'The sun's out.' The bacon begins to burn. I hurry back to the cooker and place the bacon neatly over two slices of doorstop bread before passing it to my father.

He takes a bite. 'This is the best thing I've eaten in years. You not having one?'

'No, I had some toast with the girls.' I can't tell him that I'd literally throw up if I tried to eat bacon or indeed anything right now. I grab my black tea and take a sip while watching him enjoy his food.

There is a knock at the door and before I've even reached the lounge, Rosie has already opened it. I hurry and pull her back. 'Rosie, what have I told you about answering the door?'

She looks at me as she pokes a finger in her mouth and chews it.

'You always call one of us. Anyone could be behind that

door. It could be a stranger that has come to take you away. I've told you about people like that, haven't I?'

Rosie nods. PC Bickerford is on her own today. She bends down to Rosie's level. 'Your mummy is right, you know. Always good to be safe, kiddo.' The PC winks and smiles.

'Come in.' I lead her through the lounge after she's wiped her feet and Dad is just finishing his sandwich.

'I thought it best that I come today and update you in person. We spoke on the phone and you know I said we found someone, possibly a woman who was on the beach at the same time as you in Polperro, I've brought a printout for you to see. The camera belongs to a local business that barely captures anything but she is caught on it for literally a passing second. The woman fits the description that the witness gave. She is the same woman that was on the beach. I mean, she might not have anything to do with what happened to you and we're definitely only treating her as a witness.'

'Take a seat, please.' I pull a chair out for her. 'Would you like a drink?'

'Not for me thank you.' She places her police hat on the kitchen table and sits down.

Dad leans against the worktop and I sit close to her. 'Can I see the picture?'

She opens the folder. 'It's a screen grab from CCTV, so don't expect much.'

She places the A4 sheet of paper in front of me. I recognise the path, I walked down it. I scrunch up my eyes in the hope to see a clearer picture but it doesn't help. It's so grainy, I can barely make out anything but the figure of an average woman. She has a bust line but is covered in a dark jacket with a hood up that is baggy, which doesn't help narrow down her build. As the CCTV was high up, the clearest view is of the top of her hood.

'Are there any better pictures?'

'I'm afraid not. We have interviewed a fair few people and this woman was seen at the beach, too.'

'Do you have any more CCTV, anything at the car park or by the café that I went in?'

'There was CCTV at the café but she wasn't on it. There is none currently in operation at the car park. We are waiting for a download of all the details from the machine. We're hoping that whoever did this to you parked there too.'

'When do you think you might get that?'

'Tomorrow, hopefully. We're waiting for the company to respond.'

'Any news on the car?' I swallow, wondering if I should tell her about the car turning up at Archie's nursing home and the fact that I thought it was Laura's, then I hold back. Right now, Laura and Natalie are helping me and I don't want to jeopardise that by bringing the police into their lives. I can't prove it was Laura's car either, in fact, I don't think it was. Besides, Dad is also standing there. He doesn't know that I was followed to the nursing home and he'd be concerned that I went off snooping alone last night.

'No. So far, we have nothing on the car. Your description was too vague. There are so many cars that fit the description we wouldn't know where to start. Have you had any more messages?'

Again, I glance up at Dad. The message I received last night was as clear as it gets. *Last warning. Go home.* 'No.' I have to trust that the answers are coming, and that Natalie and Laura are on my side. In fact, if I pass everything I have to PC Bickerford, it will set me back. Everyone will clam up. Natalie might not help me and I'm back to square one.

'We think that the person sending you these messages and stalking you is a very fixated troll. You have to be so careful online these days. We won't give up but even with the social media appeal, we don't have much to go on. All I can say is, if you hear anything else, call us straight away. Whatever you do, don't put yourself in any danger. If this person messages or calls you again, let us know. Given the circumstances, I'll organise a couple of drive-bys tonight and if anyone is loitering around, we'll catch them.'

'Thank you. Knowing that the police will be close is a weight off my mind.'

'You're welcome. Try to enjoy the rest of your break. Right, I best get back to the station.' She pops her hat back on and stands.

After I see her out, I head straight back to the kitchen just as Dad is making another coffee.

'We best get ready to go out. Let's go to the beach café and get some ice cream on the seafront. The girls are already getting ready.'

He smiles. 'I'll get myself dressed and we'll head out.' He abandons the half-made coffees. 'The police don't seem to have much.'

'No. Did you see that woman while you were hanging around?'

'I wish I did. I was too busy looking for you.'

After he leaves me alone in the room. I slump against the fridge-freezer and exhale. What am I doing? I glance at that message again and shiver. Everything will be okay as long as I stay out in the open or with Dad and the girls. Whoever is threatening me is only after me and I won't give them the opportunity to hurt me again.

My mind flashes back to the CCTV screen grab. The woman in the picture gave me no clue at all. I couldn't get a feel for this woman's build or age, and, of course, her features were concealed. I'm in the dark.

Bethany and Daisy – I didn't like the way they watched me run down that hill last night. I don't trust them. I hit the worktop and bite my bottom lip. Maybe I'm reading too much into them. But my instincts tell me something isn't right and I shudder. Daisy has been really pleasant, maybe it's the nicest people you have to watch out for.

I check my phone again and there's another message.

You're still here. Big mistake! There's no going back now. You've lost your chance.

'Are you ready? Millie and Rosie are waiting by the door.' Dad rubs his hands together.

'Yep. Let's go and have some fun.'

I swallow the need to cry down and follow him into the living room, where I help the girls with their trainers and I wonder if I really have made a big mistake, but the truth is worth it. It has to be, otherwise why am I doing this? As I replay the message in my head, I shiver. I'm getting close to the truth and whoever this is knows that. They will not scare me off. My girls are safe with me and I'll make sure they don't leave my side. We are safe. The more I tell myself that, the less I'm starting to believe it.

FORTY-THREE

NATALIE

The weather appeared calm for the first time in days. Natalie hurled a pebble into the sea. She wondered if Laura would mind that she'd left her alone in her bed, the same bed that she couldn't bear to sleep in anyway. After several shots of whisky, she'd led a staggering Laura to her bed before settling down on the couch.

She squinted as she stared at the low sun. If Laura felt half as bad as she did when she woke up, she'd need the paracetamol and water that Natalie had left on the bedside table. The lack of messages on her phone told her that she hadn't stirred yet.

As she gazed at the deep blue horizon line, she kept replaying what Laura had told her. The thought that some man had hurt her in the past made her blood boil. The girl needed to know the truth, just like Rachel did, but Natalie knew that Laura was scared to tell Bethany who her father was. Come to think of it, she'd never even noticed Laura with anyone else in this town. She wondered if her friend had a mother, or siblings. It's as if she appeared from nowhere back then but as she said, she'd been running from abuse. She wouldn't want her ex catching up with her but it was strange that she didn't seem to have any family.

There was no getting around what Natalie had to do and throwing all the stones in the world wasn't going make the day any easier. She dropped the last two pebbles onto the beach. In the distance, she spotted Kate with her family, buckets and spades in hand. It was time for her to make an exit before Kate saw her. Right now, she had nothing more to tell her, but she soon would.

Hurrying past the Pier Café and along the streets, she stopped outside the Old Smuggler and peered through the windows. As always, Rachel and Mary were setting up for the day. The pub opened soon and she needed to see Rachel before then. The woman who was once her friend had her hair tied back with a blue spotty scarf while she pushed a mop back and forth; water and soap suds sloshing on the dark tiles. Rachel had left the sleeping baby next to the bar while she prepared the cash register for the day. It was for the best that Kyle was nowhere to be seen while Natalie broke the news.

She tried the door but it was locked.

Rachel ran over and unlocked it. 'Hi, Nat, we're not open yet. You okay?'

She nodded and smiled, taking in the shape of her soft-edged face. Her usually slim figure was slightly rounded from recently carrying a baby and her hair seemed pinker than ever as her topknot bounced with her every move. Did she have Alan's eyes? They were slightly almond shaped, more like his mother's.

'Can I help you?' Rachel placed a hand on the door frame.

She realised that she'd been staring.

Mary appeared behind her daughter. She scrunched her nose at the acrid smell of disinfectant as she inhaled. 'You need to go, now.' She went to slam the door closed as she nudged Natalie out, but instead Natalie wedged her boot in it. A clump of wet sand dropped onto the coconut mat, messing up the newly cleaned floor.

'I'm not going anywhere. You can't run away from the truth any longer.' She pushed her way in. Rachel ran over to her baby and grabbed the sleeping infant up in her arms as she sidled towards the back door. 'Don't go, Rachel. You'll want to hear this.'

'What's going on, Mum?'

'Nothing. Just take the little one and go upstairs. I'll sort this out.'

'Shall I get Dad?'

Natalie felt herself weaken at hearing Rachel call that man, Dad. 'Rachel, please don't and don't be scared. I would never hurt you, ever. That's not why I've come.'

Sorrow filled Natalie's heart. All they ever wanted was a child and Alan had fathered one all along. She should feel resentment at Rachel but all she wanted to do was hug the girl. Everything she had she would have given away to have what Mary had in Rachel.

'What's going on, Mum?' Rachel said again.

Mary stepped forward and pushed Natalie hard. 'You have to leave. We can talk about this later. You can't be here right now.'

Natalie opened her mouth but the words weren't coming out. She glanced back at Rachel, then at Mary, then at the tiny baby in Rachel's arms – Alan's grandchild. 'Your mum has been lying to you all these years.' Her voice crackled so much, she wondered if the young woman had heard her properly.

'Mum, why is she here?'

A tear drizzled down Mary's pink cheek, drawing a wet line through her powdery make-up. 'Nat, please don't do this. It'll ruin us.'

'She's...' It was no good. The moment she said what she came to say, there was no taking it back. Did she really want to ruin everyone around her? Kyle had slipped up with Laura but that didn't make him a bad father. He loved that girl with all he had and Mary had cheated on him too. That man was going to suffer.

Natalie didn't recognise herself in the mantelpiece mirror. It was as if she wasn't present, like she didn't really exist. What had Mary taken from her? She'd stripped her of her self-worth. Natalie had nothing left to lose, but she couldn't go through with it.

'I shouldn't have come.' As she went to turn, she knocked the mop out of the bucket spraying soapy water up the wall. 'Damn, I'm sorry about the mess.'

'Wait.' Rachel passed the baby to Mary and caught up with her before she could escape out of the door. 'What do I need to know?'

'Rachel, stop it. Let Natalie leave.'

Rachel blocked the exit. 'Don't think I don't know what you and Alan have been up to behind Dad's back all these years, Mum. Half the town knows. Bethany knows. Daisy knows. All my friends at school knew as it's been going on forever. This is what it's all about, isn't it?'

The baby began to cry and Mary bobbed the restless infant up and down on her hip.

Natalie rested her bottom on a chair. 'You knew all along.'

Rachel nodded. 'It's nothing. What Alan and my mum were up to, it didn't mean anything, did it, Mum? Please tell me you're not leaving Dad?'

'I'm not, love. It was all nothing. Please leave, Nat. You've done enough damage.'

She wanted to escape this situation so badly but her legs wobbled with nerves. They were numb to the idea of escaping what needed to be said. If she walked out now, Mary's life wouldn't change. There would be nothing to set in motion the release of all the lies that needed to come out.

'Wait. I'm not stupid. There's more to this, isn't there?' Rachel asked.

'Are you going to tell her?' Natalie bowed her head.

'Tell me what? I need to know what you're both hiding.'

'There's nothing to tell.' Mary shook her head, a panic-stricken look spread across her face.

Her voice filled the room. 'Alan is... was your father.'

A tear ran down Mary's cheek and the baby screamed louder, its little hands reaching for her hair. 'No, Nat is fixated. She thinks that you might be his but you're not, love. Kyle is your dad.'

'But the dates—' Natalie tilted her head.

'Kyle is her dad. I did a test and that proved it. You have to go now.'

After everything, Mary still couldn't utter a true word.

'Oh yes, the test that you failed to show me the results of. There's more too. Your mother is hiding loads more secrets. Lies, lies and more lies. Do you remember hearing about the baby that went missing all those years ago? Jessica? She was just a little older than your little one is now, Rachel.'

'That seriously has nothing to do with Mum, now please leave.' Rachel moved out of the way and took her crying baby from her mother.

She wished she'd never mentioned Jessica, but she'd committed now to everything coming out and she'd also promised Kate that she'd help.

'Imagine it, the precious baby in your arms right now. One minute she's safe, the next, you turn your back for a second and your baby is gone, forever. That's what happened to baby Jessica. Your mother kept information about that case hidden all these years, only I heard her telling someone what she knew. Imagine if your baby was killed and someone could have helped the police at the time. Look at your baby and imagine how painful that would be.' Her voice boomed out.

Rachel stared, a tear drizzling down her cheek.

'Stop it, Nat. Kate's father killed that child. It was all his fault. He was drunk. He fell asleep and that child fell into the harbour and got dragged out to sea.'

Natalie could see that Rachel was upset and she hoped that she'd given her enough to think about. Maybe the girl would now order her own DNA test. She knew where to find Natalie when the time was right for her to talk about the situation.

'Okay, this is going nowhere. Your mother saw Archie disposing of Jess's hat on Banjo Pier and she clearly told someone else as I overheard her. Those words came out of her own mouth. If she was there, what else did she see? Laura and I visited Archie and he told us everything.'

Mary exhaled. 'Archie doesn't know what day it is.'

'Is that what you're pinning your hopes on? The truth is already out there.'

'Rachel, take the baby up, please.'

'But, Mum...'

'Just do it.'

'Shall I get Dad?'

'No. I need a private word with Nat. I've never heard so much bullshit in all my life. Just give me ten minutes, love.'

Rachel grabbed a bottle and began feeding the baby in her arms. 'If you're not up in ten minutes, I'm coming back down to check on you.' She moved across to the door that led upstairs.

'Why did you have to do that?' As she said those words, Natalie felt the weight of Mary's gaze.

'Why, why? It's all about you, like it has been forever. You and Alan played me for a fool. Even now, you won't tell the truth about Rachel. I'm going to the police, to tell them what you said about Archie. Laura thinks I should too.'

'So, this is all about poor little Laura. Laura the victim. I'm sick to the back teeth of hearing about poor little Laura. I guess now that you're best buddies you'll get the sob story. I saw you with her last night, walking by the harbour.' Mary untied her headscarf and let her hair fall forwards to frame her face.

'So, that has nothing to do with you. It's great that I have a real friend to help me through the grief and pain, not like you.'

'Have you ever stopped to question everyone else's truth around here? Laura moved here because a bad man is chasing her. We talk, Kyle and me. Yes, I know he had a fling with Laura and he told me everything. I guess you don't know who Laura was sleeping with when she first moved here. I guess you also don't know that she lost a baby because of what her ex-husband did to her. You also wouldn't know how bitter she was when she saw anyone else with a baby. When I was walking Rachel in her pushchair one day, I found Laura walking off with her but did I say anything? No. I felt sorry for the woman. Of course she said she just wanted to hold my baby but I know she wanted to take her. That woman was and still is crazy.'

Natalie's mind was awhirl with everything. Had the woman she'd left alone in her flat done something to Jess?

'Oh, she had the briefest of flings with Cody when she moved here. Laura didn't care that Cody was with someone else. She didn't care that Kyle was my husband. Laura doesn't care about anyone but herself. It's easy to paint me as the bad one, but we all have a bit of bad in us. Life isn't black and white.'

'Is Bethany Cody's daughter?'

With pressed lips, Mary smiled and shrugged. 'Just when you think you know everything, you realise you know nothing. Please, Nat, stay away from me and my daughter. You're upsetting everyone. Opening up all these old wounds isn't good for anyone.'

A sickness churned in Natalie's stomach as she felt the buzz of her phone. She pulled it from her pocket. Laura was calling. If Laura had accidentally hurt that baby, Cody could have helped cover things up and maybe, just maybe, Archie dropped that hat in the sea to help them. Maybe that poor old man has had to live with the crushing weight of what he kept hidden. Natalie darted out of the pub and inhaled sharply as she stepped onto the pavement.

Glancing back through the window she saw that Rachel was back without the baby and she and her mother seemed to be arguing. Arms up in the air, Mary slamming her hand on the bar, Rachel pointing a finger. She'd started something now and there was no going back. If Kyle found out about that conversation, he'd come to her shop. The man would be upset and angry and Natalie had to have her answers ready for him. In fact, now Rachel knew, it was inevitable.

FORTY-FOUR

KATE

The breeze coming from the sea gives me a chill around the ears but Millie, Rosie and my dad don't seem to feel it because of all the fun they're having. I smile as Dad plays with the girls, it's like he's become a child again.

'Do you all want some chips?' I ask.

'Yay,' Rosie screams.

'I think I'll pop to the beach café to grab some lunch.' I need to take a few minutes to check my phone and try calling Damien again.

Dad brushes sand from the very little hair that he has left and laughs uncontrollably as Millie jumps on him while telling him to be a horse for the tenth time that day. 'Hey, girls. Grandad might need a break. Can you make a sandcastle while Mummy gets lunch? I'd love some chips. What's better than chips by the seaside?'

The girls scream again. It makes my heart swell to see them this happy. That's all it took; sand, the tiniest bit of sun and a few chips. No one is bored but I do suspect that my dad might need a nap. I manoeuvre myself off the blanket that has been weighed down with the girls' toys.

'I'll be back in five then.'

I stand and brush my clothes down before strolling along the beach. I try to call Damien again but he still doesn't answer. Maybe he still needs more time, the least I can do is give that to him. When I enter the café, the warmth hits my face. I order four portions of chips and wait.

As I hand the money over, I see that my dad is now staring at his phone and the girls are running around on the beach. They're getting closer to the sea. A lump forms in my throat as I see Millie bend down to reach the lapping wave. Before I know it, I have the bag of food dangling from my wrists and I'm trudging through sand.

'Millie,' I yell, but I'm too far away for her to hear me. I see how she kicks the water with her toe and proceeds to stand there as the wave laps at her feet. Rosie laughs and begins to sprint towards her sister. In my mind, she is running so fast, she'll run straight into the sea and a wave will take her out. My heart bangs at the thought of having to go in. However much I tell myself that seawater is just water, that doesn't take away the fear that is filling my body.

I drop the chip bag and within seconds, I reach the girls. 'Get out of there now, Millie. What have I told you?' I yank her back and grab Rosie at the same time.

'I just wanted to touch the water, Mummy. We weren't going in the sea.'

'We're going back to the cottage. Go and pack your things away now.' By this time, my dad is hurrying over too.

'I don't want to go back. Want to stay on the beach.' Millie's bottom lip folds over her top and she crosses her arms. Rosie has started to cry and both of them whine about not going back to the cottage.

'I don't care what you want right now, you can both sulk all you like. What you did was dangerous and you're going to have plenty of time to think about it.'

They have to know that I make the rules to keep them safe and seeing them so close to the sea sent shocks through my body. I glance back, knowing that Jess is out there, somewhere, and there's no way on earth my girls are joining her. They are too precious to me.

As the girls sit on the blanket looking as miserable as the grey cloud being pushed through the blue skies, they stare into their laps.

'I was watching them, Katie.'

'You.' I stare directly into his eyes. 'I left you for a few minutes and when I look back, you're on your phone and Millie and Rosie are virtually in the sea. I trusted you, Dad.'

In my mind, I'm back to that day. Dad wasn't watching Jess and just now, he wasn't watching my precious daughters.

'I was keeping an eye on them. I could see them all the time and they weren't in the sea.'

'Jess lies dead in that sea. I don't want that to happen to my children.'

My dad takes a deep breath as if choking back a sob.

'What was so important it couldn't wait until I got back with the chips?'

'I just needed to ask Danny next door to check on the house.'

Rosie is now crying like the world is about to come to an end and it's his fault. He wasn't watching them and now I'm the bad guy. I stride over to get the chips but a feisty seagull already has its beak in the bag. Running over, I shout and the bird squawks as it flies off. For a second, I feel an immense sense of guilt. In the cave, the sound of a seagull saved my life, now I'm shouting at one like a person deranged on the beach. Brushing the bag down, I hurry back. We can take the chips to the cottage and eat in the warm. So much for a lovely family day out. Everything has been ruined.

'Right, pack up,' I tell them again.

Dad comes over to me and speaks quietly. 'I'm sorry, Katie. Look at them, they just want to eat their chips on the beach. We can all sit together.'

'But they...' I wanted to say that they need to know not to go near the sea and if I don't follow through with what I said, they won't take me seriously but he doesn't give me a chance.

I thrust the bag into his hand and he gets down on the blanket and hands the polystyrene boxes out. Maybe I was over the top. Millie wasn't in the sea, she was just touching the water and Rosie, even though I thought she might run straight in, she stopped at the shoreline. Dad was watching them. Again, the problem is me, it's always me. Swallowing, I kneel on the blanket and take my chips as I look at my sad girls.

'Mummy's sorry. I just love you all so much, I couldn't bear to lose you but the sea is dangerous. Promise me you'll always be careful.'

'Promise, Mummy.' Rosie hiccups her last cry and seems placated by the chips. Millie is already tucking into hers.

'Now, let's eat before the food gets cold then we can go back into the warm.' Dad speaks in a jolly over-the-top way and the girls smile.

'Can we make an octopus when we get back, Mummy? Grandad said he'd help us.' Millie wipes her red eyes with her sleeve.

'Of course. I'll get the craft box out of the car when we head back.'

As I tuck into the chips, the saltiness and grease are most welcome. I feel as though I haven't eaten for a week as I shove them in. My phone vibrates in my pocket. I forgot to check it when I headed towards the café. As adrenaline pulses through me, I snatch it up, hoping that Damien is ready to talk.

You know what happens when you take your eye off them for a second?

A chip almost lodges in my throat as I scan the pier and the beach. There is no one around but someone has been watching me. We need to get back to the cottage, where my children are safe.

'Right, we need to make that octopus out of all the empty cartons we can find in the cottage?'

Before I can say another word, the girls are already up on their feet ready to go, even Dad looks like he'd rather be back inside now the wind has picked up. With a thrumming heart, I shepherd them off the beach and back towards the cottage. 'I'll be there in a minute. I'll just grab the craft box out of the boot.'

'Okay.' Dad holds their hands and walks ahead.

As I open the boot and grab the box, I gaze around one more time but I can't see anything out of place. I think of what PC Bickerford said, that it looked like the person behind all this is some pathetic person trying to scare me and hurt me. They've developed an obsession with me online and in real life and I allowed that to happen by coming here in the first place. I try Natalie's number but my call is immediately cut off. She and Laura were meant to be helping me and I don't have much time left. As I hurry back to the cottage with the box, my stomach drops as I spot another oil patch on the road, right outside the cottage. The person watching me must have been parked here when they messaged me a few minutes ago.

My stalker is getting ever closer to me and I'm nowhere nearer to getting closer to who they are.

FORTY-FIVE

KATE

As I place the craft box on the kitchen table, I push through its contents. There's glue, paint, sticky tape and a huge collection of stickers and random things, like pom-poms. The array of bright colours almost gives me a headache. Rosie slams against the chair in her haste to start. She drops an empty cereal box on the table.

Millie runs downstairs with the cap from Damien's deodorant bottle and two empty toilet rolls, shrieking with delight at what she has found.

Now we are safely back in the cottage I try calling Natalie again. Blood pumps through my body and the boom sound running through my head is unnerving. Her phone rings several times and then she answers. 'I can't talk right now.'

'Why, what's happened?' My heart is bursting to hear what she has to say. I can't wait until later. I'm running out of time.

'I said I can't talk. We'll speak later.' Her voice sounds hoarse, like she's been crying. She hangs up. Something's happened and the urge to know what that is has lit up all my senses. I need to get out of here so that I can find her.

'Mummy, we need a water glass for the paintbrushes.' Millie is pulling on the hem of my jumper.

'Can we use some sugar, for the sand? The octopus will sit on sand,' Rosie shouts.

'Where's Grandad?' I should talk to Dad, fill him in.

'In the toilet.' Rosie helps herself to the pom-poms, shifting me out of the way.

'Millie, spread this paper over the table first.' I hand her an old newspaper. She knows the drill as we do this all the time at home. She takes it and the girls begin to do as they're told, carefully placing the paper down.

I hurry upstairs. The bathroom door is closed so I wait, hoping to hear the chain flush soon but it doesn't. In fact, I can hear him walking up and down. 'Dad?' I tap on the door. He's not answering and I'm anxious to go out and track Natalie or Laura down.

With a whoosh, the door opens and the air itself almost sucks me into the bathroom. In his hand is the stick that tells him that I'm pregnant. 'I found this.'

'I...' I can't answer him. Damien should have been the first to know, not my dad. I've been hoping all day that he'd pick up the phone so I can speak to him rather than text.

'Katie, love. You got attacked this week and you're pregnant. You need to get checked out. I'm really worried about you.'

A tear slips from the corner of my eye and weaves its way down my face.

'I know. I didn't know I was pregnant until yesterday.' Tears fill my eyes and I can't contain my sadness any longer. 'All I want to do is tell Damien and he won't answer my calls. I lied to him. I told him we were coming here to honour Jess's memory, to say goodbye. He has to forgive me, I love him. Everything I've done, it's been for Jess. I can't abandon her even though she's dead. I can't rest until everything comes out.'

'Oh, Katie, I've accepted everything. It was my fault and I have to live with my mistake.'

'No, Dad. There's more to it and I'm not leaving until I know everything.'

He leans in and places his arms around me, and I let him. I have missed him for so long and he's the only person in the world who shares the burden of Jess's accident with me. Damien will never understand, not like my dad does. I can't believe I shut him out of my life for so long. I should have been there to help him with his drink problem. I abandoned him.

'Come on, Katie. Everything will be fine, I know it will.'

'No, I brought the girls into this and it's not fair.' Whoever is out there, playing me like a game will not let me win. I think of the message sent to me while we were on the beach. It's not safe here. 'We need to pack to go home. Tomorrow afternoon we leave and on the way back, we'll stop at the police station to speak to PC Bickerford one more time? I've had it with this place and I want to go home to Damien.'

I will show the messages to the PC, tell her everything I know or have heard and I'll do the right thing and leave the police to do the police work. I can keep in touch with Natalie from Leicester. Right now, I need to think about the baby I'm carrying and saving my marriage, if that's at all possible. Once trust is broken, there's no going back. Damien will never believe anything I say again.

'Of course. Whatever you choose to do, I'm here.'

I stroke my stomach. 'If it's a girl, I want to call her Jessica.'

My dad's eyes glass up with tears and he shakes them away. 'I think that's a lovely idea.'

'Or if it's a boy, I like Jesse, like Jesse James.' I hope Damien approves.

'Grandad, hurry up.' Millie's voice makes me jump.

'Right, I best get these empty toilet rolls to the girls. You coming to help?'

I nod. 'Yes, do you mind if I take a shower first. I've got sand everywhere?'

'Course not.'

With that he leaves me alone in the bathroom. I exhale and sit on the toilet seat, taking a moment to process all that has happened. There's so much I want and need to do, but I'm now stuck in this cottage and we're going home tomorrow. Maybe it's for the best. I message Damien to let him know.

I log on to Facebook and see that I have a message notification. Quickly pressing the buttons I need to press to get to the *Remembering Baby Jess* messages, I see that Will Wilcox has reactivated his account and he's typing. The three dots wiggle then stop. My mouth is so dry, but I can't move, not until I see what Will has to say.

I click on his profile and his profile picture is dark. When I pinch out to get a better look, a shiver runs through me. It's a picture of Willy Wilcox's cave. I scroll down his wall – nothing. Then a message pings.

With a tremble, I manage to click on it.

All you had to do was to not say a thing but you couldn't help yourself. The truth was yours to have and you blew it. You blew everything and now you will know nothing. I said I'd vanish and now I will. Everything is going to shit and it's all your fault.

No, this can't be happening. The profile is once again taken down and all I see is the outline of a grey head in a grey box. Will has gone forever. I'm confused. I know Will told me not to say anything but then I was attacked in a cave. That was a game changer. Then came all the 'go home' messages on my phone and the creepy stuff on Instagram about the sea. That message on my car window. How dare this person tell me I shouldn't have spoken after they tried to kill me.

There's another feeling welling up inside me and it's sent the grief and anxiety packing. I'm livid. My knuckles clench and I realise I'm grinding my teeth. Grabbing a towel from the rail, I turn on the shower, press the material hard into my mouth and I scream into it.

I don't know what to do. I'm itching to go out there and show this message to Natalie. Maybe it's her or Laura or Cody. I feel like people here are watching my every move. They're all in on it. Whoever this Will is, he was never going to tell me the truth. Then I think of Archie. Maybe he's not as forgetful as he leads everyone to think.

Stepping into the shower, I allow the warm water to wash away the sand, the tears and the greasy chip fat from my fingers. Through the water and soap, I catch the light of my phone from the corner of my eye. Without any hesitation, I turn the shower off and step out, drying my hands before I snatch the phone. It's another message. Will is back.

I'm sorry. I shouldn't have said that. I'll contact you soon to meet up. Please don't leave.

I answer immediately.

How do I know I can trust you?

A response pings straight back.

You don't, but you can. If I see anyone else there, you will never hear from me again. You will never know what happened to Jess.

I reply.

I'll be there. Where? When?

Biting my bottom lip, I flinch as a strip of skin tears. It feels wrong to go but my messenger doesn't seem threatening any more. I get the sense that they want to finally unburden themselves. Damien would be livid but I have one last chance to know what happened. Shaking my fears away, I've already decided. I am going to meet this person and I'll finally find out who Will is. All I have to do is await the details for our meet up.

For now, I need to go downstairs, play arts and crafts and pretend that nothing is wrong while I wait for the message. I can do this.

Am I scared? Yes. I'm terrified, but the truth is bigger than my fear.

FORTY-SIX

NATALIE

'Nat, where have you been? I was worried.' Laura swilled down some tablets with the water she'd left for her.

'Have you slept all this time?'

She nodded. 'I'm so sorry for passing out last night. What a state to get in to.' She paused and sat on the settee in her crumpled clothes. The smell of stale alcohol filled the small room so Natalie nudged the window open.

'That's okay. We did have a few too many.'

'I had to call Bethany, asked her to open the shop up. Where did you go?'

Natalie felt like a stranger in her own home as Laura leaned back, relaxing in the space where she normally sat. 'I went to the Smuggler, then I walked for ages, hoping to clear my head.'

'You went where? I thought you weren't going to go there. We talked about that.'

'No.' She shook her head. 'You thought it was best that I don't go there. I went straight in and I told Rachel. I told her that Alan was her father.'

Laura raised her eyebrows. 'Wow, and how did she take it?'

'How do you think?' The vein next to her left eye began to twitch, something that happened a lot when she was tense.

'Nat, have I said or done something wrong? You look angry.'

Maybe it was the biting of her inner cheek, her furrowed brows, or even the fact that she was gripping her keys so hard that a trickle of blood had trailed down the back of her hand.

'Say something, you're worrying me.'

She slammed the keys onto the coffee table and turned to face the window. Staring down at the street, she took a few deep breaths. 'Why did you walk off with Rachel in her pushchair when she was a baby?'

Laura stood and stomped towards the kitchen. Natalie knew her coat was in there. She followed Laura and closed the door, trapping her in.

'Nat, move out of my way.' She pulled her coat over her shoulders.

She wasn't going to let Laura leave until she had answers. Mary had caught her off guard and she still needed the truth, for Kate. She'd made a promise and she was going to keep it, not like her lousy cheating husband when it came to their wedding vows.

'No, you are going to sit in that chair, at that table, and you're not leaving this room until you've told me everything.'

'Why are you doing this? Nat, you're scaring me.' Tears flooded her cheeks and she trembled that hard, the bracelet on her wrist jangled.

'Sit.'

Without needing to be told again Laura pulled out the chair and sat with her arms folded in front of her.

'Now tell me about Rachel.'

Laura sobbed so hard tears dripped into the crease of her neck. Natalie placed the kitchen roll in front of her.

'Go on.'

'Will you let me go if I tell you?'

'Let you go! I'm not keeping you hostage. I just want to know what happened.' Natalie wanted to know if the woman in front of her was capable of taking or hurting Jess.

'When I first moved here, I wasn't myself. You know I told you about my ex-husband? I came here to start afresh. I'd spent several months in a refuge and a room came up to rent just as I got offered a job in an art shop. Finally, I felt things were coming together. Before that, life was awful with the abuse, the hurt. It felt as though I'd been living in a war zone.'

A glazed-over look filled Laura's face. 'They say there's a moment when you click, when you really see the abuser in front of you, when you stop trying to excuse or defend them.' She paused and placed her hands on the table, where she began to play with a chip in the wood. 'I was pregnant before I left him and I wanted that baby more than anything. I wanted someone who would love me no matter what, someone to care for. When you've been abused like I was, you feel like you have no one in the whole world and I didn't have anyone until Bethany came along. Anyway.' She wiped the tears with the back of her hand. 'He killed the baby inside me. He caused me to miscarry. By this time, I'd already named her. The baby was always a girl in my mind. She was always going to be called Bethany. I'd already imagined a life with her as her mother. I'd pictured us on the beach, me taking her to school, us going to the cinema to watch Disney films. I imagined a whole life and that was cruelly ripped away from me in a few seconds.' She sobbed hard.

Sadness ripped through Natalie as she took a seat opposite her. What was she doing, making Laura relive all this because of something Mary had said? She snatched a piece of the kitchen roll and handed it to Laura. What she'd done was made her friend feel trapped and abused all over again by forcing her to relive the pain, but if Natalie had to, she'd beg her to tell her the truth.

'I know this is hurting you. Please, Laura. What happened after?'

'I saw baby Rachel. Mary was talking to old man Pritchard at the time. He was laying out his catch in boxes on the harbour path. Rachel was sleeping and she looked like a tiny china doll. I don't know what I was thinking, in fact, I barely remember pushing her towards your shop. The next thing I remember, Mary grabbed the back of my T-shirt, yanking me back, all in a fluster. She called me a few names and took Rachel's pushchair off me. I was only pushing her. I wasn't going to take her.'

'You say, you couldn't remember pushing her away?' If what Laura was saying to her was true, it might be possible that she took Jessica and failed to remember.

Laura shook her head. 'I know what you're thinking. Some sad woman who lost her own child, tried to steal one belonging to another woman. Well, you're wrong. I didn't hurt Rachel and I didn't hurt Jess.'

'I didn't say that you hurt Jessica, intentionally. Maybe you can't remember.'

She slammed her hand on the table. The salt and pepper shakers rattled against each other. 'I'd remember a baby suddenly appearing if I took one. I'm not mad, you know. I simply pushed a baby's pushchair a few feet away from her mother. That's all there is to it. I apologised and I begged Mary not to say anything. She knew what I'd been through and I guess she believed that I wasn't a danger to Rachel. That was it. We left it at that and nothing like that ever happened again.'

'When was this?'

'Does it matter?'

'It does to me.' Natalie huffed out a sharp breath.

'When Rachel was really tiny, I can't remember exactly when. Is that it, can I go now?'

'So, let me get this right. You weren't pregnant when you moved to Looe?'

'No, I'd just lost a baby.'

'What was the deal with you and Cody?'

She shook her head and stood. 'That is none of your business.'

Natalie stood and stepped towards her friend, placing a hand on one of her shoulders. 'Please, Laura, I need to know what happened.'

'Why? Why on earth do you need to know who I was sleeping with? Okay, but if you breathe one word to anyone, I will kill you and that's a promise.' She swallowed. 'Cody was seeing someone at the time and she was already pregnant with his baby, that's why he stayed in Looe. It wasn't because his dad needed help. He chose me to talk to, me to confide in. He didn't plan to be a dad, in fact, he didn't even love Daisy's mum but he stood by her, right up until she died. I provided him with an ear to listen to and some comfort. I was lonely myself at the time and guess what, it just happened. We slept together once after a few drinks. We were young and stupid. Then I found out I was pregnant with Bethany. When I started showing, he guessed. Cody knew she was his but we agreed never to speak about it and I wanted that too. Like I said, Bethany has always been mine and mine alone and Cody didn't want to complicate his life. That arrangement suited us both.'

'I'm sorry.' A thought flashed through Natalie's mind. She pictured Laura telling everyone she was pregnant then Jess disappeared. Was she really pregnant or had she spotted an opportunity when she saw baby Jessica with her sleeping drunken father? She'd already taken a baby once, maybe she did it again.

Everything felt wrong. Whatever had happened, whatever she'd done, Natalie would stick by her friend. It was obvious all along now. After all, Laura was the only person she had left in the world.

She'd work out what to do about Kate later.

FORTY-SEVEN

KATE

Thursday, 27 October

I've been awake most of the night, staring into the darkness in the hope that I will receive a message from Will. My heart pounds. If I don't hear from Will soon, we'll be packed up and home, then it will be too late.

Gently, I release my leg from the entangled quilt and my toe touches the carpet. This house creaks when anyone moves about in it and I don't want to wake Dad and the girls.

I creep across the bedroom, feeling my way in the dark until I reach the door. Turning the handle, I grimace at the slight click as the door opens. The cottage is silent except for my dad's snores coming from the living room.

I check my phone again, just like I've been doing all night long.

Maybe those messages were just a ploy to waste what little time I have left. It infuriates me that Natalie didn't call me back, despite all the messages that I've sent her. She's abandoned me too.

A message appears in my inbox. It's ten past four in the morning and now he's messaging me. Will knew that I wasn't getting any sleep tonight.

Six a.m. Jessica's bench. If you're not alone, you'll never hear from me again.

Six, perfect. I can get to the bench, find out what I need to know and then be back before Dad and the girls wake up. I swallow. This could all be a trap. Maybe whoever killed Jess is going to do the same to me. Right now, I'd do anything to know what happened to her. When I get to that bench, I'm going to be ready for them. I head to the kitchen and grab a tin of beans. It's not much of a weapon but I will pound it over their head if they try to hurt me. I pop them in my wrap-over bag.

I slip on my clothes by the light of the moon flushing through the gap in the curtains. After, I peer through, searching for the navy-blue car but there isn't a car like it parked up.

I have to believe that I'm finally going to find out what happened to Jess.

FORTY-EIGHT

KATE

I close the kitchen door gently, hoping that Dad or the girls didn't hear a thing. It's still quite dark and there's a calmness about the place. The only movement I catch is that of a cat darting across the car park before ducking under a fence. The sea gently laps onto the beach.

I have my phone and that tin of beans in my bag. Right now, I feel stupid. A tin can is a poor weapon of choice and I wonder what was going through my head. Should I have taken a knife? No, the last thing I need is to be caught out carrying a knife. Besides, I feel as though the messenger wants to unburden themselves, that's what I keep trying to tell myself. A nervy flutter travels through my body. I want this to be over. I can't take much more of feeling like I'm living this close to the edge.

In the distance, I can hear the sound of boats and people jostling around. No longer is the silence of sleeping people having that haunting effect on me. This town is about to burst into life for the day. Maybe Will has a boat and is about to go to work, which is why I'm here so early. It could all be as innocent as that. As I duck through a cut, I can see the harbour. Nearly there.

Footsteps shuffle behind me and I struggle to swallow as I slowly turn my head. My heart begins to judder just as I glance back but it's only a woman walking a dog. She waits until the terrier has finished peeing against a lamp post, then she passes me without even glancing my way. It might be dark but it's bustling out here.

The lights on the front twinkle as the breeze catches them. A nervous sick feeling gathers in the pit of my stomach. I grab my bag, knowing that I can use it to whack someone with if I'm attacked. The bench is in sight but I stop dead.

For a moment, I'm taken back to that day; the day that Jess disappeared. My screaming voice filled the harbour as I demanded an ice cream like some spoiled brat. I could see that my mother was stressed, dealing with me, Jess, and my drunken father but for a few seconds, I wanted her attention all on me. I was sick of her tending to Jess all the time. Since my baby sister had come along, I made it hard for her as I lay on the floor, legs kicking out and arms hitting her. Later was not good enough. I wanted her to do something for me, right now. I didn't care about Jess. I wipe the tear away that has gathered in the crease of my nose. Everyone blames my father but I blame me. I killed Jess. I carry that burden with me every day and it gets heavier and heavier. If I'd never played up for that ice cream, Jess would be alive and I wouldn't be here in Looe, putting myself in all sorts of danger. I'd be at home, enjoying my family, my job and my grown-up sister. I wouldn't be so obsessive over the girls. My all-consuming thoughts wouldn't be of them being taken by strangers. They'd enjoy a more normal life of being able to have play dates and go to parties. I'd have Damien. If I could go back, I would.

Sometimes I think I'm the only one left that cares about Jess now and when she was alive, my biggest wish was that she'd never been born.

Tears now flood my face and I can't stop them. I didn't want

Jess. This is all my fault. Maybe I secretly hoped that Jess would be taken or she'd get hurt and die. All this sadness and regret, it's too late. *Pull yourself together, Kate.* All this blubbing isn't me. It's the hormones, it has to be and I feel so sick. I spy the bench but still no one has arrived. If I sit there, I'll feel like a sitting duck so I'm going to wait here against the wall of the ice-cream shop, hiding out the way a little. I have to remember that someone hit me over the head in that cave and I won't put myself out in the open.

A boat chugs away, all lit up and ready to fish. Lights bob in the water, some boats have already left. I hear a man call out to his mate to untie the boat. They soon go too.

I check my phone. There are no more messages and it's just gone six. Will is late and right now, I doubt that he will turn up. I flick over to the Jessica page on Facebook and I stare at her delicate features and that little ladybird rattle around her wrist. When we got home, I searched for it, but I could never find it.

Several more minutes pass and as I'm about to give up, a hot bolt of pain passes through my head. I yank my bag and fling it against my attacker hoping that the tin can will hurt them but I can't see properly and the lack of impact tells me I missed. I catch a glimpse of the back end of the car. It's the dark-blue vehicle that has been following me. Without warning, a dark sack completely clouds my vision and I'm manhandled towards the road. I reach out, pushing and shoving but it's no good. My head is spinning and the darkness of the sack is disorientating and the musty smell is nauseating. I can't tell which direction I'm being dragged in. I try to grab my bag again and aim the tin at whoever has me but the strap is tangled over my shoulders. I'm thrust head first into something tinny and they have my bag. My hands are being tugged behind my back. The tender skin on my wrists burn and tear as the coarse rope is wrapped around them. I try to scream but the sound comes out muffled. I'm confused. My head; it's like lightning has struck. The sick thrum of blood pumping bangs through my head and I can't hear anything but that.

I'd kept safe. I'd stayed back, out of sight, watching that bench but Will had stayed one step ahead of me, like he always has done. This was his plan all along.

I'm going to die!

FORTY-NINE

NATALIE

Natalie woke to the sound of banging at the shop door. 'Laura?' Rolling off the settee, she grabbed her dressing gown and stepped into her slippers. Hurrying down the stairs and through the shop, she glanced through the smeared windowpane, taking in the skewered view of the harbour. Daisy's bike was locked against one of the railings. She spotted Cody and his daughter on the boat as it pulled out, heading to sea.

Whoever was knocking had gone. She checked her watch. At half seven and barely daylight, she doubted that anyone could be that desperate for an ice cream. As soon as she reached the living room, she grabbed her phone and checked her messages. There had been so many from Kate that she'd ignored. She switched it off and threw it back onto the coffee table as she tried to shake the guilt away.

For the first time in years, she reached across to the sideboard and pulled out the two cigarettes she'd left there since packing the habit up several years ago. Popping one between her lips, she lit it and inhaled, coughing only slightly. How good it felt to have nicotine coursing through her veins once again.

She thought back to the afternoon before. In confusion,

Laura had left but a few hours later, she'd returned and they'd talked further. Natalie had to protect her friend. No woman should have to relive a past like that.

Another hammering sound came from the shop door. She stubbed out the cigarette on the glass table, vowing to clean it up later, then once again she hurried downstairs. She only hoped that it wasn't Kate. She wasn't ready to speak to her yet, not until she had her own story straight. The shadow of a person leaning against the wall at the side of the door sent a shiver through her. She flicked the slide locks and stepped back as she opened the main door.

'Why, Nat, why?' Kyle stepped back, hands on head as he furrowed his brows. 'You told my daughter that she isn't mine. How could you do something so vindictive?'

'I'm not being vindictive. Rachel needed to know the truth.'

'I don't know who you think you are, but I am Rachel's father. That is the truth and you, you upset her and you upset me.'

'I didn't mean to upset her. I'm sorry, Kyle, Mary had been sleeping with my husband for years. I didn't know, but you did. Why do you put up with it?'

'You know stuff all.' The man took a deep breath and shook his head.

Natalie stepped back and huffed. 'I know you can't be happy about it. The whole town knows about Mary and Alan. I can't grieve after I saw all their disgusting messages about what they're going to do to each other on Alan's phone. It had been going on over twenty-five years. Had I known all this when he was alive, I would never have forgiven him. He would have been out that door so fast—'

'Nat, you know nothing about me and Mary. You wouldn't know that we have the kind of relationship where we don't mind the other having something on the side.'

Natalie went to speak but no words came out. That was the last response she expected.

'What I care about is you upsetting my daughter and telling her that I'm not her father. I raised that little girl. I've been to all the parents' evenings, the school sports days. I've stayed up with her through the night when she's had flu, tummy aches and nightmares.' He shook his head. 'You've never had kids, you wouldn't understand any of that – the bond between a father and a daughter. You came into our pub with the intention of ruining my family and I will never forgive you.'

The very thing that Natalie thought would get Kyle on her side had backfired. He didn't care about the one thing that had torn her apart, Alan and Mary's affair.

'You know feck all. You and Laura, stay away from me and my family. If I so much as see you near my pub, I'll call the police and report you for harassment.'

Anger ripped through Natalie. She roared and charged towards Kyle, knocking him onto the pavement outside the shop. Kyle stared back at her, silenced by her outburst that had floored him. She gasped and stepped back. What had she done?

Kyle stood and brushed himself down. 'Stay away from my family. Last warning.' With that, he left.

Natalie stumbled to the floor, doubling over as tears began to spill. As she wiped her face, she caught sight of something glistening on the pavement. Bending down, she picked up the bracelet, a delicate gold piece that had the word Mum engraved on it.

As she went to place it in her pocket to deal with later, she came face to face with Kate's dad, his grandchildren holding a hand each.

'Where did you get that?' one of the little girls asked.

She held up the bracelet. 'This, I found it on the floor. Right here.'

'That's Mummy's bracelet. We bought that for her.'

'Kate is missing and you have her bracelet. What have you done with her?' the man shouted.

FIFTY

NATALIE

'I just found the bracelet here on the path.' Natalie passed the bracelet to Kate's father.

'That's convenient. You've got her. What have you done with her?'

'I swear. I haven't seen Kate today.'

'I don't believe you. Is she up there in your flat? Have you had enough of trolling her? She trusted you.'

Natalie held an arm out. 'She's not there. Go up and have a look.' Defeated she placed her head in her hands and sat down on the step, listening as Kate's father charged through the door that led to her private quarters. His grandchildren cried as he charged through. Doors slammed and the man kept calling Kate's name.

Everything could be fixed with a phone call. After all, Kate had been trying to call her non-stop. If she called her now, Kate would definitely answer and all this would go away. She pulled her phone from her pocket and pressed Kate's number but the tone was dead. Taking a deep breath, she swallowed. Something was seriously wrong.

Kate's dad thundered back down the stairs. Natalie waited, a nervous humming in her chest as the man approached her from behind, puffing and panting.

'Kids, sit here.' He led the children to the step and Kate's dad sat next to Natalie. 'Where is she? I swear if you've done something to her, I'll never forgive you. I won't lose another daughter. Where's your boat?'

Natalie shook her head. 'I don't have a boat. I haven't done anything to Kate. She came to me for help and I was trying to help her.'

'Help her? From where I'm sitting, you could have lured her here to hurt her.'

'I wouldn't do that.'

'Where is she?' he shouts.

Natalie flinched. 'I don't know.'

'And I'm meant to just believe you?'

She shrugged. 'I don't know. I can't prove anything. I like Kate, I wanted to help her.'

The man exhaled and scratched his head. 'Tell me what you know.'

'I thought I knew something but it turns out I don't know much at all. Did she tell you about her visit to see Archie?'

The man nodded and leaned over, running his tense fingers through his thin hair. 'Yes. Did she tell you about the cave, that someone hurt her?'

'Yes.'

'How do I know it wasn't you that tried to kill her?'

'Please, you have to trust me. I would never hurt Kate. I wouldn't hurt anyone.' Her bottom lip quivered as she looked into the man's eyes. She hoped that he could see how genuine she was.

'If I find out that all of this is your doing, I swear—'

'You won't. All I want to do is help you. Look, give me a

minute to get dressed properly. You've got a good one in Kate and those children need their mother back. I'm not the enemy here.' She glanced at the little girls. The slightly older-looking one was comforting the younger one. 'Do you want me to help?' She didn't want to assume that her presence would be welcome, not with Kate's bracelet being found by her shop.

'Yes, please.'

'What time did she leave the cottage?'

The man shrugged. 'I wish I knew. I woke up and she wasn't there. It could have been anytime in the night. I need to find her. What if something bad has happened?' His fingers trembled.

Natalie placed a hand on the man's shoulder. 'We're going to find her. In the meantime, you should call the police, let them know what's happened.'

A few minutes later, Natalie hurried down wearing a fresh pair of jeans and a warm coat. It was going to be a long day. As they hurried through the maze-like streets, they peered through every shop window and called Kate's name. It was starting to feel more hopeless by the second. A fresh breeze whipped through the wind tunnel roads.

'Grandad, I'm cold,' the older girl said.

'Okay, Rosie. I need you to be a brave girl as we need to find Mummy.'

'Is she going to be okay?'

The man kneeled down while doing Rosie's top button up. 'Of course she is. When we find her, she'll need a big hug from her two favourite girls.'

A lump formed in Natalie's throat. They'd both tried to phone Kate over and over again but it looked like her phone was completely off. With her bracelet being found on the pavement, Natalie wondered if there had been a struggle. Cody's boat had just left the harbour. Cody and Daisy, Archie, Laura, Kyle and Mary; they were the key to unlocking the secret of what happened to Jess. The cover-ups, the lies and the entwined relationships that had preserved the secret were now coming out. The threat to them was real.

'Girls, hold each other's hand, okay?' Kate's dad turned away, leaving the girls for a moment so that he could try calling his daughter again. His frustration evident in the frowning that turned his face red and blotchy.

They took the turning along the street where the Smuggler was positioned. Rosie gripped her sister's hand as they stared through the window of a shop adorned with buckets of large shells. Natalie's stomach turned as they got closer to the pub. There was no way she wanted to bump into Kyle again today. She glanced through the window and saw Rachel behind the bar. The girl caught her eye and looked away. A couple of customers were sitting at the bar with a breakfast that the young server had only a moment ago placed on the table. She turned and walked away. Kate wasn't in there.

Hurrying, she reached the end of the path and waited for Kate's father to catch up.

'Kate, Kate.' The man kept calling her name, frantically searching through shop windows and checking his phone. An influx of tourists walked by, some taking to stepping into the road, others entering and leaving shops. The weather wasn't putting people off in the slightest. An elderly woman chugged along in a scooter forcing Natalie to step back. Most of all, she felt helpless. They'd been looking for nearly an hour and there had been no sign of Kate.

Kate's dad rushed over. 'Where next?'

'What do you mean?' How was Natalie supposed to know where they needed to go?

'You know what she's been up to more than me. She's been

talking to you, and that woman who owns a shop, Laura. No one I ask has seen her around here.'

Natalie followed Kate's dad around the next corner, avoiding a couple with a dog.

'We should head to Laura's. It wasn't open when we passed but she might be in there now.' Natalie wanted to see Laura anyway, to see if they were okay.

'Which way?'

'Here.' Natalie pointed down a back row of houses.

'Millie, Rosie.' Kate's dad turned around and charged through a group of kids, before running. 'Rosie!'

Natalie jogged after the man, back along the street as he called and called for his grandchildren. When they turned the corner Rosie was sitting on the kerb, her hands over her face while a woman was kneeling and giving her an ice cream.

'Rosie.' He grabbed the little girl, lifting her up and hugging her close. 'I'm so sorry I left you. Where's Millie?'

Tears poured from the scared little girl's eyes as she pointed to the shop with the shells in the window. 'We were looking at shells.' The ice cream was starting to melt down her hand.

'Is she okay?' the woman asked. 'I saw her alone and crying so I gave her my ice cream.'

'Have you seen another little girl? They look alike. She was with her sister, Millie.'

The woman shook her head. 'No, she was alone.'

With Rosie in his arms, Kate's dad ran across the road and barged into the shop.

Natalie followed. 'Have you seen a little girl?'

Kate's dad added. 'She has reddish brown hair, four years old?'

The shopkeeper lowered his spectacles and shook his head. Natalie stayed by the door, holding it open. Her heart sank. First Kate and now little Millie.

Kate's dad pushed his way behind the counter, nudging the

shopkeeper aside as he shouted Millie's name. He placed Rosie on the floor and after searching, they left.

Outside Rosie's cries caught everyone's attention. She tugged on Natalie's top and held up her empty ice cream cone.

'We'll get you another one in awhile, sweetheart,' Natalie said.

Natalie grabbed her phone to call the police but her hands were uncontrollably shaking. 'Someone help us. Someone call the police.'

Kate's dad held his hand up as he held his phone to his ear. 'Police, you have to hurry. My granddaughter is missing as well as my daughter.' Kate's dad relayed their current location to the police. 'Yes, we'll stay here until you arrive. Please hurry.' The man gripped his crying granddaughter as he leaned against the wall of the shop, looking like a man who'd given up hope.

Natalie stepped a little closer to him. 'Are the police on their way?'

The man nodded as he kissed the child's head. 'I lost her and I lost Jess.' Tears began to slip down his face and he hiccupped a sob. 'I've let Kate down. She will never forgive me for this.'

Natalie stood in front of him and looked straight into his eyes. 'This was not your fault and we are going to find Millie. I promise.'

'She's gone.' He shook his head and gripped Rosie's hand.

'I'm scared, Grandad. I want Millie.' The little girl began to sob.

'I'm sorry, I'm so sorry,' the man kept muttering as he held the distraught child.

Natalie wiped a tear away and took a few deep breaths until the trembling subsided. Time was of the essence and she didn't want to waste a second. 'I'll carry on looking. Can I put my number in your phone?' She held out her hand.

Kate's dad handed his phone over.

'What's your name by the way?'

'Harry.'

'I'm going to head to Laura's shop, see if Kate has been there today.'

'Thank you.'

'It's called Laura's Treasure Trove. After that, I'll come straight back.'

She'd tried to call Laura but there was no answer. The only thing Natalie could do right now was to help the family so that's what she'd do. At least she had been with Kate's dad all the time. She couldn't be suspected of taking Millie. Whoever had taken that little girl had done so right under their noses.

Her phone buzzed and a message from a private number came up.

I need to speak to you now. I know who took Kate and I'm scared. They're coming for me and I don't have much time. Please meet me where the old phone box used to be, by Archie's nursing home. I'll be there at eleven. They said, if I tell anyone, Kate and Millie die. Don't tell a soul. Mary. X

Her heart revved up and she nearly choked on the invisible mass in her throat. Who are the *they* that Mary speaks of? What trouble had they all been in over the years that had built up to this?

As she turned to go, she spotted a familiar face walking through the streets looking puzzled. The red-haired man spotted his crying little girl and ran over. Natalie watched for a few seconds as the man's body language changed from confused to angry in all but a few seconds. He started shouting at Kate's dad. It was time to go.

Running through the streets, she arrived back at her shop. She got straight into her car and with shaking fingers, struggled to turn the key. The car screeched as she selected a gear and drove off. Whatever she thought of Mary right now didn't matter. If Mary, Kate and Millie were fighting for their lives, Natalie would help and not only that, she had to do everything she could, regardless of the danger it would put her in. That little girl needed her and she wasn't going to let her down.

FIFTY-ONE

NATALIE

She skidded to a halt outside the phone box. There was no one there. The old rusty door squeaked as she opened it. Natalie peered around wondering if the noise had alerted whoever had sent that message to the fact that she'd arrived. The phone hadn't been connected for years with most people now using mobile phones but there was evidence of kids hanging around. Cigarette ends and a couple of empty cider bottles were strewn outside and the inside had been sprayed with pink and green paint. There was a piece of paper stuck at eye level. She snatched it and read.

> *Follow the walking trail behind the post box until you get to the clearing. I can't be seen with you or we all die. Hurry, we're scared and there's no one else I can trust. M.*

Snatching the note, she left the phone box. As she stepped onto the muddy walkway that led through the dense trees, something told her to turn back. Nothing about what she was doing felt right. Why was Mary using another phone? She wondered if Kyle had taken to reading her messages since everything kicked off. If Mary knew something about Jessica and she was running scared, Natalie wouldn't turn her back on the woman, despite their differences. She checked her phone again. Laura still hadn't tried to call her back, which was odd, but maybe she'd failed their friendship.

Branches whipped in the gale and one slapped her across the face. A drip of rain landed on her forehead. The weather was set to be much the same as it had been, chopping and changing all week. The sooner she was back in Looe and all this was resolved, the better.

She reached the clearing, the one people occasionally parked in but this place wasn't a tourist spot and the weather was definitely putting the dog walkers off. She leaned to the right, narrowly missing the hurtling twig that flew past her head. Wind whistled through the clearing. She caught sight of the car parked up on the muddy verge. She recognised the navy-blue Citroen but she thought that it had been sold years ago. She also wondered why on earth Mary would be driving it.

'Hello,' she called out. She gulped. Kate had been followed by someone driving a dark-coloured car.

After transferring her weight from foot to foot for several minutes between checking her phone, she walked over to the car and glanced in. There was nothing unusual about it. Nothing on the seats, nothing in the centre console. There was a tiny sack on the back seat, a random tin of beans and an empty bottle of water. A blister pack of tablets and two spoons lay on the floor.

'Mary.' She ran around, checking the ditches and behind trees but Mary was nowhere in sight. Maybe she'd come too late. She grabbed her phone. It was time to call the police. No signal. She had one back on the trail. Hurrying back the way she came, pushing through leaning branches, stepping over decaying logs, she was nearly there. Holding her phone high above her head, she could see that one bar was appearing. She'd call the police, get back in her car and let them deal with it but then a bolt of pain stunned her, sending her slipping in the mud to the ground where she bashed her nose on a log.

'You had to keep digging, didn't you? You killed Kate,' a voice bellowed as it was hauntingly carried in the wind.

As she went to turn her head, another blow came down and just before the world went black, she knew that Kate and Millie were dead. The person doing this to her didn't know the meaning of the word mercy. It was game over.

FIFTY-TWO

KATE

A car hums outside the building I'm being kept in and I can't see. However much I try to wriggle, the drugs I've been given in that drink and the pain in my head both make escape impossible and he knows it. All I know is that my captor is a man – I think. The voice is warped as I take in what is being said through my covered ears. It's like I'm living a nightmare. I kick out and my foot crunches on the wall and all I want to do is cry.

I wriggle and kick. My captor's footsteps move away from me and it sounds like they're searching for something. Objects clatter to the ground as they open drawers and pace around. I hear something fall close by so shuffle a little to my left until my tied up hands touch what feels like a block of cold. My sweaty hands release the corkscrew of a Swiss Army Knife. My heart pounds. I have a tool and I'm going to use it. I need to save my daughter and if I have to kill my captor I will. I'd do anything for my child.

There's a smell, like sweat and it's not mine. Hot breath catches my cheek. He's there, right beside me. I feel sick but I breathe in slowly through my nose and I sit on the knife.

'Millie is a perfect child, so perfect.'

Tears dampen my blindfold. This person has my child and I'm stuck here. I kick out and roar behind the gag. I need to get out and get to Millie, now.

The doors close. My captor is going now he's parked the car up. I hear the lock click and I know I'm alone again. Fumbling behind my back, I manage to release the knife.

I take my chance and start to saw. Flinching, I realise I've caught my wrist with the blade but I carry on, trying to be more careful this time. Nothing can stop me now. I need to get out of all this, if I don't, he will kill me and take Millie.

Jolting up, I'm startled by a bang coming from the car. I'm not alone in this hellhole of a lock-up.

Heart pounding and mouth dry; even with a tremble I carry on sawing. The rope is getting looser and bingo, it slips off my wrist to the ground. I untie my feet, remove the gag and blindfold.

Glancing around, I try to work out where the bang came from. 'Hello.'

More banging.

The navy-blue car that took me sits proudly in the middle of the large lock-up. Oil droplets adorn the concrete floor and there are tools and fishing equipment everywhere. My eyes stop on the crowbar. Without hesitation, I smash the car window and take my bag. I reach in for my phone but the battery has been removed. Running to the back of the car, I strain as I lever the boot until it opens.

A muffled scream comes from inside. I slip the blanket off the wriggling person and stare into the terrified woman's eyes. 'Natalie.' A trail of dried up blood comes from her nose.

She muffles out some more words so I reach in and remove the gag from her mouth.

'We have to get out of here. He's going for Millie.'

As I free her, she places a hand on my wrist. 'I'm sorry,

Kate. She's missing. The police were called just before I was hit over the head and thrown into this boot.'

Nothing has ever hurt so much. The little one I carried for nine months, the screaming baby that I pushed from my womb, those invisible binds that tie a mother to a child are now broken and I can feel it. I'm never going to see Millie again and that is a pain I cannot bear as I double over and let out the most primal yell ever. The pain of loss runs deeper that any physical pain and nothing can make it better except saving Millie.

'My father was meant to be looking after them.'

'It happened so quickly. We were searching for you.'

I frantically gaze around the large unit. 'Where are we?'

She wipes her sleepy-looking eyes. 'I don't know.'

'How long ago was this?'

Natalie shrugs. 'Not long.' She yawns. 'He forced me to drink water and...' She slumps in the boot, gibbering on about my daughter and the shops they looked in and she mentions Damien.

'You saw Damien?'

Natalie murmurs.

'Natalie. Did you say my husband was there?'

The woman yawns and nods.

He came back for me. I have to get out of here. More than anything I need his strength but at the back of my mind, I fear that he'll be even more upset with me now. I lost our little girl. I don't have any time to waste. The best thing I can do is get out of here. I search Natalie's pockets for a phone but I can't find one.

I crash into the metal garage door, hoping to break the lock but it's not budging. Wedging the crowbar into the minute gap, I try to lever the lock but I can't.

My focus catches everything, then I spot a long window but it is too high up to reach. Rain clashes against it and I have no idea how high the drop is on the other side. Ladders?

I spot a set of steps leaning up behind an old engine. Forcing them out, I yell as I free them. After placing them against the wall, I grab a hammer and an old coat before climbing up. There are no openers, which means I'm going to have to smash it open. With one mighty blow the glass crashes, now I have to get through that window and find Millie. Knocking out all the bits of glass, I peer through. There's about a ten-foot drop from a ledge and at the bottom, concrete. I swallow and take a deep breath. Everything hurts and my head pounds like never before. Fatigue numbs me and I wonder if I will make it without spraining or breaking an ankle. That's a risk I have to take.

As I take another deep breath, I listen to the sounds outside and I can hear the seagulls. It's like they're telling me to get a move on. For a second a shiver runs through me. It's like Jess is with me. I throw the coat over the ledge then I feed my first leg through. After that, I follow through with the second leg then I perch on the ledge. If I was standing on the pavement below, this drop would look like nothing but from here in my injured state, it looks like I'm about to drop to my death.

I have to do this. My child's life depends on it. I won't let what happened to Jess happen to Millie. I close my eyes and count to three then I feel the breeze lift my hair as my body goes down.

As I fall, I roll onto the pavement, flinching as a pain shoots through me. I don't know where I am. 'Help,' I call out but the place is deserted. The only thing I can do is run. As I take a right past the units, I can see the harbour. I'm up on the hill, past Laura's house. Half hopping and running, I hurry down as fast as I can, hoping that I'm not too late.

FIFTY-THREE

KATE

Within minutes, and sodden from the rain, I'm scurrying down the steep hill, past the bookshop and into the town. I glance up and down, searching for a crowd. If Millie is missing there must be a search party going on. I frantically push people out of the way until I get to the cottage and hammer on the door. It's empty.

Where can my father and Damien be?

Rushing back into town, I head towards Laura's shop but that too is closed up. The Old Smuggler, maybe they're there. The closer I get, I notice that there is a crowd and PC Bickerford is asking people questions.

'Kate.' The PC looks my way and leaves the man she was speaking to.

'There are some lock-ups, up that hill.' I point in the hope that she knows where I mean. 'He took me and he took Natalie. She's drugged and in the boot of a car.'

'Who took you, Kate?'

I shrug and shake. 'I don't know. Whoever it was, they blindfolded me and I escaped out of a window. They took Millie just like they took Jess.' The enormity of what I've just said makes my voice quiver until I can no longer hold back my sobs. The PC turns away from me and begins speaking through her radio.

I can't see Damien or Rosie anywhere. I place my hand over my stomach and sob. I love my daughters. My legs give way and I fall to the ground.

Laura totters over in her high-heeled boots, splashing in puddles before she finally reaches me. 'Kate! What happened to you?'

'Please help me?' I grab her and she helps me up. When I get to my feet, I almost fall over but she keeps me propped up. She takes off her thick coat and forces my stiff arms into it before doing it up, shielding me from the wind and rain.

'Come here.' She places her arms around me. 'Everyone is out looking for Millie.'

'Everyone was out looking for Jess and they never found her.'

'We will find her.'

'Someone kidnapped me and they have Millie.' Tears flood my face and I can't breathe. I hyperventilate. 'I'm never going to see Millie again.' My voice is quivering that much I wonder if she can understand what I'm saying.

I spot Damien as he comes around the corner gripping Rosie so hard, she's almost being dragged along as she cries.

'Damien!' I leave Laura and hobble over to him. As I go to hug him, he steps back.

'I came back to talk and look what's happened. You leave the same man that lost your sister in charge of our children so you can put yourself in more danger. You lost Millie, Kate.'

'Where is my dad?'

'I, err, we had an argument.'

'Where did he go?'

'I don't know.'

'What did you say to him?'

'What did you expect me to say? You lost my daughter, never mind. I can't believe you left our children with him.' Damien sighs. 'I may have said a few things but all I want is to get Millie back. Forget him for now. Where the hell have you been all day?'

The reality hits me. Damien is right but that doesn't stop my heart from aching to have my dad here. I can't believe he didn't stick around to help, despite how angry Damien must have seemed. Millie is missing. That's all that should have mattered.

'I...' My legs give way and I lean on the wall of a shop. My head is spinning and the path is warped. I can't breathe. The world is going black so I close my eyes before I pass out.

'Kate.' He steps over towards me and takes a hold of my bleeding hand. 'What's going on?'

I sit on the pavement, the water instantly soaking through to my bottom.

'Mummy,' Rosie cries as she hugs me.

I hug her like never before and I can't stop the tears from falling.

'Kate, I'm sorry. I shouldn't have gone off like that. We need to find Millie together. We will find her.'

'Someone took me and now they have her.'

'Who did?'

'I don't know,' I shout. 'Tell the police officer to find Cody.'

Damien takes Rosie and leaves me alone for a few seconds while he tries to get the PC's attention. Laura comes back over and sits by me.

'What could they want with Millie?' I shout, trying to wrack my brain.

'I don't know but all these people are looking for her. They blocked all the roads off as soon as it was reported and no boats have been able to leave. The town has come to a halt.'

I shake my head. 'That's more than they ever did for Jess.'

'They've learnt, we all have.'

'Yet you all still keep secrets. Everyone in this town knows what happened to Jess and no one has said anything.'

'That's not true, Kate. I don't know.'

'Do you know where my dad is?'

'I saw your husband arguing with a man in his sixties earlier. He told the man to leave and never come near you or the kids again.'

My dad – I thought he'd changed but he lost Millie. For that, I can never forgive him. I should have known better than to trust him, especially now that history was repeating itself. A shiver runs through me. If the person that took us comes back, they might try to finish Natalie off. She was trying to help me and look how it turned out.

'Everyone who comes near me gets hurt. They'd all be better off without me.'

'Nonsense, Kate. You're the strongest woman I know. Look how you've fought to find out about Jessica.'

'And what do I have? No more information and a missing daughter.' My sobs come thick and fast. 'I left Natalie in a lock-up unit of some kind and wasn't able to tell the police where, but it was just past your house. Could you help them? Go and tell them. Natalie needs help.'

She hurries away and Damien comes back over, leaving Rosie with the police officer.

He kneels on the pavement. 'I'm sorry, Kate. I should never have left you then you wouldn't have had to rely on that man. I should have been here, helped you look into things more, but I didn't.'

I reach across and stroke his face. 'Damien, I'm pregnant.'

He's taken aback and for a moment he can't speak. This isn't the way I wanted to tell him but right now, I want him to know.

He holds me closely and strokes my hair. A thought passes

for my dad. I wanted him to be so much more and I never wanted Damien to leave me. We're all to blame. Dad and I are worse, we should have known better. I wonder where he is right now. If there are roadblocks, he'll still be in the town somewhere.

I stare at the crowd. People are asking questions, muttering to each other. I spot Bethany and Rachel huddled at one end of the street, both trying to placate Rachel's crying baby. Daisy hurries over to Laura. A woman with a microphone nudges her way in. The press are here too.

PC Bickerford starts jogging my way but her concentration is broken as a man bursts through the crowd. 'There's a woman standing on the pier with a child.'

I nudge Damien out of the way. 'It has to be Millie.' I'm up on my aching legs and feet. Before I can even exhale, I run as fast as I can.

'Kate, stop.' PC Bickerford tries to chase after me but her shorter legs are failing to keep up. I need to get there before anyone else. I will beg and plead for this woman to let my child go. My heart bangs. Archie stood on that pier with Jess's hat. She went in there, I know she did and whoever killed Jess is now going to do the same to Millie. Why would anyone do this to me? I hear Damien shouting but I don't even turn back. My little girl needs me and I won't let her down like Jess was let down. I am not my father.

FIFTY-FOUR

KATE

I sprint to the end of the pier and my eyes lock on Mary's. The woman sits on the banjo-shaped end and her and Millie's legs dangle over the edge. A flash of the past hits me like a train. Millie's red jumper is as striking as Jess's red hat. My daughter is shivery cold as her eyes plead with me to save her.

'Come one step closer and we're both going in.'

I stare down at the turbulent sea below and I know my little girl would die if she went into that cold, choppy water.

'Please, you don't have to do this. Please let Millie go. She's scared.'

I know now that she is Will and everything she's done is nothing more than an elaborate lure to end my search for Jess. Something doesn't add up. Why would she bring me here in the first place? My head hurts and I'm not thinking straight.

'Tell the police and everyone else, if they come any closer, we're jumping.'

I hold a hand up, telling everyone to stay back. PC Bickerford's mouth is wide open and PC Barnes has joined her.

Mary grips my child with such force, I can see tears running down her little cheeks. Millie is too scared to make a noise or move and my heart is breaking to see her like this.

'There's no other way out. All I wanted to do was start a new life, replace the one you ruined. Why did you have to come back, Kate?'

'You messaged me.'

She let out a huff and shook her head. 'You ruin families, first your own, then mine. Go away, Kate.'

'Please, I'm pregnant with Millie's brother or sister. We're a happy family and she needs to be with me and her dad. You have a granddaughter who you love, a lot. Please think of my children. We all need each other. Millie needs me.'

The wide-eyed way she looks at me gives me the chills and her blonde hair is billowing in the breeze. 'I am thinking of my child. I can't think of anything but. You ruined everything. The past was in the past but you came along and whipped everything up. This is all your fault, Kate.'

Rachel pushes through the crowd. 'Mum, please come down from there. I love you. We love you. Don't do this.'

Mary turns her head back, the warmth of her skin tone framed by the darkest of thundery clouds. My heart begins to hammer. If they go into the sea, I will follow. My worst nightmares are coming to life.

'Look what you started, Rachel.' With pressed lips the woman smiles at her daughter.

'Mum, I'm sorry.' Tears streamed down Rachel's blotchy face.

'Rachel, what is she talking about?'

'You don't get it, you don't get any of it.' Mary slaps her free palm on her head.

A crash of sea spray sloshes against the pier, soaking my little girl and she shrieks. It's like my heart has stopped but I have to keep trying to get through to her.

'What don't I get?'

'No, no, no.' Mary keeps repeating those words as she shakes her head and sobs.

A huge gust of wind bellows and another wave crashes against the wall, splashing over me too. I can barely feel my shivering body or trembling fingers.

'Mary, please come down. It's too dangerous for both of you.'

'Mum, please.' Rachel goes to step closer.

'Stay back.' Mary's manic stare is enough to stop Rachel from taking another step. 'Do you really want the truth because the truth stinks?'

I nod as tears slip down my cheek. Is the truth worth all this? I ask myself that question and I think that maybe it isn't. Millie's life is at risk and I could have prevented that. I wish I was back at the cottage packing to go home with Damien and the girls after having a lovely family holiday. Sobs come from deep inside as I imagine snuggling up with him, in our bed at home, cuddling the girls as I tuck them in for the night. 'Yes.'

The woman stares into the dark sea. 'I can't keep this secret any longer. Rachel died. We loved her more than anything.'

'Mum,' Rachel cried.

'Why Jess?' I press her for more.

'It was an accident. When Kyle and I saw Jess with your father, we took our chances. Kyle took Jess, then he took the boat back out immediately, while you were in the ice-cream shop with your mother, and I took the car and met him along the coast. We transferred her into the car and into our lives, and everyone thought she was Rachel. I left Jess's red hat behind and old Archie picked it up. While I was getting into my car, I saw Archie on the pier, holding the red hat before dropping it into the sea. We didn't plan it, you have to believe me. We didn't want Cody to believe that his dad had done such an awful thing but we promised we'd keep his secret. Now, I've lost two children.' She shook her head and stared at Rachel. 'I fell in love with little Millie here and I wanted to start all over again, be a mother and look after her.'

'Millie needs me, she needs her sister and her father. Please climb back over. If she falls into that sea, she'll die. If you love her like you say, you'll let her go.'

Rachel is sobbing so hard. The girl runs as fast as she can off the pier and into Bethany's arms.

Jess is still alive and Cody thought that Archie had accidentally killed her all those years ago. Rachel is Jess, I know that now. All these years I thought she was dead. The look on Mary's face is deep. I need to keep her talking while I think. When she stops, she stares out at the sea in a way that makes my stomach lurch. 'What happened to Rachel?'

'Mummy,' Millie whimpers.

A guttural roar escapes her lips and her whole body shakes in a way that I've never seen before in a person. My heart bangs away and another wave crashes over the side. My pain has gone, I'm too numb to feel.

'She wouldn't sleep. She cried and cried all night. It was because she was...' Mary paused. 'She was poorly. I couldn't shut her up. The only way she'd stop crying was if she was in our bed. I'd had a couple of drinks. She slept and slept after I lay her next to me. We all slept. Me, Kyle and Rachel. Then she was—'

'I'm sorry, so sorry.' My heart was breaking. She had buried this truth too. I know where this is going.

'I crushed her. I killed my baby and only a day later while Kyle and I were still working out what to do, Jess was there, like a gift from heaven. She was the answer to our prayers. We did nothing but love that baby with everything we had.'

I need to keep her talking. 'I can tell how much you love Rachel. Everyone can.' What else can I say apart from, let my daughter go? 'Did you hit me in the cave? It doesn't matter. I understand why, I just need to know.' My arms ache to hold Millie in them.

'Yes, I didn't know what else to do. I love Rachel. She's mine and I knew you'd break my family up. I'm sorry. Why did this have to happen? We were happy, we were all happy until you came here.'

Glancing back, I see Damien standing midway along the pier and the police begin to approach. I shake my hand at them. They have to go back or this woman will jump, taking my child with her. They don't stop and as Mary turns, I see the look of horror on her face as she pulls my little girl into the sea. Screaming, I stare for a moment and all I see is Millie's red jumper crashing in the waves.

Damien runs up to me, shouting my name but I stand on the pier wall and without hesitation, I throw off Laura's coat and dive into that sea, ready to die to save my daughter. The swirl drags me in and deep and I feel like my breath has been pulled from my body. The icy fingers of the sea pull me in all directions and I'm blind to my surroundings. With all I have I flap and swim up, but where is up?

Reaching around, I feel my way, trying to grab Millie's red jumper but I get crashed against the wall and it knocks the wind out of me as I'm thrown under once again. In my mind's eye, I see Damien and as I close my eyes and succumb to my end, I imagine holding him tight and telling him how sorry I am. I lost this battle, I lost Millie and our baby. I lost my chance to get to know Jess. I love her so much and I'm sorry for being jealous of her. It's my fault.

Now it's time to let go. I can't fight the perilous sea any longer. *I'm sorry.*

As I'm about to give up, my fingers brush on Millie's jumper and we reach the surface. My daughter swam with all she had. All the time I spent in the pool teaching her, making her strong, had paid off. She needed me, of course, but she helped herself too but she's weak now.

I can do this. I'm a swimmer, a lifeguard, a teacher. I doubted myself because of fear but I've already faced my worst fears. A rope dangles down. Reaching up, I grab it as I hold Millie. Another wave crashes me against the wall. I take the impact, saving my fragile little girl, then I wrap that rope around her tightly and watch as she gets pulled up.

Steps, I remember passing them as I ran down the pier. I swim with all I've got underneath the waves until I think I'm close. With chattering teeth, I stumble onto the first step and see Damien calling me from the top. He runs down and pulls me up the rest of the way. When I reach the top, I lie on my back, a shivering mess staring up at the darkened sky. Rain begins to pelt and I welcome it. I'm alive. I swallow it as it gathers in my mouth and it quenches my thirst in a way water never has before. My salty lips are a reminder of what I've been through. Hurrying to sit up, I see that Millie is being wrapped in a foil blanket and led down the pier by a paramedic. Damien helps me stagger to her and when I get there, I wrap my arms around her as we both shiver together.

She's crying and scared, understandably. If I didn't have to be strong for her, I'd be sobbing like that too. PC Bickerford meets me with Rosie and my other little girl throws her arms around me.

In the distance, I see my dad standing against the wall of the lifeboat station. He bows his head and turns to leave. Letting go of my girls, I start to run in his direction. He needs to know about Jess. As I reach the station, he turns on his engine and car lights, then he's gone.

FIFTY-FIVE

KATE

PC Bickerford comes over. 'Head over to the ambulance. I'll need you and the little one to get checked out before we speak.'

I wipe the tears from my eye. My father has gone carrying the burden of the blame on his shoulders. I want to call him but my phone doesn't have any battery. Damien doesn't have Dad's number. I have no way of contacting him to tell him about Jess. The moment I knew that Millie was missing, I knew how my father must have felt and I can see why his drinking got worse and why he and Mum lost their zest for life. That could have been Damien and me. I'm thankful that my daughter is safe now.

'Thank you. Please tell me you found Natalie.'

The PC nods. 'We found her. She's been taken to hospital to sleep the tablets off but she's fine. We've also picked up Mary's husband. He was trying to leave in his other car and he got questioned at the roadblocks. There was an altercation and he was arrested and he did confess to taking you and Natalie, but he's said no more.'

Damien helped Millie and Rosie into the ambulance and

I'm slightly relieved to see both of my girls smiling at the attention.

'Do you mind if we speak for a moment?'

I can't stop shivering. She nods to a paramedic who passes me one of those foil blankets. 'No, I'll let Millie get all the attention first. I can wait. Did they get Mary out?'

PC Bickerford shakes her head. 'They're searching now but given the conditions, I can't see that she survived.'

I should hate her. She tried to kill my daughter but all I can think about is the accidental death of their own baby, the real Rachel. In the throes of immediate grief, they saw Jess and never looked back. As far as I can see, they've never been cruel to Jess. They brought her up well and she seemed happy. I hate what Mary did and what she became, but I wish she were still alive to answer to everything.

'Can I just reel some things off? I'm a bit fuzzy and I don't feel that good.'

'Of course. We can go through everything in more detail when you've had a rest and been checked over. Are you sure you're up to it?'

'I want to talk. I was hit over the head early this morning outside Natalie's ice-cream shop, then I was thrown into the boot of a navy-blue Citroen with some sort of sack over my head and then I was forced to drink water that must have been drugged.'

I scrunch my brow as things got hazy for awhile and I'm struggling to recall the order of everything. 'I was taken to a lock-up. Then the driver came back and parked the car inside. At that point I was gagged and blindfolded but I found a knife and managed to cut the rope around my wrists and ankles.' I realise how badly my teeth are chattering as the PC tilts her head and squints to make out what I'm saying. 'The man who trapped me had to be Kyle. Do you want to know their secret? Mary told me.'

'Yes. We still don't know why they did what they did. Natalie Thomas was found at the Penroses' workshop, but she hasn't spoken to us yet. What did Mary tell you?'

'Rachel died as a baby. While I was at the end of the pier, Mary said that she rolled onto baby Rachel while she was in their bed. They woke up and Rachel was dead. She and Kyle saw Jess that day when she was left with my father. One of them took her away in the boat immediately, while the other drove around the coast to meet the other. Jess became Rachel and no one ever asked any questions.' I can't remember who did what or exactly what Mary said. My thoughts are fuzzy.

'And then you received those messages?'

'Yes.'

'Why would Mary send those messages? She wouldn't want you to know what they'd done.'

I wrap the blanket tighter around my body as I stand under lamplight. 'I don't think she sent them. Someone else knew everything. Natalie overheard something... you'll have to ask her the details. Natalie wasn't my messenger.'

White-hot pain flashes through my head and my stomach is gargling. I feel awful and all I want to do is go back to the cottage, pack and then go home.

'Mummy, your turn.' Millie enjoys being carried by Damien and Rosie reaches up and holds her sister's hand. There's so much love between the two of them. I swallow back a tear. If only I was as caring towards Jess that day.

'We'll speak later. For now, get checked over.'

I nod and head over to Damien. 'What did they say?'

'This little one has no water in her lungs. She swam like a pro, didn't you, Millie?'

Millie snuggles into his chest and buries her face.

'I'm so proud of you, sweetie.' I lean in and kiss her, then I bend over to kiss Rosie. I never want her to feel left out.

About fifteen minutes later, I've been checked over and

Millie and I are going to hospital. They want to know that all is okay with the baby and they want to observe Millie for awhile. Damien stands over me, a hand on my shoulder as we wait. I bite my nails while he frowns and placates the girls. I've only known about my pregnancy for a couple of days and Damien has only known for a few hours but both of us know that if anything has happened, we'll be heartbroken. If this little life has clung on through all that it's been through, it deserves a chance.

'Kate, I heard what happened. They've just let us moor the boat up.' Cody stands outside the ambulance as we all wait. 'Oh, I'm sorry. This is a really bad time.'

'Damien, can you and Rosie bring the car to the hospital while we go in the ambulance?'

He nods, understanding that I need a moment with Cody. Millie lies back on the bed and pulls the blankets over her while I sit at the end.

The man I thought was behind all this deserves to know the truth about his father.

'Archie didn't hurt Jessica. All he did was find her red hat. You've been carrying that burden for years now, you can move on.'

Daisy spots her father talking to me and she runs over. 'Dad, are you okay?'

I can see he's not. 'I think your dad will need a stiff drink after this. Mary made him believe that his father killed a baby. Archie was a hero and you both deserve to drink to that. He saved a toddler from a car and had nothing to do with what happened to Jess.' This is the first time I've seen the man in front of me look sad and speechless.

He holds a hand over his mouth. 'Thank you, thank you so much.' He grips my hand and presses his lips together. 'I need that drink, Dais.'

Daisy smiles as she leads her father away. He glances back

at me and waves. I've seen everyone now and the only person I'm missing is Rachel. No doubt she will know of Kyle's arrest and Mary's death. She also knows about me. If I had the energy to stand, I'd walk straight out of this ambulance and find my little sister but I need to know that my baby is okay. I wonder if it was all too much as she ran away from the pier. I swallow, wondering if she'll ever want to see me again.

FIFTY-SIX

KATE

Millie has had the all-clear but they're keeping me in for a few more hours. Things are looking good but I have hypothermia. The shivering has been that bad, I feel as though I've torn ligaments. As soon as the adrenaline wore off, it hit me like a train. I don't know how Millie bounced back so quickly.

I had to force Damien to leave in the end. If he'd had it his way, he and the girls would have been sleeping in that hospital chair next to my bed all night. He's left me a box of chocolates, which have been most welcome. Well, they would have been had they not kept sticking in my throat. I yearn to speak to Rachel but I can't. My phone has had it. Damien promised to get me a new battery but I won't have it back until tomorrow. I need to know that Rachel doesn't hate me.

The curtain around my bed flutters and I stare. 'Jess.'

'It's Rachel.' She fiddles with the ends of her pink hair.

'Rachel. I'm sorry it had to come out like this. I'm sorry about your mum and dad.' I have to remember that Kyle and Mary are all she's known. My eyes tear up. It's been emotional and my hormones are playing havoc with me. 'I never gave up on you.' My bottom lip trembles.

She steps in and throws her arms around me. 'I knew it was you. It was me who sent the messages. I brought you here.'

I pull away. 'You're Will?'

'I was Will. Mum found out and saw the messages on my phone. I tried to warn you to leave but then she deleted the profile.' Rachel wiped a tear away. 'I found out she'd been messaging your phone and Instagram after that. I can't take it all in. I didn't think it would lead to this.'

'How did she get my number?'

'The cottage you're renting, it's ours. Your number was on the booking form.'

'How did you know that you might be Jess?'

Tears stream down her face. She sits on the chair and leans back. 'I found a baby photo marked up with my name. It was a photo of my mum holding a baby wearing only a nappy.'

'And.'

'The baby she was holding had a birthmark on the back of her ankle. I don't have a birthmark. Then I found something in the attic.'

She reaches into her bag and pulls out a little ladybird with a strap and Velcro strips on the edges. 'I saw that you posted a picture of Jess wearing one these wrist rattles. I must have had it on my wrist on the day I was taken. Deep down, I've always felt that something wasn't right. I was led to believe that Archie accidentally killed Jess; that he was holding her and dropped her off the pier during one of his funny turns.' She paused and looked down. 'We were all told to keep it hush as the poor man was ill. I remember arguing with my mum about it in the beer garden awhile ago. I kept telling her that Archie wouldn't have done that. I know he had that amnesia thing going on after the accident that confused him. The more Cody and my mother spoke to Archie about Jess, the more he believed he could have done it. It's all a mess and I don't know what to do.'

'That's what Natalie overheard.'

Rachel scrunches her brows.

'We'll take each day as it comes. Can I see you tomorrow?'

I realise I don't know my sister and she needs time to take everything in. However much I despise Mary and Kyle, they've been her parents for her whole life and it's going to be impossible for her to let go of them. She'll also be mourning for Mary. She also knows now that her parents hurt me and Natalie. I don't know how she's going to process everything, but I hope that I will have the chance to get to know my sister. I haven't spent all these years and nearly lost my life for nothing.

'I... I don't know.' She sniffs and wipes her nose. 'I haven't stopped crying since I left the pier, then the police told me that my mum—'

I place my hand over hers. 'I understand.' She doesn't respond. Instead she stands and leaves. In the distance I hear her let out a hiccuping sob and she's gone. I feel hollow. What I hoped to find was the truth. Now I have it. I've found my sister. She's alive and I have a niece. I lived through the unimaginable but all I want to do is cry.

FIFTY-SEVEN

NATALIE

Natalie smiled, the kind of smile where a person still frowns. 'Thank you for being here.' She sat on her settee as Laura passed her a cup of tea. A few hours in the hospital hadn't been a pleasure but now it was all over. Laura had filled her in on everything.

'I'm sorry I didn't answer my phone earlier, when you were trying to call. I was feeling miserable about my life, about everything really.'

Laura had helped Kate and she'd been there for Natalie after the ordeal. The tablets that Kyle had forced Natalie to take had kept her in a deep sleep for a couple of hours.

'I'm sorry too.'

Laura tilted her head. 'Why?'

'I thought you might have taken Jess.'

She shook her head. 'I suppose when you found out that I tried to take Rachel in her pushchair – I mean Jess – I can see why you might have thought that. I'm sorry too.'

'You don't need to be.'

She shrugged. 'No, maybe not. But I should have been more open with you. I should have known that I could trust you.'

'With what?'

'You know. Cody is Bethany's father. I owe it to Bethany to tell her the truth. She might hate me for awhile but I've seen what secrets can do to a person. She deserves to know everything.'

'You're doing the right thing.'

'I think so too.'

'Laura, do you want to get out of this town and go on a girls' holiday when all this has blown over? I've never been on one of those and I think we both need a getaway.'

'I'd love that.'

As they sipped their tea, Natalie couldn't help but think about baby Rachel. No wonder Mary didn't want her to go on about seeing the DNA test results. Rachel didn't even have her DNA. Natalie swallowed. Everyone now knew the story, it had been rife on social media and the search of Kyle and Mary's old garden in Polperro was causing a stir. Had their Rachel, the baby who got buried under a sleeping parent, been Alan's daughter? Maybe she'd never know.

FIFTY-EIGHT

KATE

Saturday, 29 October

We've moved to a bed and breakfast. As soon as Damien got back to the cottage with the girls, he couldn't bear to be in it, knowing that Kyle and Mary owned it. I'm glad I didn't have to stay there any longer. Too many memories. I finally managed to call my dad to tell him the news after Damien got me a new battery, but he was drunk. Again, I blame myself. All I want is my dad back in my life which is why, when we get back, I'm going to help him to sort his life out. Things were said in the heat of the moment. I hope he sees that. He has us now and I like to believe that he thinks we're worth making an effort for.

In her own time, Rachel could go and see him if she wanted. I still call her Rachel because that's what she wants.

My phone rings and I answer immediately. 'Nadine, I'm out of hospital now. We'll be back home in a couple of days.'

'That's okay. I wasn't checking to see when you'd be back at work. I wondered how you were. We were all worried when you messaged to say you were in hospital. How are you, lovely?'

'I'm getting there. The baby is a tough little thing but please don't tell work yet. I should be the one to tell them when I get back.'

'My lips are sealed. It's your news to tell but I'm really happy for you.'

'Thank you.' I pause.

'You okay?'

A little choke noise escapes me. 'Yes, it's all a lot to take in. Rachel hasn't really spoken to me since the hospital and I wish she would. There's something she doesn't know and if she did, she might hate me.'

'I'm sure she wouldn't.'

'When she went missing all those years ago, I hoped that she'd vanish. I was so jealous of her I was almost glad when it all happened. That's horrible. I was a horrible child. I felt like the universe had answered my prayers when she went but after, I thought I'd caused her to vanish because I'd wished for it.'

'Kate, darling. You can't do this to yourself. That doesn't matter so forget it. Most siblings get jealous when the new baby comes along. It's normal. I hated my brother for years but now, we get on great. I swear I thought similar things. Look at how you fought for the truth all these years. You're a person who cares. You did it out of love. Yes you were jealous but you loved Jess more than anything, even going as far as nearly dying to find out what happened to her. If that isn't love, I don't know what is. You're the loveliest and kindest person I know, Kate. I mean you save babies from the pool that aren't even drowning.' Nadine lets out a slight laugh.

I'm sobbing so hard I can barely reply. 'I owe you so much.' Damien and the girls are approaching with a basket of petals. 'Dammit, you've got me bawling my eyes out already.'

'Sorry. I have to go as reception calls and the boss is coming. Speak soon.'

I hang up.

'Shall we scatter those petals?'

The girls nod. They know that we're scattering them for a baby that died in the past who was called Rachel. I hoped my Rachel would turn up but I can't see her. Laura and Natalie step towards me. I think of Natalie being trapped in that car and drugged for hours. My heart bangs as I wonder what Kyle and Mary were going to do with Natalie and me. We'll never know. I imagine they would have just escaped with Millie and left us to come around and escape the lock-up. Kyle had pleaded guilty overnight to various charges relating to their dead baby, the taking of Jess, and the taking of Natalie and me. He blamed my assault in the cave on Mary but they both planned it, I know they did. They both planned everything once they knew that Rachel knew the truth.

Before we go home, we're heading to Polperro. I need to thank the lovely people who saved me a few days ago and I owe the woman who works at the pub a hoodie. The police booked hers into evidence.

We all take the walk together onto the pier where we'll throw the pink rose petals into the water and spend a minute remembering baby Rachel. Millie grips my hand. I know this pier is a scary place for her after all that has happened. We talked about it this morning and she said she wanted to say goodbye to the baby.

The police are still looking for baby Rachel's body. They're searching a cottage just up from Willy Wilcox's cave, a place that my Rachel used to play in as a child with her friends, that's how my sister came up with the name she messaged me with. The Penroses' used to live in Polperro when Jess was taken, in one of those beautiful hillside houses overlooking the sea. I stare along the pier and in my mind I still see Mary sitting with my daughter on the wall of that stormy pier and I shiver. Mary's body was found a few hours later and regardless of what she did, I'm sad for Rachel.

Cody is already standing on the pier. He bows his head slightly as I approach but he doesn't say anything. Daisy stands with Bethany, her arm linked in her friend's. I glance back, that's when I see Rachel approaching, her baby in a sling against her chest. She's trying to run but the breeze is catching her skirt. One hand is holding it down, the other is dragging a baby-changing bag along. 'I'll just give her a hand.'

I run towards her and take the bag. 'Let me help. I'm so glad you came.'

She stops dead and without warning, she places an arm over me, our faces meeting. 'Thank you for finding me, for coming.'

'I'd do it all again to have you back in my life. I've always missed you and I always loved you.' Wet tears land on my neck as I hug my little sister. I stroke the baby's soft hair too. My niece. Who knows what the future holds or how things will pan out, but for the first time in years I feel optimistic. I'm going to embrace everything life has to offer with Rachel, and I will be the strength she needs right now. 'We'll get through this, I promise. I've never asked what my little niece is called.'

Rachel tears up. 'Katherine.'

I tear up too. The young woman in front of me has lost everything she knows in pursuit of the truth but I hope that gaining me was worth it. Nearly losing my life, twice, was worth everything to have her back.

'Thank you for coming back for me.'

'I never gave up and I'd do it all again.' I hug my little sister.

The girls hurry over and Millie shyly grins. 'Aunty Jess, can I see the baby?'

My sister nods and crouches down letting the girls have a peek at sleeping Katherine.

'Girls, it's Rachel.'

Rachel shakes her head. 'It's okay. They can call me Jess. Only them though because they're my special little nieces.' She beams a huge grin at them and I know they like her and they'll soon love her like I do. I finally feel like my family is complete – except Dad. A person can't have everything so I have to count my blessings.

EPILOGUE

KATE

June, the following year

Our home is decorated in banners and bunting and the food is laid out on the large kitchen table. I place the last plate of cakes down and throw open the bi-fold doors. No longer is the garden nothing but a stretch of patchy grass with a broken playhouse at the end, we have a new patio and furniture. I'm happy that we're ready for our guests. My stomach flutters as I play with my mum bracelet. I've called Rachel a lot and I'm thrilled that she's finally coming to stay with us. The girls can't wait to play with little Katherine who's now walking. I also can't wait for her to meet baby Jesse, he has our nose, I'm sure of it.

Damien comes in holding the sleeping baby. 'I just called Mum, the girls are having too much of a good time at the park so they're going to be a little late.'

Yes, I now let the girls spend time with family and friends, and it feels wonderful.

A year ago, Damien's mum wouldn't have even had the girls

on her own because of me, but now she takes them to the park a lot. They've been to her house to make cakes when I was working and they loved it. I've changed so much and Damien is much happier too. I don't think he'll ever totally forgive me for putting myself and unborn Jesse in so much danger, but he loves me and he knows why I had to do it. For once, I feel as though we are stronger than ever. There is one lie that I need to clear up. Now might not be the best time but it's the right time for me. 'Damien?'

'What?' He smiles.

'There's something I need to tell you.'

He frowns and swallows. 'What have you been up to now?'

'Nothing, I promise. You know last year, before Looe?'

He nods.

'I didn't save a baby. I jumped into the pool and saved a perfectly safe baby because I misread the whole situation and my boss gave me a warning.'

He held his breath. 'And that's it?'

I nod. 'That's it.'

'Come here.' He pulls me close and kisses me on the forehead. Jesse begins to stir.

There is a knock at the door. I brush the icing dust off my summer dress and hurry to open it. 'Nadine.' I hug her. We've become best friends over the past few months and I don't know what I would have done without her being my sounding board through all this. She's comforted me while I've cried, she's picked me up with afternoon teas and pub lunches. When my maternity leave is up, I can't wait to go back to work and spend my lunch breaks eating cake and joking around with her.

'I brought you wine. If anyone needs a glass, you do, my lovely.'

'And I can drink it.' I laugh, pointing at my little post-baby paunch. I rarely drink but today I will enjoy a glass with my family and friends while we celebrate Jesse's safe arrival.

A host of others turn up. Damien's work colleagues, some of mine, our friends from past and present. Damien's extended family and their families. The garden is filling up and I'm thrilled that the sun is shining. Nadine laughs like a machine gun as she flirts with Damien's right hand colleague, Danny. It's a joy to watch.

The girls hurry through the door with Damien's mum and they instantly drag her to the garden to join in with the fun. It was kind of her to take them out while Damien and I set everything up. Little Jesse can be a handful but I wouldn't have it any other way.

I'm getting seriously nervous now. There's been no sign of Rachel, Natalie and Laura. They said they were coming and they haven't sent me a message saying they'll be late. I check the time. It's only twenty minutes. They're not coming. It's all too much for them.

I also check the message I sent to my dad. When we got back from Looe, I found a broken man, drunk on both vodka and self-pity. I know he's working hard to stay sober again but something inside tells me he's slipped. He hasn't called me with a progress update and I haven't been able to help him as much after just having Jesse. He's never met his long-lost daughter in person and I'm upset he didn't reply to my invite.

'Kate, everyone's wondering why you're not out there enjoying the party.' Damien places his arm around me.

'I'm just waiting for Rachel.'

He gave me one of his pressed lips smiles, one that tells me he's sorry for me. 'Maybe she's had an emergency.'

'Or second thoughts.'

'No, love. It's a lot to take in. She's had a hard few months with losing the woman she knew to be her mother. Kyle is in prison. She's lost a lot too. Finding the body must have been hard for her.'

They eventually found the bones of a baby buried in the

woodland next to Archie's nursing home after Kyle confessed to burying his baby there. I haven't said too much about it to Rachel as I don't want to upset her. 'You're right. Maybe this was too much.'

'Finding out that the baby was murdered is something else. It's a lot for her to process.'

I agree with him and hug him close. Kyle had cracked and also told the police that he had lost his temper with the little one in a fit of drunken rage after Mary told him that she'd given birth to Alan's baby. The bones don't lie and they back up his story. I guess that he told all because he couldn't live with his crime any more. And, I wonder if Mary believed her version of events because it was easier to digest.

An engine hums as a large people carrier pulls up onto the drive. Natalie and Laura get out of the front seats, then opens the back where Bethany, Rachel and baby Katherine all get out. I shriek with joy as I let go of Damien and throw the front door open. We all hug and kiss before I lead them through to the garden. After introductions, they relax and join in the party.

I hurry over to Rachel. 'I was so worried you weren't coming.'

She smiled. 'I had to stop and change a nappy, then we had a flat on the motorway of all places.'

'I'm so happy you're here.' I take Jesse off Damien. 'Meet your nephew, Jesse.'

She places Katherine down on the floor and the little girl toddles over to Bethany. 'Can I hold him?'

I pass my little one over to his aunty and she stares at him like he's a shiny jewel. 'Oh, he's a beauty. Hello, Jesse.' She sits on the floor and calls Katherine back over. 'Come over here, Kat, and meet your baby cousin.'

The toddler smiles and sits next to her on the grass while I hold Damien's hand. He squeezes it. 'Do you want a glass of wine, now?'

I nod. 'More than anything.' My dad isn't coming.

Natalie comes over to me, a bottle of cider in her hand. The frown lines in her forehead run deep.

'Are you okay?'

She half smiles but that smile soon went as she shook her head. 'I know you heard about Rachel, being my late husband's baby.' She went silent.

'Yes, I'm sorry.'

'I hate that man for what he did to me. He had an affair that lasted over twenty-five years and I was in the dark. How does a person do that? I can never forgive him, not even now he's dead, but that baby didn't deserve to die like that and I know if Alan was alive he'd be heartbroken at this news.' Natalie glances at Jesse who is lying on his back on a blanket while everyone fusses over him. 'Mary knew all along. I've been sobbing my heart out since I heard. I wasn't going to come but Laura said it would be good for me. I don't know what I'd do without her.'

I don't know what to say so I lean in and hug her hard. She's a victim in all this too.

'There's nothing I can say that will make the pain go away,' I say to her. 'But you have a good friend there and I bet you get on with Bethany too. You have good people around you.'

'Thank you. I know.' She shakes her head and exhales. 'Bethany and I have become quite close. She fell out with her mother for awhile when Laura told her that Cody was her father, but they're close again now. Cody is slowly coming around and Daisy has accepted she has a half-sister. It's been hard on her but telling the truth is the right thing to do. I have faith that everything will work out.'

'I've never thanked you properly. I just wanted you to know how I appreciated the things you did for me. I know you doubted that you should help at times but you did and you risked your life. It means everything.' I'm tearing up now.

'We helped each other. Right, I need another drink before I blub.' She walks off, leaving me alone.

I smile across at Rachel. 'Hey, Rachel.' She comes over. 'I'm sorry that Dad hasn't turned up.'

'You did warn me.'

'I have some photos to show you later, of Mum.' I swallow.

'It must have been tough on you all.'

'It was.' I take in her long pink hair and her high cheek-bones. It's hard to marry what I see in front of me with the baby at the harbour side. I catch Damien staring at the path alongside the house. I move to see what he's looking at and my dad stands there, hunched over in a crumpled shirt holding two boxes of chocolates. As he comes forward a little, he looks at Rachel. I've shown him a photo of her.

'Is that our dad?' Rachel squints and holds her hand above her eyes to block the sun.

I nod. A tear slips down my dad's cheek as he takes her in. I run over and hold his hand, leading him towards her. 'Rachel, this is Harry, your dad.' He's not perfect by any means but he's ours.

Who knows, maybe we can all heal each other, or maybe I'm just being idealistic. Either way, I'm prepared to give it a go if he and Rachel are.

Damien grips my hand. I have my rock by my side. I have my sister, my children, my dad and my friends. My family is now complete. That's all a person really needs. The rest will fall into place.

A LETTER FROM CARLA

Dear Reader,

Thank you for choosing to read *Find Me*. I adored writing this book and I hope that you enjoyed reading it.

If you enjoyed *Find Me* and would like to keep up to date with all my latest releases, just sign up at the following link. Your email address will never be shared and you can unsubscribe at any time.

www.bookouture.com/carla-kovach

The combination of lovely childhood memories and the beautiful landscape led me to believe that Looe and Polperro were the perfect fit for my latest. The fact that I could draw on a little bit of pirate legend was even more of a bonus.

I took a research trip during Covid restrictions but the world-class hospitality that I received was second to none. Experiencing this wonderful location first-hand was an absolute delight. I tried to take in what my main character, Kate, would see, which meant I walked on the beach, I ate at the chip shops and I marvelled at the many trinket and art shops. While there, I allowed Kate into my head and her story grew and grew.

I should point out that my characters are purely fictional as is the pub and the ice-cream shop. There were no scary people lurking around every corner and it really is one of the best places on earth to take children.

Whether you are a reader, tweeter, blogger, Facebooker, TikTok user or reviewer, I really am grateful of all that you do and as a writer, this is where I hope you'll leave me a review or say a few words about my book.

Again, thank you so much. I'm active on social media so please do contact me on Twitter, Instagram or through my Facebook page.

Thank you,

Carla Kovach

facebook.com/CarlaKovachAuthor

twitter.com/CKovachAuthor

instagram.com/carla_kovach

ACKNOWLEDGEMENTS

It's time to credit all the wonderful people around me who made this book happen.

Helen Jenner, my fabulous editor has been brilliant in shaping this book. As always, she's been there from the bud of the idea to the fully grown flower and I remain grateful every day that she wants to work with me. Massive thank you to Helen.

Team Bookouture are a tower of support. I'd like to express my many thanks to everyone, from the rights team to the lovely people who work in accounts. It's always a delight to hear from them.

I adore the cover and for that I have to express gratitude to Jo Thompson. The cover is the first thing that people cast their gazes on and I'm thankful to her.

Publication day is special in every way, and that's because of the amazing publicity team. Noelle Holten, Kim Nash, Jess Readett and Sarah Hardy all work hard to get the new book news out there. I'd like to extend a massive thank you to them and their constant supply of enthusiasm and positive energy.

I'm hugely grateful to the bloggers and readers who share reviews, share the love, and tag me. The fact that they use their precious time to do this is heart-warming. I'm hugely grateful for their selflessness in doing this.

There are two communities that I have to give my ongoing gratitude to, The Fiction Café Facebook group and the Bookouture author community. The happiness that I receive from being a member of both is priceless.

Beta readers, Derek Coleman, Su Biela, Brooke Venables, Anna Wallace and Vanessa Morgan, all read my earlier draft and for that, I'd like to say a big fat thank you. Special thanks to Brooke Venables who writes under the name Jamie-Lee Brooke, and Phil Price who are also authors. I appreciate their motivational support in our little bubble. Long live the writing buddies group.

During my research I stayed at Little Pudding Cottage in Looe and I'd like to express my gratitude to the owner, Clive, for his hospitality. The views from the cottage were inspiring and it made the perfect research spot. In fact, I had my character, Kate, climbing that steep hill at one point.

During my trip, I frequented The Pier Café, Pier Café One and The Beach Café in Looe. All were a delight to eat at and the staff were lovely as was the food and coffees. Also, I have to thank the cafés of Polperro, which was one of the most magical towns I've ever visited. Again, I felt welcomed with every step.

When I visited Polperro, I didn't find out enough about Willy Wilcox's cave so I had to ask the Looe and South East Cornwall Facebook group and the admin, Claire Martin, was happy for me to ask away. I'm thankful to everyone who helped with my questions. As promised, I'll send a copy of *Find Me* to Looe Library. Any mistakes on tide times or how the sea comes in are all my own.